# MORNIN

C000182319

Tharun James Jimani is also the author of *Cough Syrup Surrealism* (Fingerprint! Publishing, 2013). His short story, *An Absurd Romance,* was previously published in *Music of the Stars and other Love Stories* (Scholastic, 2012). *Mornings After* is his second novel.

# MORNINGS AFTER

*Tharun James Jimani*

# BLOOMSBURY
NEW DELHI • LONDON • OXFORD • NEW YORK • SYDNEY

First published in India 2016

© 2016 by Tharun James Jimani

ISBN 978 93 85436 46 8
2 4 6 8 10 9 7 5 3 1

Bloomsbury Publishing India Pvt. Ltd
Second Floor, LSC Building No.4
DDA Complex, Pocket C – 6 & 7, Vasant Kunj
New Delhi 110070
www.bloomsbury.com

Typeset by Manipal Digital Systems
Printed and bound in India by Thomson Press India Ltd

To find out more about our authors and books visit www.bloomsbury.com.
Here you will find extracts, author interviews, details of forthcoming
events and the option to sign up for our newsletters.

*To passing fancies*

# PROLOGUE

'Arriving at each new city, the traveler finds again a past of his that he did not know he had: the foreignness of what you no longer are or no longer possess lies in wait for you in foreign, unpossessed places.'

-Italo Calvino, *Invisible Cities*

Bombay, if she were to speak, would probably not quote Italian neorealists, or even register their names if you chose to drop them in conversation. She'd likely not borrow from works of literature that read like a former day Lonely Planet Multicity Guide on speed. Bombay, for all her abrasive chutzpah, is at heart a giver, not a taker; a listener, not a talker; the apparatus, the medium even, but not the high. But of course people don't understand cities the way cities understand people. Bombay will hug to her bosom, take to her grave, tales of love and despair, of life and longing, because cities are really just the secrets they keep. And because cities—and Bombay—are not dreams or abstractions or joy or melancholy, the easiest way to put yourself in a city's shoes may just be to put yourself in the shoes of its residents.

Take Sonya and Thomas, for example, who are slowly settling into their respective silhouettes on the bed. The particular sex act they were engaged in till a few moments ago was of a somewhat unconventional nature, placing an unfamiliar requirement upon Thomas: to be delicate, reassuring, tactical. These are not traits that have been in short supply previously but they have also never been summoned for under duress in the few weeks they have known each other.

'How're you feeling?' he asks, his arm around her.

'About what?' she says.

'What do you want to do now?' he asks.

'You decide.'

'We could watch a movie on the laptop?'

She shakes her head. 'Ask me something,' she says.

'Ask you what?'

'Anything. Tonight, for one night only Thomas Mathews, you have been granted permission to ask me anything at all and I will answer honestly and to the best of my knowledge. Any subject, any question. Go.'

'Any question?' he asks.

She doesn't reply but he can feel her mouth break into a smile against his neck.

'Ok,' he says, 'ok, of all the men you've been with, how do I compare?'

'What, like a personality competition?'

'In a manner of speaking,' he says and turns to her. 'In terms of size. How do I compare *size*-wise?'

'You really want to know?' she asks.

'Yes,' he says, 'no. Yes.'

'You compare ... *favourably*,' she says, and closes her eyes, finally having twisted and turned and narrowed down her Sonya-shaped impression on the bed to its exact coordinates.

# 1

When Thomas and Sonya met again, they were still strangers, of sorts. They had met only once before on a suitably rainy night, a couple of months ago on Om Beach in Gokarna. He had just arrived, and she was at the end of her tether, plagued as she was by emails from work and sand between her toes, in her clothes, in her hair, even her keyboard.

'Yearly ritual,' she explained.

She was leaving next morning, she had informed him, but gave him her number anyway. Old soul that he was, it is likely he took that to mean something, though he didn't think it likely that he'd purchase a phone any time in the near future. So Whatsapp they didn't, text each other they didn't, and if it weren't for the internet, chances are they'd have been strangers, *proper*, if-when they did meet again.

She knew him in that strangely familiar way the twenty-first century knows everybody. Bored at work a few days after she returned home to Bombay, she had looked him up one afternoon, not out of any fascination for the man, but out of that most basic of requirements for satisfactory workplace procrastination: things to google. Sonya had finally run out of things to google. She couldn't quite remember the full name of her journeyman acquaintance but something had stuck: a word, a phrase. Something about childhood or fatherhood or violence, something statement-like, something *sweeping* that he had dropped in conversation, something about his novel. He had said he was a writer, 'of sorts'. At least that much was true, she thought as she pored over generally favourable reviews of *Kill Them All,* and determined to order a copy from Flipkart. His profile on Goodreads also mentioned an earlier anthology of short stories, *The Ferment of Clarity*, but that appeared to be out of print, or stock, or both.

He knew her a little less stoically, less factually. He remembered her vividly, or parts of her, the *idea* of her, in fragmented pixels, like an image still loading on dial-up: her hair and her voice, the way she'd look around after saying something rude, or pretentious. The distinct impression that nobody called her on her bullshit before she did. There was an easy irony to her he found surprisingly engaging, and depth he suspected she liked to keep to herself. He remembers thinking they had crossed paths before, that this was continuum. He remembers thinking it would never work, and immediately chastising himself for assuming there might be an 'it'. He had only realized later, a few days after she had left, that he would need to find out for himself if this were true.

The emails only started coming in a considerable while after this realization; or to put it more accurately, he had only visited his inbox after one inquisitive email ('Your blog is much funnier than your novel. Why'd you stop writing?') had been followed by another, a couple of days later, apologizing for the intrusion ('I didn't mean to pry.'), and a third, sent a week after, inquiring if this was in fact even the right email address, if she was bothering somebody else entirely with what must seem like a schoolgirl crush (which wasn't the case at all, she had clarified). He had, as he would admit in his preliminary return correspondence (a little too readily, she would chide him in days to come, 'You lonely old man!'), been thinking about her, but it had never crossed his mind to call.

Because calling somebody—he had explained in a hastily post-scripted mail—a physical intrusion, even if only in the form of sound waves, seemed a touch too intimate given the brief nature of their acquaintance. 'Do you also lug around a typewriter during your travails?' she had replied, to which he responded with the news that her city was the next stop in his impressionable itinerary. He didn't know how long he would stay, he had stated, but he didn't think it would be for very long.

Though Sonya was disappointed that Thomas hadn't reciprocated her attempts at banter, the news precipitated much IM-ing between her and Anjali, who had been forwarded every correspondence so far, as well as subjected to significant quantities of wine-fuelled musings on the pros and cons of bedding a writer. Neither woman was impervious to the charms of the written word, but they were both in agreement that a writer who appeared not to write any more stood considerably diminished in terms of desirability. But these deliberations had taken place, and conclusions had been arrived at, in the cozy glow of hypothesis: *If* they ever met again; *if* there arose the possibility.

Previously, they had both agreed that his novel lacked a certain *gravitas* that may be overlooked in the light of the regrettably youthful age of the author; he was barely their age when it was published, much younger when it was written if the book jacket were to be believed. But the news of his imminent arrival in her city, and the hours of entertainment his blog had provided her with—both Sonya and Anjali confessed to having read it in one sitting, twice; starting with the most recent entry and working their way back to the oldest post, *and* the other way round—upset their strenuously arrived-at conclusion by inserting that damndest of variables in their carefully crafted equation: that of potential. How does one, in the inherently skewed mathematics of mating, account for something as unpredictable as Potential?

So while Anjali and a severely smitten Sonya slaved away at an enforced electronic silence (and this was just as hard—or harder—on Anjali, for what greater misery than backseat misery?) calculated to buy them some time, Thomas went diligently to work at erecting a Grand Gesture that would have been the equivalent of a thousand ships launched in more romantic times: a new entry in his recently more-trafficked blog, on the cons (and cons only) of the muse.

The drought, you see, had nothing to do with a lack of inspiration, and everything to do with the lack of an audience. So write he did, vaguely and obtusely, about the magic of chance meetings, of passing fancies, and the necessary narcissism of the wordsmith. It wasn't his best work, or even very good as she would point out when they met (It was 'too self-referential, meta to the point of being a little retarded.'), but it did the trick. It tilted the questionable swing of Potential in his favour—there was something there, she thought; something worth nurturing, worth saving.

Still. We live in times of absolute accessibility and closure. And men—bumbling fools that they are—are inadvertent masters of that little space between delusion and reality that we have all come to know and love as the 'grey area'. So, much as Romeo set the tone for their romance with that suicidal tryst under Juliet's balcony, Thomas planted the seeds of Sonya's later discontent by preferring to wallow instead of fight. Thomas's great mistake was not that he didn't invest a couple of rupees in the nearest phone booth and inquire about Sonya's silence, or even that he didn't mail her again with a transparent excuse like 'Long time, is everything ok?' just to remind her of his existence, but that he left it all to chance. Thomas did not *take initiative*. He merely squeezed what he could out of the one thing to happen to him in several months that made him *want* to write, and embarked on a two-day binge.

One may argue, as Thomas would in the not-distant future, many times over, that this was a test—and confirmation—of serendipity, and that it worked out quite well for them after all; just as one may argue as Sonya would, just as frequently, that it was a sign of Things To Come, of taking her for granted—what if she hadn't visited his blog again? Could he not have at least forwarded her the link? But psychoanalysis is for the overly involved. For the moment, a blogpost was all the encouragement Sonya needed, the customized ping of Google Reader was the very beat her heart skipped, and in a moment of non-deliberated (Anjali would have liked her to confer), unadulterated abandon (Anjali would have liked her to wait), she replied: 'Call when you reach.' And call he would.

# 2

She swept around the debris of the previous night, lifting a chair leg here, putting away a hastily unbuttoned shirt there. She worked the broom in short, staccato strokes, deftly avoiding under-the-tables and behind-the-curtains, neglecting corners with practised ease. Thomas had taken to calling her 'Didi' like Sonya did, though he suspected that she was uncomfortable with the arrangement. She was probably a few years younger than Sonya, at least a decade his junior, though her eyes betrayed a world-weary detachment that followed her around like a fart. She picked up what was left of a half-smoked joint and considered lighting it. Thomas closed his eyes, not wanting to embarrass her.

A few minutes later, she was back, spirit visibly reconciled with body, armed with a mop and a bucket of water. She held his stare, challenging him to look away. Thomas attempted a smile and immediately worried it came out as a sneer—or worse—a come-on. He held Sonya tighter, and kissed her on the forehead. She was still asleep, their legs locked in a complicated tangle that had him wondering where his waist ended and hers began. Didi untied the knot in her hair and tied it back into an efficient bun. He watched, helplessly fascinated, as she expertly lifted her saree over her knees and sat down to squeeze every last drop of water out of the mop. She would stand up in a second, he knew, and run the mop over the floor, careful to leave it just wet enough for Sonya to notice. Just another ghost that needed to make its presence felt for survival.

Of course, he only knew this because this was their morning ritual. Every morning of the week gone by, Didi had played out her little dance for her audience of two: Sonya and Thomas under the sheets, sometimes locked in embrace, most times nude. Sonya, like a disrespectful theatre-goer, opened the door for her at seven every morning and promptly went back to sleep, not nearly as interested as Thomas was in the movie of Didi's life. He watched, charmed by this slip of a girl who wore sometimes sombre, sometimes flamboyant sarees that had clearly been paid for with the currency of charity, and cleaned other people's houses and washed and folded their clothes month upon month for less than an evening's worth of drinks at The Bend.

Didi put a folded hand to her mouth in a gesture of 'coffee?', eliciting a nod from Thomas. She left the room, door ajar. He watched her in the mirror, lighting up the stove in the kitchen, framed by a stack of dirty dishes and a criminally underused spice rack. Checking to make sure she had her back to him, Thomas stepped out of bed. He climbed into his boxers and hurried to the toilet, choosing instant bladder relief over modesty. Besides, she had seen worse, prone as Sonya and he were to bouts of passion in the morning, secure under the cover of the duvet, oblivious to company. Pissing, he wondered why Didi didn't register as a human being; why her presence did not put them off activities people normally reserved for private moments, like fucking, or arguing. Not that Sonya and he had ever argued.

Back in bed, Thomas realized he had been unfair to Sonya. She was good to Didi, paying her over the odds and letting her take with her what was left of breakfast. But what were the odds for domestic chores, for cleaning up somebody else's mess? How does one put a price on hands that delve casually into commodes and heads that bow permanently in one's presence? He remembered reading in an article that sexploitation of domestic help was so common that the majority of housemaids in India expected their masters to make a sexual advance in some form or the other. He wondered if Didi had ever been groped by an errant boss, if she had ever mentally castigated Thomas for a misinterpreted look or word. He remembered recently masturbating to a '*desi* maid sex' video, and felt guilty. He also realized that he was not middle class enough to ever be attracted to domestic help in real life, and wondered if that wasn't worse somehow. He decided it probably was.

Thomas desperately wanted Sonya to wake up. Her coffee was cold, as were the soles of her feet. She rubbed them against the top of his feet, warming them, still asleep, as she had done every morning of the few days they had spent together. He found himself hoping fervently that this was a quirk that had somehow magically developed as a result of their sleeping together, by the chemistry and fit of their bodies, that it was not something she did with all her men. Then he hoped that there hadn't been many men before him, that there hadn't been another too recently, or better (and impossibly) yet, ever. He placed his hand on the dimple on her back, and reminded himself that they had only known each other a short while, that he was a soi-disant traveller, a journeyman, and she, this, *them*, was a pitstop. There is no *us*, he told himself.

He looked again at her face, the wry squiggle her mouth morphed into when she was fast asleep, the swell of her right breast, misshapen and cramped by the proximity of their bodies. He could still smell their sex when he lifted the covers, taste the aftertaste of their togetherness as he took a sip of her now-cold coffee. He wondered if Didi caught it too, the beachy, musty whiff of Sonya's being, the tangy salt of her core. He wondered if poor people—servant class—smelled of poverty, if Didi smelled of resignation and despair. He wondered if their bodies spoke in English when they made love, if they tasted of roti and watery sabzi, or of avocado and Rosé wine like Sonya's did. He decided he needed a cigarette.

On the terrace, the Bandra air filled his lungs with possibilities; the eight o' clock sun felt good on his skin. Below, men returned flushed from jogging or the gym in shorts that were too tight for middle age; a group of women were assembled around the vegetable-walah at the end of the street voicing incredulity at the price of karela or bhindi. Thomas looked at the apartment buildings around him and wondered how all the young people who lived in them had managed to avoid stepping out at this time of day altogether. Straight ahead loomed a hoarding for one of Bollywood's biggest hits of the past few years, *Missed Call*. The poster, which featured the country's bona fide male matinee idol climbing out of a swimming pool in fluorescent green Speedos, had triggered much mirth between Thomas and Sonya.

Though Thomas had only been in Bombay ten days, the city was beginning to feel like home, like he might be able to retire his backpack for a while. It was the first city he had set foot in in a long time, but the morning orchestra of scooter engines and auto rickshaw horns was already growing on him—no longer an irritant, just the sounds of a different jungle. He checked on the goldfish he and Sonya had picked up at Pali Naka, squinted at the old man in the building opposite, feeding grains or rice or something else entirely to the pigeons that congregated in mid-flight around his balcony every morning. He knew Didi serviced a number of flats in the area and wondered if she worked for him too, if she had watched him grow old. She had known Sonya almost three years, he knew, and had held her hand through two break-ups and an abortion, hangovers and chicken pox. She knew how Sonya liked her eggs, and, probably, the timing of her period. She knew which of her shirts to wash by hand, and remembered to pick up zucchini on Salad Saturdays. He wished he knew Sonya a little more, a little longer, a little better.

Thomas watched as Didi hung up clothes to dry. She tackled the terrace like an obstacle course, hanging a tee-shirt here, a dress there, careful to avoid spots that were too exposed to the sun. He wished desperately to make conversation, to acknowledge her presence, her service. But what does one talk about with the help? Somebody else's help. Would she be impressed that he was a writer, or consider it elitist and self-indulgent? Would she care for the existential plight of the characters in the novel he was writing, or deride them for their propensity to navel-gaze in the shade of their privilege? He didn't know but he wanted urgently to find out.

He didn't, however, ask her about the perceived shortcomings of a certain section of people of Sonya's generation, the ones driven by possibly misplaced artistic aspirations and an inflated sense of self-worth, bankrolled by their parents. He held back from asking her about what she made of their tendency to internalize society and play their lives out on social media, the very irony he was trying to capture in his work. He wanted to ask her if art could only be borne out of hardship, if she had a novel inside of her, crying to be let out. He wanted to ask her if she grudged Sonya her education, her access to the best schools and colleges and the subsequent five-zeroed pay packet. Did she think she could have done better, made more of it all? He wanted desperately to ask her if Sonya's past lovers were taller, broader, more muscular. Were they intellectuals? Bankers? Doctors? Were they nicer to her, she to them?

'Didi,' he said, 'naam kya?'

'Radha,' she told him, and surveyed the strategic positioning of the laundry one last time before going in. He stayed a little longer, content to play observer to a world that was making no demands of him yet.

Back indoors, Sonya was awake, checking her emails on her Blackberry. She had avoided going in to work these past few days but today she had spreadsheets to pore over, meetings to sit through. Thomas watched her steel herself mentally for the onslaught of mediocrity, the unrelenting march of the mundane past the gates of her person. Someday, she had told him, she would quit her job to write her novel. To travel, to think, to breathe. Today though, today, she would grapple with colleagues and clients and taxi drivers and tea boys, smoke umpteen Marlboro Cloves, and lunch at her desk and write 140-character epitaphs for her younger self, ditties to what once was and could have been, just like every other day.

'Good morning,' she said. 'Stay for breakfast, no?'

'Where else would I go?'

'Are you getting bored of me?' she wanted to know.

'Not any more than usual,' he told her.

'That's funny,' she said, "'cause I can't stand the sight of you.'

'You disgust me,' he countered. 'I die a little every time I'm inside you.'

'I have to ask myself if you're alive at all when you're inside me.'

'Go easy,' said Thomas. 'You're going to scar me for life.'

'That's the plan,' she confided. 'The plan is to leave a lasting reminder.'

'I'm quite content just being another notch on your bedpost,' he said. 'I'll leave without a sound.'

'You couldn't if you tried,' she replied.

'I should hope not,' said Thomas, and kissed her.

Didi walked in without knocking. They pulled away from each other, too awake and too sober to not care. The women talked, and Sonya climbed off the bed, sheet wrapped around her, to inspect the morning's work. She took a round of the premises, her back exposed to Didi who followed mutely behind, and showed her out. Through the paper-thin walls, Thomas could hear Sonya opening the newspaper, humming to herself. He thought to himself that he was a lucky man, that they were all lucky in their own ways, even Didi. Then he told himself that was probably not true.

# 3

Thomas applied the finishing touches to his hair—a ruffle here, a pat there—and stood back to appreciate his handiwork. He wasn't balding like so many men his age but despite not having got it cut in a few years now, his hair had mysteriously stopped growing in length a couple of summers ago. Sonya buzzed behind him, redoing perfectly made beds and taking surreptitious peeks out the window, throwing a rhetorical question or two his way about the appropriateness of the playlist he had put together for the evening and the 'ice situation' (Should they order more? Should they separate the cubes so they wouldn't congeal and form one unhelpful, unbreakable, icy mass?), all the while easing herself into a little black dress that they had picked out together from a little boutique on Waterfield Road. He thought to himself that she was holding up better than he had expected.

He wondered how it was that something as basic as covering one's body, preserving one's dignity, took so much out of Sonya. Whether morning or night, for work or for leisure, the amount of accompanying physical activity that went into Sonya getting dressed was a thing of wonder. She wasn't uncomfortable in the nude like so many women he knew—they had certainly spent a lot of their time together without their clothes on—and he knew from the way she didn't suck her stomach in when they sat around playing Scrabble or arch her back while they made coffee and omelettes that it was not a lack of discomfort borne out of their familiarity, or history. She was comfortable like a child, like a Goldingesque creature. Sonya was in her element in the nude because the body in itself held no sexual implications for her. She was yet to discover shame.

It was a struggle for her to get dressed, and more so to dress appropriately, because it seemed an imposition to have to cover oneself up at all. So she delayed and deliberated, stayed liberated, till she was left with the tiniest of windows in which to execute the task. At which point, she would make it as multi-disciplinary a process as possible—reply to emails and call her mother and reread a favourite paragraph— juggling as many things as she could so that the tight embrace of her brassiere and the enforced intimacy of polyester trousers between her legs were just another minor inconvenience to be overcome on the way to work or the pub or the cinema. He would normally lie back and enjoy the show but today he felt just as nervous as he watched her answer the phone, putting it on speaker mode and tending to her eyelashes with a stick of Colossal Kajal.

Sonya and Thomas had spent a good part of the previous couple of days assuring each other that things would be fine, that they would be just fine. Lies had been told, illusions made to prevail. But that hadn't always been the case. Thomas had initially been vaguely enthusiastic at best about the whole idea. Sonya herself had broached it with caution. The circumstances were thus: Thomas and Sonya had been living together for just over three months. For much of this time, they had done what any two people newly in love would have done and shut the door on the world outside.

After the first couple of weeks spent exploring each other in the privacy of their home, they had set about exploring the neighbourhood. Sonya took great pains to explain the osmotic qualities of Bandra to Thomas, to point out the colonial cobbled streets that led them to St. Andrews Church and the graffitied tributes to India's first anti-hero that adorned their walls. Often, they had breakfast at The Bagel Shop and went for walks around the premium greenery of Pali Hill, settling down to share a smoke or read at the first convenient spot, Sonya sometimes checking in with work and sometimes deciding not to. They had cocktails for lunch and got drenched in the rain and made out in the 24/7. They bought a pair of potted petunias and smoked a joint outside Toto's and couldn't keep their hands to themselves except to tear into Ramu's piping hot dosas on Carter Road and thought they spotted Jackie Shroff in an open-top speeding past Bandstand. They scored some MD off a dreadlocked kid outside Bonobo's and danced to dubstep like they were into it and attended an exhibition at Pali Village Cafe that left them cold and never ventured outside Bandra, never went anywhere farther than a rickshaw ride away from home. They spent their days like they were on holiday, Sonya determined to play guide and Thomas happy to oblige. One delighted in the pure physical pleasure of the new, while the other rejoiced in the exorcism of the old, in the replacement of old memories with the recent. They didn't talk as much outdoors as they did at home.

They had also not managed to find time to immerse
Thomas into Sonya's real life. It was a thought that weighed
heavily on Sonya's mind every morning, but always avoided
causing any real damage. By luck or by design, something
would get in the way—an early sitting, a lunch meeting in
her part of town, something or the other she could always
manage to put off doing or do online or make do with a quick
appearance and head back home where Thomas would still
be asleep and she would slip in beside him and wake him as
though the world hadn't turned a bit while she was gone.
But that wouldn't be the case much longer. Sonya had been
assigned a new team, and they would be starting straightaway
on a monumental due diligence, the thought of which made
Sonya's heart weep.

She had got used to living the way they had been living,
finally getting to do the little things she had never had the
time for earlier. Suddenly, she could remember the crazed
days of working like they were only yesterday, the long train
rides across town and the cold panic at looming deadlines
and the countless con-calls and the endless meetings and
the distress sales of so many Sunday evenings. It made her
want to cry. She had only just started getting into it, and the
movie was already threatening to end. Not wanting to appear
foolish or dramatic by expressing her concerns to Thomas,
she arranged to meet Anjali for a drink one evening.

'I just can't get bored of this guy,' she laughed nervously
into her drink at Ivy. 'What's wrong with me, man?' Anjali
leaned back and looked her over, and said, 'You seem really
happy.'

Sonya liked the sound of that, and wondered again how
Thomas and Anjali would get along. She knew her friend had
tired of asking to be introduced, and had only given up on the

subject lately as a sort of retaliation. They had in fact stopped talking altogether, Sonya realized guiltily, and determined to catch up more with her friend's life as soon as she could figure out what to do with her own problems. 'Do you want to meet Thomas?' she asked.

They were already down a couple of bottles of Sauvignon Blanc when Thomas appeared, still in the shirt he had been wearing when she left him. It felt perfectly natural to lift her head to let him kiss her till she wondered about it a moment later, and thought she caught a look from the bartender as Thomas pulled up a chair. He had been trying to write, he said, and had lost track of time. He could really use a drink, he said, before noticing Anjali. He extended a hand, and shook hers warmly. She laughed and made a gurgling noise that set Sonya off too, and Thomas had the distinct feeling of being ambushed. Sonya seemed to notice and put a hand in his hair, and whispered, 'We're a little drunk.'

For the first time that night, Sonya noticed that Anjali's low-cut summer dress and peacock earrings set off the mango of her face like a frame ordered to size. As for her, she had simply thrown on one of Thomas's tee-shirts—an old green thing that had the Marlboro logo emblazoned across its chest in Thai—over a pair of elephant print chill pants she had picked up in Gokarna, and rounded off her ensemble with a pair of navy blue Cloggs, or as Anjali had once described them, 'the standard issue footwear of those who have given up on life.' Sonya smiled to herself and squeezed Anjali's arm in a sudden burst of affection for her childhood friend. She wanted desperately for Thomas to feel the same, and wondered if he could tell. Anjali duly spilled her drink, ordered another and left soon after, citing work and inebriety, much to Sonya's disappointment.

'I don't want you to judge her, ok?' said Sonya. 'She's a lightweight but she's Superwoman. I can't tell you the shit she's gotten me through; she's my oldest friend. I love this chick.'

Thomas appeared to have fixed his gaze on the group at the next table but he pressed her shoulder the way he knew she liked to be touched. He could have reached for her in the darkest darkness and still found her exactly where she ought to have been. How much more in tune, how synchronous, bodies were than minds. A meeting of the minds required a degree of kindness that he had been unaccustomed to giving or receiving for a long time now. Bodies were easier; bodies only needed bodily attention. Bodies spoke in picked-up affectations, and mastered rhythms, and clothed themselves in old lovers' hand-me-downs. There was nothing they could do with their bodies that hadn't already been imagined.

'I wasn't judging,' he said, 'but do I detect a spark there? Curiosity, maybe? A little girls' school hangover?'

Sonya scoffed. 'What's the matter with men, Thomas?' she asked. 'When did we start sexualizing everything? Why does everything have to go *into* something, fit nicely into little slots?' She looked at Thomas and laughed. 'Don't look so terror-struck, baby,' she said. 'Just making conversation. You know women can do that, right? Oh, and a pox on he who comes betwixt BFFs!'

They ordered another round, stayed a little longer, and headed for home on foot.

The air was abuzz with rumours of rain as they walked hand in hand. So much earth clung longingly to their feet with every step that she began to feel heavy and had to stop. 'You should get some beanbags for the flat,' said Thomas. She laughed. She looked again at the crude, hand-drawn advertisement on the wall behind her ('BEANBAGS,' proclaimed the writing, followed by a phone number) and said, 'You haven't noticed these ads before? They're not selling beanbags; it's street-speak for hookers. That, my friend, is the phone number of a certified, anything-goes, Bandra pimp.'

Thomas seemed unconvinced and prodded her forward.

'Have you ever been with a hooker?' asked Sonya as they proceeded homeward. 'Have you ever had to pay for it, Writer-man?'

'I've had my share of dry spells,' said Thomas, carefully, 'but I've always managed to stop just short of paying for it.'

They walked in silence for a bit, till they turned the corner towards Sonya's flat. 'Remember that NGO I told you I volunteer at?' said Sonya. 'They work with little girls. Daughters of sex workers. A lot of them missed school or were never enrolled in one till the organization picked them up. I help them make up at school with a little extra tutoring. It's almost maddening how positive those kids are, despite everything they've seen.'

Thomas seemed content to follow her up the stairs in silence. 'Anyway,' she said as they went in, 'I'm supposed to be putting together some flyers for them to raise funds at an event. Can you help?'

Sonya watched Thomas take a long gulp of water and distribute what was left in the bottle neatly between the two glasses of whisky he had laid out on the kitchen counter. As he offered her one and sipped from the other, Sonya wondered if she was imposing. This was the first time she had asked him to be involved in her life; it was the first time she had asked him for anything. 'I'm not nearly qualified to save the world,' he said and that should have been that but she thought she detected a touch of arrogance in his voice. It wasn't surprising in that Sonya already knew that Thomas functioned almost entirely on the back of a brittle but significant ego; she also thought that she had figured out a system to manoeuvre around it without crushing his spirit.

'It's just a couple of catchy headlines and some straightforward copy,' she persevered. 'I'll get somebody from our marketing team to slap on a couple of images. You won't believe what typing in 'poor happy Indian children' on Shutterstock will throw up. And you wouldn't be doing it for free. My firm is sponsoring the event, and I'll just be paying you what we would otherwise pay an ad agency. You said you were looking for some freelance work, right?'

Thomas nodded and mumbled something about finding the time as he lit up a cigarette. Sonya lowered herself onto the bed, balanced her glass on her stomach, and closed her eyes. She could feel the drink being lifted off her body as she slipped gratefully into sleep.

Watching her, Thomas wished he could think as clearly as Sonya, that he were less prone to abstractions and more— he searched for the right word—*capable*; capable of the nitty-gritty that made all the difference between a life lived and a life led. He wished he were in ownership of a thought process that led simply from A to B, and didn't go missing for a few days on a euphoric binge with E or a doomed romance with K. When Sonya decided to do something, she did it. No amount of rumination or digression or consequential ping pong could stand in her way. He had observed her like a scientist these past few weeks, run tests, made notes on her humanity. She clenched her fists when she wanted to make a point, he had noticed; her jaw would set in defiance, her upper lip curl down in a pronounced droop that made him want to kiss the clefts under it and drove him mad with desire. He wondered if she knew that he admired her almost as much he adored her. He wanted to tell her that her body wasn't always enough, that sometimes he wanted to kiss her indomitable spirit and make love to her mind. He decided instead to finish the rest of their drinks and try and come up with something clever to drum up resources for the progeny of the eternally persecuted.

Sonya woke him up the next morning in established fashion, smelling of last night and tasting of coffee. 'Thank you for the flyer,' she said. 'I've sent it to the designer.'

'I didn't mean to impose,' she added as Didi burst into view in the hallway, efficiently and unobtrusively going about her business. Thomas nodded at her as he followed Sonya into the kitchen for no real reason other than the ineffable joy of trailing in her wake. 'I've been thinking,' she said, 'there's actually a shitload of content-writing work we outsource to some agency or the other. A lot of it is just proof-checking, editing, drafting a couple of whitepapers here and there. I could just route them all through you. You'd have almost-steady work and I'd save the firm a lot of money. What do you think?'

Thomas tried to muffle his response in the nape of her neck, and, feeling her stiffen, knew she deserved better. 'I really appreciate what you're trying to do,' he said. 'I promise I'll think about it. Now what plans have we?'

Sonya was already laying the breakfast table when Thomas returned from his liquor run. 'We've got eggs, toast, and news,' she announced testily. Thomas took his seat, mentally resigning himself to whatever fresh hell lay in wait for him. 'So I texted Anjali last night, saying the two of you should hang out, etcetera,' Sonya started, 'and well, she invited a few more people and I invited a few more people, and now it's blown out of all proportion into a party.' Thomas dug into his toast, maintaining his trademark—if steadily growing uncomfortable—silence. 'The party will be here,' continued Sonya. 'This is where we usually throw parties, and it's been my turn for like, well, since you got here, really. But it will be a mess, you know? Everybody will just crash here, and somebody or the other will throw up somewhere, and ...'

Thomas didn't have the heart to look up, but he could tell he was giving her a hard time. He made up his mind.

'I'm sorry I've been old-manning you,' he said. 'Let's do this. Party sounds great.' Sonya clearly expected more reluctance and seemed for once to be at a loss for words. 'You want me to be there, yes?' he said, and she nodded. 'Was there something else?' he asked.

In that instant, Sonya knew what it was to be committed, caged, to be in an adult relationship; even if—as she would point out to Anjali later—she was the only one living a lifestyle resembling anything like that of an adult, as far as she could see. She was the one with the regular income, the flat, the one responsible for the bills, and lately, even the cigarettes and alcohol. So why did she feel so guilty?

'A friend of mine might be coming around later,' she said. 'Sudhi.'

Things were just getting interesting, thought Thomas. Nothing had changed in the few years he had been away; society and people and lovers and the loveless were all still fucking about in the same dirty petri dish. 'Your ex?' he asked.

'Yup,' she answered, 'he's all out of weed. You don't mind, do you?'

Thomas didn't have any reason to mind, at least not technically. He had no doubts about how Sonya and he felt about each other, and in any case, he had heard enough from

Sonya about Sudhi and their prolonged on-again, off-again relationship of five years to know that she had put it well and truly behind her.

They had met at some inter-collegiate event; they had met too early. They had applied to the same business schools after, applied for the same jobs and moved to Bombay with a blueprint for the rest of their lives only to fall out of love and grow bored of each other while they were still looking for a place to rent. They had continued to sleep together every now and again for a while, an arrangement born out of convenience more than anything else in this high-speed, high-maintenance city, till Sonya started seeing somebody else. That had been a year ago.

Watching Sonya now, Thomas found himself wondering if the two of them still remembered each other naked, if Sudhi could just close his eyes and summon images of them together for his personal enjoyment. He knew enough about the familiarity of the flesh to know it was all in the head, that one time was as many as any. But it was still a pregnant sort of predicament; one he felt certain he could learn from if he would only disengage. How contrarian, he thought, to be called upon to maintain status quo, to preserve and not to bring crashing down.

'Again,' he said, 'I don't mind stepping out and leaving you to it.' Sonya seemed to be considering this, and Thomas was thrown. What could he say?

'No,' she decided, 'I would like you to stay. I've already told him you'll be here. Besides, you do stay here, right? However temporarily? I haven't just been *imagining* this.'

It was a valid point, Thomas knew, but these weren't the circumstances in which he would have liked to discuss it. 'This is as real as I've had it,' he said cheerfully, 'but let's talk about your imagination another time.'

Sudhi turned out to be a harmless sort of mid-twenties, at least upon first impression. He was taller than Thomas, clearly more athletic, and donned one of those non-committal goatees his generation appeared hell-bent on adopting as its own—not quite tended to but not an afterthought either. Thomas would never understand cultivated carelessness; he truly belonged to the last great decade of real excess. Engineering degree, MBA, corporate job: Thomas thought he had Sudhi all figured out, especially when he walked in with about three litres of fizzy beverages to go with his bottle of bourbon. Thomas had just inserted two trays of salmon, freshly marinated in lime and olive oil, into Sonya's make-do grill when he announced himself, evidently at ease with the politics of the doorbell by virtue of not using it at all. To be fair, Sonya never actually locked her door when she was home. 'That smells nice,' were his first words. 'Makes me wish I wasn't allergic to fish.'

Sonya came rushing out of the shower with her hair in a towel and another around her body, muttering apologies. Sudhi leaned forward in an almost-hug, a gesture Sonya took a moment to reciprocate by which time he had already pulled back and pushed out a hand instead, all of which culminated in a weak jab at Sonya's stomach and a weaker pat on Sudhi's back. They laughed and Sonya promised to get dressed and be back in a *jiff*, a harmless abbreviation that caused Thomas more annoyance than it probably demanded. He poured the three of them drinks and passed one to Sudhi.

By the time they sat down to smoke, Thomas had already disassociated himself from the conversation. He would listen, he would imbibe, but in the manner of all old friends meeting each other after a while, Sonya and Sudhi didn't offer many talking points a third party could contribute to. The smoking

corner at India Bulls Centre had become a lot less fun since
Sonya started playing hooky from work, Sudhi informed them
with a playful nod at Thomas. Thomas knew that Sonya and
Sudhi had been recruited by the same consultancy straight from
B-school, but she had somehow failed to mention that they took
smoke breaks together. The famously talkative receptionist they
took great pains to avoid had taken to texting Sonya about her
marital woes, she offered in return. They laughed, exchanged
office/B-school (Thomas couldn't tell which) gossip.

Realizing he could safely switch off, Thomas contemplated
the loss of their exclusivity. He studied posture, compared
looks, tallied physical contact. He realized that his cock
was standing up in urgent acknowledgement of the scent
of Sonya's hair, still wet from the shower, and wondered
if it was having the same effect on Sudhi. It felt strange to
have another man in their home, to be restricted by his mere
presence from touching or fucking. He wondered if it would
be alright for Sonya and him to excuse themselves, lock the
door behind them, and indulge in a spot of love-making.
Probably not, he decided.

He wondered if his ardour wasn't—at least in part—
connected to some latent competitive spirit, the thrill of
coveting and conquering in plain sight. He hoped that not all
men thought of their women in such commoditized terms,
that Sonya wasn't sizing her lovers up as they sat side by
side, each a model of what the other might have been in a
radically different life, like characters created for a body-
swap movie. He concluded that this line of thinking was a
sort of information bias on his part, and that Sudhi was likely
neither as plain nor Thomas as different as Sonya had made
them out to be, probably out of compassion or infatuation or
both.

'So what do you do, Thomas?' asked Sudhi when Sonya nipped out to borrow rolling papers from the pothead next door.

Thomas had been dreading the question since Sonya started suggesting he meet her friends. He didn't want to embarrass her but neither did he want to give Sudhi the satisfaction of knowing that he was feigning ambition.

'Nothing,' he replied. 'You stay nearby?'

He used to, Sudhi said, only a couple of kilometres away. But he had to move because Sonya and he had been spending too much time together, he said with a wink, and 'feelings' were getting hurt. Whose feelings, he wouldn't tell, but the implication seemed to be that they were Sonya's. *Women*, he seemed to be saying. Women couldn't separate the physical from the emotional.

But now, he said, they had a 'healthy relationship', and he was staying in a swanky new flat that overlooked Wankhede Stadium. He had to skip a meal here and there to afford paying the rent, he confided modestly, but it was worth it for the address alone. Thomas had never heard anybody use the word 'swanky' to describe their own residence before.

'Odd career choice from our man here,' Sudhi said before taking a hit off the joint Sonya had just spun around to him. 'Never met a man who does *nothing*.'

Thomas had disliked Sudhi within a few seconds of meeting him, but he hadn't quite known why. It was the two-facedness, he now realized, the change in tone when Sonya was around.

'He's a writer,' said Sonya. 'He doesn't do *nothing*. He's published a novel, and now he's working on another one.'

Thomas didn't want Sonya to fight his battles but he didn't mind either; he only hoped she wasn't discomfited by the hollowness of her claim. If she wanted to maintain the fantasy of her lover as the creative crusader, that was fine by him though he wasn't about to help her along by embellishing it in any way.

'It's a dead art,' said Sudhi and rubbed his thumb and index finger together. 'There's no money in it, no? Writing won't pay the taxman.'

Sonya squeezed Thomas's hand but he continued to smoke in silence, and thought he detected a hint of hurt in Sonya's voice when she spoke next.

'He also works in advertising,' she said. 'He takes on freelance writing work.'

Sudhi nodded, inspected his Rolex with some elaboration and made to leave.

'We should do lunch,' he declared, standing up. 'My treat.'

'Barbeque Nation,' said Thomas. 'Friday.'

Sudhi bent his knees, bowed his head and brought his hands together in a Namaste that made Sonya cringe visibly. Thomas nodded and went back to a book he had started on the previous night as Sonya saw him out.

'I'm so sorry about Sudhi,' Sonya said when she returned. 'I told you he's a little … *square*.'

Thomas didn't reply. He didn't see why she should have to apologize for Sudhi; Sonya, uncharacteristically, mistook his stoicism for hurt. She pulled off her shirt, climbed on to his lap and kissed him.

'Let me make it up to you, okay?' she whispered. 'Why did you set up a lunch date with him for fuck's sake?'

'It's no big deal,' said Thomas and kissed her back. 'You heard the man. He wants to do lunch.'

He had unclasped her bra and was starting on one of her breasts when Sonya placed a hand on his mouth, leaned back, and said, 'Why does nothing matter to you, Thoma?'

Thomas unattached himself from Sonya and watched as she slowly worked herself into a reluctant temper.

'Why didn't you shut up that moron? He insulted your calling, your philosophy, your whole way of life. What's a bigger deal than that?'

He thought she sounded more guilty than angry, but he had to be sure.

'He was right, Sonya,' he said. 'Writing *is* a dead art. It doesn't pay the bills. And I certainly don't pay the taxman.'

Sonya climbed off Thomas and planted herself in front of the mirror. Thomas thought she winced a little; she certainly didn't appear happy to be looking at what she saw. She pulled on her shirt, patted back her hair and tied it loosely into a bun.

'I guess there's also the little matter of actually writing anything,' she said quietly.

Thomas stood up to touch her but she backed off. He put a hand under her chin to draw her face towards his but she brushed it away. He moved a couple of steps forward and backed her into the wall. Holding down both her hands, he tried to kiss her again and inched himself closer. It was an attempt at reassurance, he knew; whether he was offering or seeking, he wasn't sure. She relented for a moment, letting him kiss her, touch her, feel her, till she pushed him away again.

'You're hurting me,' she said, not entirely literally.

Thomas moved away and asked, still facing her, 'Are you ashamed of me, Sonya?'

A smile played on his lips that Sonya thought looked almost cruel, but only momentarily. Without perhaps realizing it, she filed the moment away in her head as footnote to some future calamity, some inevitable disappointment that could only be made sense of in the light of ... what? *Precedent*?

'Is that why you wanted me to take on all that writing work? So I'd have a job? '

Thomas, forever wading through myriad possible responses to any situation in his head, did not see it coming: Sonya burst into tears.

'I'm sorry,' she said. 'Is that how I made you feel? I'm so sorry. I was worried for you. Everybody at the party is going to be the same, Thoma, they're all going to want to know what you do, how much you make, where you live, the moment they meet you. The moment they meet *any*body. And I didn't want you to get hurt, I couldn't bear for you to be insulted.'

She stroked his face.

'Fuck that Anjali man, I'm just going to cancel this damn party.'

Thomas held her a moment, kissed her forehead and said, 'To paraphrase something you couldn't stop shouting only a couple of nights ago, I *am* a big boy, you know?'

Sonya laughed.

'The jokes are why I sleep with you Writer-man,' she said. 'Men don't know this, and we're not at liberty to tell, but women will take a good laugh over a big dick any day.'

By the time Friday afternoon pulled up, Thomas and Sonya had discovered a new rhythm, rolling up their sleeves

and working together with their backs to the wall like a couple
on a mission. They had spent the last few days picking out a
dress for her, stocking up on ice and mixers, making lists of
possible party disasters and how to deal with them.

People throwing up: Cover all furniture and carpeting
with old sheets.

Police raid: Unlikely.

Not enough people: Ask the pothead from next door and
his *firangi* flatmate to drop in with their friends.

Too many people: Nope, she had had this many people
over before and they were not, in fact, *too* many.

And so it went on, as they regularly assured each other
that it would all go off without a glitch. They worried for each
other—Sonya that Thomas would somehow be offended by her
friends, and Thomas that she would appear a bit of a fool to be
sleeping with this older man who clearly had nothing to offer—
and refused to acknowledge that these were real concerns. The
show would go on, and intoxicants consumed, fun had.

At Barbeque Nation, Thomas ordered the seafood platter
with a questioning glance at Sudhi, who gallantly waved
his indifference, while opting for white meat, and Sonya
announced that she would just help herself to a little of both.
Sudhi inquired if Thomas harboured any interest in the
English football league, and Thomas muttered something
about being out of touch. Whether he was referring to the
league table, or the sport, or the world at large, it wasn't
clear. Sonya busied herself checking messages in a WhatsApp
group conversation Sudhi had insisted she rejoin. The three of
them greeted the arrival of the dishes with a collective cheer.
Chairs were pulled back, forks polished and knives drawn,
and napkins unfolded ceremoniously across laps. It was time
to dine, and dine in silence, that last great dance of civility.

Sonya noticed it first, though she kept her thoughts to herself initially. Sudhi's cheeks and neck had turned a shade of red, and were quickly turning darker. Sonya thought she detected a slight inflammation under his jaw.

'This is spicier than I was expecting,' said Sudhi as he gestured to the waiter for more water. 'Have you been eating the seafood?' asked Sonya.

'No, you know I'm allergic to seafood,' he said and turned to Thomas. 'You'll love this story. Once in B-school, Sonya and I were so wasted after a night out—it was graduation night, I think, for my immediate seniors—anyway, I was just ridiculously hungry, and I thought: what harm can a piece of fish pickle do?'

He stopped to take a swig of water, setting the glass down only after draining it completely. His eyes were puffy now, sweat dripping from every pore in his face.

'Quite a lot, as it turned out,' he continued before clutching his throat, clawing at it as though at a fence or a postbox.

'Call the waiter,' said Sonya as she helped him unbutton his shirt.

The waiter was kind enough to fetch him a strip of Allegra from the pharmacy nearby and Thomas and Sonya helped him into a cab. The waiter also admitted that during busy hours, it was not unusual to use the same grill to prepare all their dishes, including fish, meat and vegetables, and that Sudhi's was a very unfortunate allergy indeed.

Sonya was still reeling from his callousness, raving that she would take Barbeque Nation to court, when they got home. Thomas offered to roll a joint while she changed, and left her to steam. When he returned, Sonya was already calmer, more collected.

'Baby,' she said after taking a couple of drags and passing the joint back to him, 'I'm going to ask you something, and I apologize in advance if I'm crossing a line.'

Thomas held her gaze, and nodded.

'I was going to leave a nasty review on Barbeque Nation's Zomato page but their page just showed up from an earlier search a few days ago,' she paused, and looked at him carefully. 'I haven't looked them up in ages and you're the only other person who uses my laptop.'

She paused again. She had the slightly glazed look of someone realizing an uncomfortable truth and not wanting to deal with it.

'There's a very pissed off comment from somebody right at the top of the section complaining about the same thing— the common grill system and how it's inconsiderate and unprofessional.'

She was tiring. She looked to Thomas for help but his eyes were set in stone.

'You want me to say it,' she said quietly.

'Are you accusing me of something?' he asked.

Sonya didn't reply straightaway.

'You said you were above this,' she said. 'You *said* you didn't have a problem with us hanging out.'

It was Thomas's turn to reflect. He stubbed the joint in a whiskey carton-turned-ashtray with some ceremony and said, 'I don't have a problem with you hanging out.' He lit a cigarette. 'I do have a problem however with you pretending to anybody that I have a job.'

Sonya's head was spinning. Was that an admission of guilt? Even if he had known about the irate diner on Zomato, she thought, he couldn't have possibly known with any certainty that things would pan out the way they had.

'Because having a job is such a terrible thing for an adult, right?' she lashed out, more angry at herself for creating excuses for him than anything else. 'It's such a damn shame to be able to pay for your own meals, yes?'

Thomas shrugged.

'*If* someone's complained about the service before,' he said, 'I didn't know about it. I may have looked them up online but I've also looked up every other eating place in Bandra because you insist on trying a new place every day. But it's good to know that's how you feel.'

And just like that, the shoe was on the other foot.

Thomas and Sonya were still not talking, except about the most practical of concerns—the appropriateness of the playlist he had put together for the party, or the 'ice situation' (Should they order more? Should they separate the cubes so they wouldn't congeal and form one unhelpful unbreakable icy mass?)—when Sudhi phoned to inform them that the inflammation had all but gone, that he had been lucky not to have consumed more of the poison. Sonya made relieved noises and switched her phone off speaker mode and put it to her ear, and made him promise to be at her party later that night.

'Yes, you can wear a scarf around your neck,' Thomas heard her say, 'or a turtleneck or a plastic bag or whatever makes you comfortable. Just come.'

Her eyes met Thomas's in the mirror and broke out into a smile, and before they knew it she had ended the call with a hurried goodbye and they were lying on their backs on the bed, laughing helplessly.

'God, we're terrible people,' she said and let him kiss her. 'I'm sorry about what I said earlier. Let's just forget this ever happened, please?'

**4**

# The Girlfriend Chronicles 2: The Breakfast of Champions

No man likes getting caught tiptoeing across a girl's living room at seven in the morning. It's an exercise in great inner turmoil, a mandatory walk of shame that must be undertaken before your induction into some sort of one-night-stand hall of fame. The surreptitious sweep of her bedroom door as it closes shut behind you; those tentative, Huxley-esque steps through domestic purgatory, hoping you don't step on her cat or—God forbid—the remote control on your way to the Other Side; and finally, finally, the operatic symphony of upper floor  flush tanks flushing and air conditioners air-conditioning seeping in through the ceiling as you pause (and all men pause at this point) in the hallway, safely outside her apartment. Of course, you tend to look back at the moment with some degree of pride if the woman whose apartment you're attempting to sneak out of isn't your girlfriend of several months.

Fatboy, still sprawled out on the couch as we had left him the previous night, caught me in mid-tiptoe.

'Dude,' he says, 'crazy night last night, huh? Good times.'

'SShhhh!' I tell him and mime my way closer.

'Where's Girlfriend?' he wants to know. 'I said I'd make breakfast.'

I gesture wildly for silence as I collect his jeans and shoes, roll them into a ball and deposit them on his lap.

'Let's go,' I whisper, '*now.*'

'What, *why?*' And then he panics. 'Fuck, did you do some weird shit last night? Is Girlfriend hanging from the ceiling with a crown of thorns around her head? I'll never understand your Jesus fetish.'

'Worse,' I say, 'she's got the Grumps.'

'The 'Grumps'?' he asks. 'What's that, like a that-time-of-the-month scenario? Water turning to wine?'

'Ok, *one*, you're going to hell,' I say, 'and secondly, no. It's her time of the *day.*'

'Oh come on,' he dismisses the notion, 'she's not a morning person; big deal.'

'SSSSSHHHHHHH!!' I shush, but I know the damage has already been done.

'Listen,' I say and cock my ear bedroom-wards for signs of danger, 'don't ever use that word around here.'

'What, "morning"?' he says. 'Seriously, you're such a drama quee ...'

The room changes before he can even complete the cliché. The smoke and the flatulence and the waft of leftover Peking Duck that permeated the atmosphere till moments ago have all made way for a terrifying, uncharacteristic wintry cold. There is a draft in the room, originating from under her bedroom door as far as I can tell. There are sounds of unrest, of bedsheets being flung in frustration, of thunder making its way up Girlfriend's body and quickly gaining momentum.

I look Fatboy in the eye and tell him I'm sorry I snogged Sara Markose in tenth grade.

'I knew you were into her,' I say. 'That was unsavoury of me.'

The draft has become a force of nature; there are icicles on top of the television, hail stones raining down from the ceiling. Her bedroom door appears to be vibrating on its hinges, threatening to be blown away. 'SAVE YOURSELF, FATBOY!' I scream as I jump over the couch and rush to her door as fast as I can. Holding on to the door knob with all my strength, I fumble around in my pockets for the key. Fatboy, equally scared but just as loyal, jams a chair under the knob. I find the key, lock the door and collapse on the floor, exhausted. 'Thanks bro,' I say. 'You're a good friend. Now, *go.*'

Girlfriend has left the bed. We can hear her coming. Her footsteps echo down the hall and across children's parks and hospitals around Bombay, sending pigeons and Catholic nuns into defeatist rapture. Their wails (and coo-roo-ctoo-coos) of despair come boomeranging back to meet her footsteps, through the open window and into the living room, but timidly stopping short at her door, bouncing off her Warhol-tinted works of art like tweens at a #Belieber tweet-off.

'This is the end,' I say as the room turns on its side. The chair Fatboy had jammed under the door hurtles forward and catches him in the jaw, sending him reeling. 'FAAATBOOOY!' I scream as I push out a leg for him to grab on to, my hands still firmly wrapped around the door knob. 'There must be something we can do,' he sobs. 'Have you tried garlic? Or a stake through the heart?' I weep as I remember attempts past—padlocks and chainsaws and sugar donuts—all fated to failure. And pain. *Oh*, the pain.

'Go,' I say, 'just go.'

'I can't, bro,' he tells me. 'I'm not leaving you behind.'

There is a sarcastic knock on the door, almost a taunt, and a body crashes against it with a force that sends me flying across the room. 'Run, Fatboy,' I yell. 'I didn't just kiss Sara Markose. I got some cheeky sideboob action too.' 'You BASTARD,' he says and kicks me on his way out.

When I come to, it's midday-bright. I can hear Girlfriend in the bedroom, going about her business, humming an old song. 'Girlfriend,' I call out, 'baby, are you okay?'

'Yes,' she shouts back, 'open the door.' I find a *Cosmo* on the floor and slip it under her door, the key pressed between an article on what men want and an infographic on the dangers of pandering to their needs. I take my spot on the couch, and await judgment.

'Is Fatboy gone?' asks Girlfriend as she steps out, all pinstriped and corporate-sexy and ready for work.

'Yes,' I say, 'and I don't feel good about this at all.'

'Oh don't be a baby,' says Girlfriend, and ruffles my hair. 'You know this was the only way. He can't boil an egg to save his life.'

---

Tags: Bombay, fatboy, fetish, girlfriend, music recco, one night stand, sideboob, The Grumps, what would jesus do?

---

# 5

Thomas and Sonya needn't have worried about the party. As it turned out, Thomas was blessed with a natural ability to own the stage if one was presented to him. Though Sonya had snorted derisively at his light-hearted ribbing in the preceding days that the party was really intended as a sort of 'grand unveiling' of the Boyfriend, an unveiling was certainly what the audience had come expecting.

Anjali was the first to arrive and immediately offered to take over DJ-ing responsibilities to which Thomas said no. The rest of them came in groups of twos and threes, hugging Sonya hello and handing her their spoils—a few bottles of Teachers, a couple of crates of beer, some hash, flowers, and a goldfish in a plastic bag that Sonya handed back straightaway (she was still recovering from the sight of their goldfish floating belly-up in its bowl a few days ago), after which they sort of paused and looked around in expectation.

'So?' some would say, still holding Sonya, leaning back to take all of her in.

'He just writes this ... *blog* ... for you?' asked another, one of the girls from HR.

Sonya rolled her eyes at Anjali.

'The whole office reads it!' she laughed.

Thomas had set up stall behind the music station, a beer in hand and a cigarette tucked behind his ear. He had placed the last of the MD on the tip of his tongue a little before the guests started arriving, and he was slowly getting there. He had only wanted to take the edge off a little, to relax, but the MD was starting to get under his skin in the heat of the cramped living room. He felt incandescent, invincible. Or was it the amphetamine that was sending the temperature soaring? Either way, he wasn't ready for conversation just yet and the music station was the least disruptive way to put some distance between him and Sonya's friends.

It worked like a charm. Sonya, busy attending to the stream of people in the kitchen, sent the seen-to guests his way, Anjali in tow. Thomas gestured politely or nodded at every new arrival before turning to busy himself with the speakers or the computer or Sonya's ipod. The message was clear: he was aware of their presence and he would join them as soon as he had attended to whatever musical emergency he was in the midst of resolving. Drinks were poured, glasses clinked, snacks passed around, as his audience pulled up chairs or leaned against the wall in loosely defined cliques in collective expectation. Thomas stood framed by the rotating red lights that Sonya and he had mounted on the wall behind him the previous night, his hair untied and hanging low below his shoulders.

The rotating lights had been a gift from her Secret Santa at the office Christmas party the previous year. Sonya had been worried that it was a little juvenile—that they were 'one

Pink Floyd song away from college hostel territory'—but the lights flitted fittingly enough around Thomas's head. Like an ironically accessorized hipster's halo, thought Sonya, before worrying that the irony would be lost on most of the people in attendance.

Observing him out of the corner of her eye from her spot by the door, she couldn't help noticing that she had done well for both of them, that Thomas had visibly improved in health and cheer in the time they had spent together. His cough persisted and his frame was still wiry but his shoulders didn't slump as much anymore, apparently liberated from the weight of having to fend for himself, of operating on survival mode, and from certain angles, she thought she detected the slightest bump of a paunch under his white shirt. The shirt suited him, as did the black denims he had on, both of which he had casually dropped into her cart at the billing line at Shoppers Stop a few days ago. He had arranged for some money to be transferred to him, he explained later; it was just taking longer than he had expected. She hadn't minded; she just wished the jeans were a little less tightly tapered. Maybe, she mused now, Thoma was going for less irony than she gave him credit for.

Sudhi was the last to arrive, a lumpy scarf draped around his neck as promised, and Thomas decided he couldn't put off social obligations any longer. He turned the volume up a notch, queued up *Ankytrixx* on Soundcloud, and valiantly made his way out of his little cocoon. Sonya, by his side in a flash, guided him around the guests, feeding him names and other assorted tidbits of information as she helped him work the room. He was attentive and interested, and Sonya was sharp enough to prise him away from these introductions before the lull set in.

In any case, most of the guests were enthusiastic, if indiscriminate, conversationalists and Thomas was treated to a hodgepodge of information he found genuinely compelling. A girl was convinced a stray dog she had taken in recently was in fact a cat and wanted him to see for himself. He looked at a picture she had of the dog-cat on her phone, and to his amazement, it really was a tough call. There was a lot of talk about air miles, enough air miles to travel the world. Two guys told him about how they had never been fans of Angry Birds, and how, despite which, they were hooked on the Star Wars version. The real achievement was that it wasn't just Angry Birds with a Star Wars skin, said one of them. Yes, agreed the other. 'See, all the birds have character-specific moves.'

Some of the guests wanted to know how Thomas and Sonya had met; a lot of people inquired about the flat and how much Sonya paid for it. A big group discussed the trending topic of the hour: 'The Torso', possibly one of Bollywood's most popular actors ever, had been found heartbroken at the scene of a murder, that of an ex-girlfriend of his nonetheless. A neighbour had heard a gunshot and called in the police, explained the girl who had introduced the topic to Sonya and Thomas, but the cops had been unable to find a murder weapon at the site or gunshot residue on the Torso's hands.

Speculations abounded about the Torso's involvement in the crime though his lawyers had whisked him away on anticipatory bail within minutes of him arriving at the police station; the internet was abuzz with rumours of his links with the underworld. But, added the girl charitably, which Bollywood actor could afford not to be connected with the mafia these days? Thomas nodded as Sonya gently guided the girl by her elbow to the window, through which the Torso peered back at her from the hoarding for *Missed Call*.

Sonya had attended the same business school as some of the guests, Thomas found out, and worked in the same building as many of the others. A few of the guests had brought along lovers or dates, most of whom, from what Thomas gathered, had also gone to the same schools or worked in competing consultancies or banks, like the trader who constantly checked stocks on his phone and intermittently expressed interest in what his date—also a trader, also on the phone just as often— had to say about the state of her portfolio.

Thomas, who had never held down a regular job for very long, mused that the office had become the new mating arena, a natural turn of events given the number of hours these people spent at work. Even the odd rebel appeared regimental in their non-conformity, like the kurti-clad girl with the buzzcut and numerous piercings on both ears who had walked out on her MBA in her last semester to pursue a PhD at Tata Institute of Social Sciences and had much to say about male privilege and the need for gender equality. She had founded the NGO that Sonya volunteered with and was impressed with the quick *turnaround* on the promotional literature. She wanted to *pencil in* a lunch meeting with Thomas to discuss future funding activities. Everybody at the party—with the honourable exception of Thomas—was on the move, was going somewhere, even when sprawled out on Sonya's couch. Nobody went to lunch just to eat.

Thomas knew of course that this was a myopic view of a group of people who seemed inherently decent and well-intentioned, that his observations were coloured by his own positioning of choice as the outlier. He suspected the MD had something to do with it as well, and reminded himself periodically to keep an open mind. Conversation and propriety naturally took on a less inhibited ebb and flow as the alcohol level peaked, and Thomas watched fondly as Sonya dragged people on to the space they had cleared in the middle of the room to dance.

She was the life and soul of the party in a way he could never be, her absence a tangible presence the moment she left the room for a refill or to check on something or the other. Somebody shifted musical gears to Bollywood, and the stentorian Gender General proclaimed the possibilities of the *item number* as a subversive tool 'when done right', of the empowering lyricism of *Sheila Ki Jawaani*. Thomas apologized and asked her to remind him of her name again, and was amused to learn that he had heard right the first time, that she had named the NGO after herself. On his suggestion, she followed him to the terrace for some air.

They sat under the water tank, by the potted petunias, and were joined by Sudhi and Anjali just as Thomas had finished rolling a joint.

'Aah the feminists of the world unite!' said Sudhi as he sat down. 'Our man here is the solution. Did you know that, *comrade*?'

Anjali giggled and helped him down.

'That rhymed,' she said by way of explanation.

The Gender General took a hit and passed her the joint.

'There are similarities between communism and feminism,' she said, 'but they're not—'

Sudhi cut her off.

'Oh spare me the rhetoric,' he said. 'Stay-at-home dads and women who bring home the bread. That's the vision, isn't it?'

He nodded at Thomas.

'This is your man.'

Anjali mumbled something to him about Sudhi mixing alcohol with his antibiotics and Thomas smiled at her to tell her it was alright.

'Did you know I asked Sonya to marry me?' he said. 'She agreed, we moved to Bombay and then she just … lost interest.'

This was news to Thomas.

'Great, *great* girl,' Sudhi continued, 'but can*not* stand the normal. Even in college, you always got the feeling she might run away any minute, to the nearest junkie conclave. The fucked-up and the freaks, that was always her thing.'

Thomas offered him some water and told him that he had probably had enough drinks for one night.

'Who made you the sobriety-police?' Sudhi countered, but his tone betrayed too much resignation to be threatening. Ashamed, he struggled up only to sit down again as Sonya appeared at the door. Sonya was in high spirits but immediately sobered up even as she detected the slightest hint of tension in the air.

'What's happening, people people?' she asked and helped herself on to the floor next to Thomas. 'I mean: *party* people,' she corrected herself.

'Oh, Sudhi was just telling us how Thomas is the poster boy for feminism,' said the Gender General, 'because he likes to *cook*.'

Thomas placed his hand on the small of Sonya's back to reassure her. Sonya didn't seem to notice.

'Not that shit again man,' said Sonya. 'Anybody who believes in the equality of the sexes, who doesn't expect women to give up their jobs after they have a baby and stay home and play mommy is a feminist.' She paused pointedly. 'That list may or may not include Thomas.'

Thomas wondered about this as the conversation changed direction.

'Isn't the idea of a husband too *establishment* for you?' piped up Sudhi. 'Why don't we all just live in a big collective, the gays and the transsexuals and the criminals and the unemployed? Let's all just screw who we want to and not pay taxes and grow pot in fish tanks and not worry about where our next meal comes from.'

The Gender General laughed.

'The point is,' she said, 'that if that's what you choose to do, you should have the freedom to make that choice.'

Anjali declared that she was going inside and stood up.

'You're a strange man, Thomas,' said the Gender General as they all made their way back in. 'I admire your Zen.'

Thomas thought she cupped his behind but he couldn't be sure.

Inside, the party hadn't abated but it was winding down. A good number of the guests had already taken leave. A couple of people Thomas didn't remember meeting danced half-heartedly in the centre of the room. The trader duo kissed copiously on the couch, next to the quiet Bihari boy with the accountant's haircut. Thomas went to the bedroom to fetch the futon he had rolled up and put away under Sonya's desk earlier in the evening. He shook awake one of the members of the group who had taken up possession of their bed and gently reminded them that the bedroom was off-limits. Somebody muttered something along the lines of that *never* having been the case earlier—meaning Before Thomas—which he chose to ignore. He switched on all the lights instead, turned off the air-conditioning, and made his way back to the hall. The MD was slowly wearing off and he wanted desperately to listen to something less aggressive than Bollywood.

The trader duo were on the dance floor now, as were Sonya, Sudhi, and Anjali. The Gender General and the accountant occupied the polar ends of the couch and he eased himself down between them. The three of them watched in silence as Sudhi kept inserting himself between Sonya and Anjali. The two childhood friends appeared to be performing some sort of *dhappankoothu*, presumably an in-joke from their college days. It wasn't particularly graceful but they were laughing and clearly having a good time.

'Notice anything?' asked the Gender General.

'Nothing I'll file away for the wank-bank,' said Thomas. The Gender General laughed and slapped his thigh.

'You boys and your toys,' she said and ran a hand over her closely trimmed hair.

Thomas wondered if he would like the feel of scalp against his face as much as he liked burying his face in Sonya's hair after they climaxed.

'See how Sonya always lets Anjali take the lead?' said the Gender General. 'They break formation every five seconds, do a little twist, and, see? *There*! It's an opportunity to change tack, to try something different but Anjali always ends up in the male role.'

Thomas thought she was over-theorizing but asked her what she thought it meant instead. He wanted to listen, to soak in.

'She's less of a rebel than Sudhi thinks she is,' the Gender General went on. 'She likes to play by the rules she's set for herself. No wiggle room there.' The song ended and Anjali made for the loo before the next one began. 'But god she's beautiful,' the Gender General added.

Sonya smiled at Thomas and blew him a kiss before steadying herself on the back of a chair. She seemed about to come over when Sudhi grabbed her arm.

'One more dance,' he shouted as Sonya made apologetic eyes at Thomas.

Sudhi's scarf had been replaced by a *dupatta* slung loosely around his neck. Every now and again, he would take hold of either end of the *dupatta*, arms wide apart, and perform a sort of Bollywood version of the limbo under an invisible bar. Thomas went back to wondering what the Gender General had in mind and bummed a cigarette off the sleeping accountant. He wasn't going to intervene unless Sonya wanted him to.

Anjali returned and announced that she was going home but Sonya wasn't ready to renounce her dancing shoes just yet. The three of them reverted to their earlier formation, and Thomas turned his attention to the Gender General.

'About what you were saying earlier,' he said. 'Maybe Sonya prefers playing the woman. We're all playing something or someone, aren't we? Maybe she's just exercising her *choice*.'

The Gender General picked up on the reference and smiled.

'There's no shame in being a woman, you know,' he added, and wondered if he had pushed it too far.

'That's your thing, is it?' she shot back. 'Flowing tresses and little black dresses?'

Their eyes met. It was the first time Thomas had held her gaze since they met.

'It's one of them,' he said, and backed down. He had been down this road before, but he didn't know if he could do it to Sonya. The General watched as he walked over to Sonya, whispered something in Sonya's ear and ambled over to the music station.

The group settled down to smoke a joint and call it a night.
Sonya squeezed herself between Thomas and the General, and
inquired if somebody would like to finish her drink. Sudhi
and Anjali dragged the futon over to face the couch.

'So what's your deal man?' the General asked Sudhi.
'You sleep with someone once and you own them forever
*kya*? Permanent hand-roaming rights?'

Sonya shifted uncomfortably.

'Just come out of the closet already,' said Sudhi.

The General laughed.

'He was just dancing,' warned Sonya.

'I know you were, sweetie,' the General replied.

Sudhi smirked.

'Wake up that *chootiya*,' he nodded in the direction of the
accountant, 'and let's all go home. I'm calling a cab. We're all
SoBo, yeah?'

Anjali nodded in the affirmative.

'*SoBo* is South Bombay,' she smiled at Thomas.

Sonya told the General that she could crash on the
couch and take the train to Andheri with her in the morning.
Thomas and she would take the futon. She had been meaning
to visit the girls anyway, she said; didn't they have exams
coming up?

After the SoBo gang left, Thomas asked Sonya and the
General if they minded giving him company while he had
another beer. The General offered to roll a joint. She said she was
'ambivalent' when Thomas inquired about musical preferences.
Relieved, and a little amused by her turn of phrase, he put on
one of his favourite *after* albums, 'Fever' by *Sleepy Sun*.

He hadn't realized she stayed with the girls her NGO had
taken in, Thomas told the General as Sonya started putting
away bottles and disposable plates and emptying ashtrays

into a plastic bag. 'I've rented two apartments in the same building,' she explained. 'Three of the girls stay with me, the others in the other flat.' Thomas stood up to help Sonya but she waved him away. 'I have a *system*,' she said. He opened a beer.

'You should visit sometime,' the General continued, 'see what life's like beyond the 'burbs.' Thomas was new to Bombay's residential politics. 'Do you have a chip on your shoulder about everything?' he smiled. 'I've also got a tattoo on my shoulder,' she said and placed the joint between her lips, 'but that doesn't stop me from having an opinion either.'

As it turned out, Sonya really did have a system. Pizza cartons doubled up as trash containers, beer bottles were collected eight at a time, and within minutes, the hall had almost returned to normal. Except for the smoke in the air which she addressed by opening the windows, and promptly lowered the music. Didi would see to the details in the morning. Sonya washed up and pecked Thomas on the cheek.

'You weren't weirded out tonight, were you?' she asked when the General left the room. He kissed her, suddenly filled with the need to compensate, to make up for crimes considered.

'At least Sudhi got one thing right,' announced the General when she came back and took in the scene. Sonya and Thomas parted in mock modesty.

'God you're obsessed with him,' said Sonya.

The General ignored the barb. 'Assuming we're all for equality and what not,' she said and looked at Thomas, 'it seems pretty unfair that there's three of us left in the room but one of us will go to bed alone.'

He had almost believed Sudhi about the coming-out thing, said Thomas, and Sonya elbowed him. 'We're all just bodies, sweetie,' said the General, and caressed Sonya's head. Sonya pulled at her hand and asked her to sit. The General turned away, desolate. 'God, I'm sorry,' she said. 'Look at us, you guys: the man, the beauty, and the butch. Only a guy could have written this novel.'

# 6

Sonya's first full day back at work was educational, to say the least. The big team meeting that was supposed to set the agenda for the next few months had been postponed. Thomas was the topic of conversation everywhere she went. Whether gathered around the coffee machine or bent over the sink in the washroom in front of the mirror, her colleagues, male and female alike, greeted her with expressions of interest and declarations of approval. Wherever she turned, they offered her pieces of information, tidbits and anecdotes, that Thomas had regaled them with at the party. Stories: some of which she knew to be false outright, and others she suspected of having been spun in desperation or made up out of compulsion.

One of her colleagues, Vivek from M&A, told Sonya about the time when Thomas, under a month-long spell of meditation during his time at a Buddhist monastery in Dharamkot, had managed to summon up crystal clear memories of his childhood, going as far back as when he was three months old. He had recommended the experience so highly that Vivek was considering making a trip there before the end of the quarter.

Thomas had told Susan from Communications that he was partially blind in one eye from dropping LSD in it many years ago, and Tamanna from the accountancy firm next door that he once dated a quantum physicist who had discovered definitive evidence of life after death and now practiced Shamanism.

They were all fantasies, and they couldn't be disproved because they had happened to Thomas and not to Vivek or Susan or Tamanna. They shied away from cross-questioning him like they would one of their own because to the untrained eye, Thomas's was a life spent in pursuit of his *passion* and this awed and frightened them in equal measure.

It was a little like when she would lie in his arms and ask him to tell her a story, Sonya thought, and without missing a beat, Thomas would cook up a cock-and-bull story using whatever resources were at his disposal at the moment. Like the time he said he had made such a huge loss in a poker game on a cruise in Goa that the only solution was to jump ship and swim to shore. But Sonya knew they were stories, that they were meant to be disbelieved almost as much as they were meant to entertain. That they could affect so profoundly a group of professionals and individuals with what was quite possibly a higher average IQ than most both surprised and amused her.

Sonya didn't mind all the fuss till they started asking her *about* him. She side-stepped their questions at first, but as the day wore on she steadily grew tired of making up excuses to avoid answering them. If Sonya appeared secretive—even guilty—in her dealings with All Things Thomas, it was because she knew so little about him herself. She didn't consider him a dirty little secret, or herself a victim, but it was true she didn't possess the kind of knowledge about Thomas's past that most of her friends would consider mandatory in a *healthy* relationship. She didn't know, for instance, where he went to school, or how many women had broken his heart before she would (and she knew she would), or just what he had been doing all these years since his last book or how he had managed to survive without a job or regular income. But she didn't know not because he was unwilling to volunteer information, but because neither of them could differentiate truth from fantasy, fact from fiction, in all the data he spewed.

Sonya didn't consider this to be naiveté on her part; if anything, it was the consequence of being the owner of an accepting, accommodating, big fucking heart. She may not have known much about Thomas, but she knew what she needed to know about them: they were two compatible adults—for as long as it might last—in an exclusive, loyal, symbiotic relationship. What she didn't know about Thomas—the history, the *backstory*; stuff he didn't know or demand to know about her either—was the excessive detail, the baggage, that soured most relationships.

The decision, on Thomas's part, to *not know*, was not a conscious one. It had happened one afternoon when they were still young and new, still a mixture of nervousness and giddy contentment in each other's presence, still waiting for the wind that would manipulate their sails in whatever deliciously unpredictable direction it cared to take. After the successful culmination of a particularly deviant bout of love-making, Thomas—not the most adept practitioner of the art of self-preservation at the best of times—wondered aloud what most men wonder about after sex so diabolical: 'Where did you learn that?'

Sonya, usually so measured in her post-coital chitchat, so considerate in her honesty, had a momentary lapse of concentration. Looking up at the man who had just brought her off, and magnificently, a second time in under an hour, this manchild who talked the big talk and clung to her like an infant to bosom during the frequent nightmares he insisted she not wake him up from, she thought: maybe she'd finally met a man who could *take it*.

'Do you really want to know?' she asked.

He didn't. No wait, he did. He wasn't sure. No, he *definitely* didn't. So Sonya, without judgment or disappointment, merely chalked it up to Being A Man, and made a mental note never to put him in that position again.

Thomas, like many writers unable to write anymore, lied compulsively, and instinctively. So desperate was he for the next big idea, the next grand inspiration, that he was in many ways his own greatest experiment—the quintessential mad scientist, letting his work seep into his life and his life bleed into his lies. Every conversation, every new acquaintance, was an opportunity to try out a potential premise, a situation, a twist. He was Trial, *and* Error. He made up such fantastical answers to the most casual of inquiries, and detailed them so convincingly (or maybe it was the abundance of details that made him so convincing), that he usually ended up believing his own fictions too, living them out, retrospectively sometimes, and sometimes simultaneously as they came tumbling out of his mouth. Over the years, he had shed so many skins, put to bed so many affectations and resurrected others, and conjured up new ones, that in the process he had created a beast so magnificent, a monster so riddled with weaknesses, that it excited and infuriated him in equal measure. For if it be true that writers, unlike the common fibber, are granted a little creative licence even in their facts and realities, it is just as true that there can be no greater tragedy for a writer than to be his own greatest creation.

If Sonya understood his proclivities more than most—certainly more than any of the other women Thomas had been with—revelled in them even, she also took the fun out of them. She neither called him on his bullshit nor encouraged it. But she also detached herself from it, watched as though from afar or from up above, as if the few inches between their bodies were the greatest distance on earth as they lay together, one pontificating, spinning webs of deceit, the other looking right through his lies and into their core. She may as well have poked holes, or held a flame to the many layers of silvery gauze that—to the discerning ear—barely held the story of his life together.

For what joy is it to tell someone a story they may very well have heard before, to have one's tales of bravado and damage responded to not with incredulity or sympathy but patience? He couldn't keep adding to his persona, his ego, if it didn't drive her to madness, to sadness and fury and excess. She seemed to think of his dishonesty as a quirk (Not even an occupational hazard, a *quirk*!), a phase, something he would outgrow. How condescended he felt, how impotent, for the story of his life to be met not with derision or desire but kindness!

Sonya was already a couple of drinks down when the General called to ask if they could meet. Sonya had asked Sudhi to join her for a drink after work on the assumption that he was the least likely of her friends to bring up Thomas in conversation but she had quickly been proven wrong. At least he hadn't wanted more information, content instead to launch into a diatribe about the entitlement of what he called 'creative types'. Who paid for the roads and the railway and the nation's *welfare*, he wanted to know; what purpose did art serve on its own other than to justify more couch-philosophizing?

Sonya gulped down her first whisky and sipped morosely on her second as Sudhi expounded on his theory that *they* were all taking advantage of people like Sudhi and Sonya, the hard working, tax-paying core of the economy.

'They claim to be revolutionaries but they think they can start revolutions from their beds,' he fumed as he accessorized the last few words with air quotes.

Sonya smiled at the thought of Thomas referencing *Oasis* in any context let alone in the formulation of a life philosophy, or indeed of starting a revolution of any sort. By the time the General made her way through the throng of lawyers and bankers and wanton 'consultants' that populated F Bar on any given weekday evening, Sonya wanted to scream.

'Oh yes, you're such an exploited lot,' said the General in the sardonic tone she reserved exclusively for Sudhi after he had given her a gist of his misgivings, 'what with your five-figure salaries straight out of B-school and your corporate retreats in Bali. Poor working-class schmucks, the lot of you.'

They were paid what their employers deemed worthy of their services, argued Sudhi. 'Typical,' he added. 'You're all in the same boat, aren't you? Only a hippie would hold my success against me.'

He may have had a point but it was lost in the flurry of giggles his unselfconscious use of the word 'success' initiated.

'I've been away for *months*,' Sonya shook her head as Sudhi stormed off to the washroom. 'You'd think my friends would have something—*any*thing—to ask me about besides Thomas. Maybe I've read a great book or travelled somewhere nice or invented something cool. But no, I'm suddenly defined by the guy they met at my house last weekend.'

The General laughed.

'If there was a Bechdel test for real life,' she said, 'half the self-proclaimed progressives would kill themselves in shame.'

'I wanted to talk to you about what we discussed yesterday,' said the General. Sonya nodded. They had spent the previous day at the General's flat, poring over her girls' paintings, some good, some worrisome. 'I think it's a great idea to exhibit their work,' continued the General. 'These girls really need something to build their self-esteem.'

A couple of guys gestured inquiringly from the bar and Sonya waved them over. She thought she had met one of them at a party a few months ago but she decided not to ask as they gratefully sat down at the other end of their table.

'Ayesha hasn't been to school in a week because she gets bullied by the senior boys,' said the General, 'and it's not just her. Most of these girls can't find it in them to forgive themselves for their backgrounds. It kills me to see them sit around moping.'

One of the guys, the one Sonya thought she recognized, asked her if she would like a drink.

'Hey *bro*,' said the General, making Sonya laugh, 'we only agreed to let you have the vacant seats out of basic human decency. If we wanted to make conversation, trust me, you'd know.'

Sudhi returned with whiskies for the three of them. Sonya and the General exchanged bemused glances as he looked suspiciously at the new arrivals.

'Anyway,' said the General, 'I'd like you to get involved. And get as many people as you can—funding, marketing, there's a lot to do.'

Sudhi muttered something about how the barkeep kept crimping on his mixer. The General asked Sonya if she thought Thomas would be interested in helping out and she promised to ask him. Sudhi, who quickly realized he could either join the conversation or get left out, pitched them a different model.

'By relying on external funding,' he said, 'you're only teaching them to depend on handouts. Try and figure out how to make it a self-sustainable, if not profit-making, venture.'

The General liked the sound of this.

'That's surprisingly insightful,' she said. 'And these kids *are* talented. Maybe Sonya wasn't entirely mistaken about you after all.'

Sudhi appeared to be weighing his options for a moment.

'Thanks,' he said reluctantly, clearly having decided to take either the high road or whatever he could get.

'I think I can convince the guys at The Bend to host the event,' offered Sonya, 'as long as you'll let them charge some kind of entry fee.'

The General slapped the table in excitement.

'Brilliant,' she said. 'We'll print out some flyers, get a little social media action going, and this might just work.'

Back in Bandra, Thomas was in the middle of plotting a different kind of redemption altogether. He had woken up with Sonya for a change, and had watched in despair as she went about her day without so much as a whiff of indecision. He made her a ham and cheese sandwich and kissed her goodbye, all the while ignoring the nagging impulse that something was slowly being wrenched away from his grasp.

The party had been a harsh reminder of the world outside, of the people and places outside their little bubble that comprised Sonya's existence. She didn't seem to be gripped by the same fear of loving and losing that he was. He hadn't felt this possessive about anyone or anything since he was a boy.

He set to work on a half-empty bottle of Teacher's and sat down to try to write. It was true that he had been writing more on his blog since he met Sonya but they were fluff pieces, comically deconstructed retellings of the time they spent together. The blog was also an attempt at normalcy: in it, Thomas's alter ego had a job and sporting affiliations and friends, just like Sonya, and he and 'Girlfriend' shared a home. It was his way of telling her that he was maybe capable of straddling both worlds too; it was Hope. The blog posts made Sonya happy—and consequently, Thomas—but in themselves, those words held no value to anyone except the two of them. The novel his agent had gone to great lengths to get an 'up and coming' indie publisher to sign up—one he had promised Thomas emphatically was going to be the next big thing in alternative fiction but appeared to have made no dent in the market as yet—languished unwritten in his mind, nearly eighteen months after the contract had been drawn up and signed. They were asking for their money back, his agent had warned Thomas the last time they spoke. It wasn't a big amount but he was in no position to repay them. More importantly, he thought, writing the novel may just be the antidote to Sonya getting bored of him.

At the time, he had gone to his agent with the best of intentions and a genuine belief that he had a story worth telling. The premise was simple: the first few years of the twenty-first century, and the technological revolution that ensued, had knowingly or unknowingly groomed a new breed of men: one Thomas referred to as the 'Beta Male'. Indigenous to urbania and reared on a steady diet of gender-bending media and class-diluting technology, they were everywhere, tugged along by the she-conomy, incapable of changing a light bulb without consulting an instruction manual, their ripped arms and perfectly proportioned torsos only any good for lugging shopping bags around malls and juggling multiple electronic devices. They sampled the latest organic diets and designer drugs without a hint of cynicism but were increasingly afraid of the dark. His novel would be vicious and satirical, a biting commentary on the infantilization of men and the demands it placed on them to stay entrapped in their childhood, an exposé of the failures of a system that valued manners over manliness and nurture over nature.

Thomas was convinced that he had stumbled upon something groundbreaking, that he would go on to write what would retrospectively be anointed a cultural milestone, that he would be hailed as the spokesperson of a generation. But publishers didn't bite. It took his agent seven months to get him a publishing deal in stark contrast to his first novel which had been snatched up within a week of contacting his agent. Thomas had already lost faith in his project by then; his conviction had waned and collected in a slough of despondence in the pit of his stomach. He wondered if he wasn't just projecting his own insecurities and experiences onto a society he had withdrawn from years ago. He suspected his views had much to do with his own upbringing and his unresolved parental issues, that they didn't possess the grand narrative qualities of a less personal idiom.

Thomas had spent much of his childhood idolizing his father. The only son of the only son of Valiyaveettil

Thoma, Thomas's father, Valiyaveettil Solomon, was a throwback to a bygone era, an era of 'Scotch'-swilling, gun-toting, thrill-seeking *Achayan*s that was barely kept alive by popular Malayalam cinema and not much else. If the Land Redistribution Act of 1970 had played Robin Hood with much of his generation's ancestral wealth, the great rubber market crash of the early nineties had robbed these merry men of considerable disposable income. But the tragedy of Valiyaveettil Solomon's predilection for pleasure arose not out of the vagaries of democracy but an acute pragmatism that made him uproot Thomas from everything he had known till he was twelve years old to send him to boarding school in Kodaikanal. Kochu Thoma's logic was simple and straightforward: Thomas would need an education, one with a *brand name*, because there would be nothing left of his estate by the time he was an adult.

Thomas would go on to spend years in the psychedelic wilderness, to party with Goa Gil and volunteer for a few months at Osho's ashram in Pune, but he would never meet a man more dedicatedly hedonistic than his father. Valiyaveettil Solomon had never worked a day in his life and spent every hour as though it were his last. Thomas couldn't remember seeing his father without a glass of the finest imported whisky in his hand, except in church which he attended religiously every Sunday morning. He had a swagger that could put Mick Jagger to shame and a temper that put the fear of God into the hearts of all living things in his vicinity. One of Thomas's earliest and most formative memories of malehood was of his father beating a confession out of one of his rubber tappers. He had tied the errant labourer to a coconut tree in their courtyard and lashed him repeatedly with a leather belt as his wife and children simultaneously begged and berated him, pleaded with him to show mercy on the head of their family. Finally, his back and face a bloody mosaic of lacerated skin and blackened bruises, the tapper admitted to having stolen a sack of rice from Valiyaveettil Solomon's warehouse and selling it to the local grocer to pay for his daughter's tuition. No more than an hour later, the grocer found himself tied to the same coconut tree, Valiyaveettil Solomon behind him, belt in hand, administering a similar brand of justice.

Thomas and his father had never been close, but they grew further apart with every passing year of his schooling in Kodaikanal. When he visited his parents during the holidays, little Thomas felt not the relief of a homesick child but the sense of injustice of one who has been robbed of his heritage, of one who has been cheated by fate and even genetics. He had hit puberty before most of his peers, but his growth seemed to stunt just as everybody else started catching up. Throughout his teenage years, he would look at himself in the mirror and wonder why his moustache didn't sprout as lushly as his father had predicted it would, why he wasn't getting any taller or broader or tougher. He was by no means an unpopular boy, and rumours abounded of him having taken not just some of the older girls but also boys to bed, but Thomas wanted nothing more than to finish school and return to his rightful place as heir to his father's fiefdom. Imagine his dismay when Valiyaveettil Solomon showed up at the gate to his freedom on the last day of school to announce that he had secured Thomas admission to a prominent Christian college in Bangalore and that they were to leave straightaway to see to his transfer and accommodation.

By the time Thomas's agent came through with a publishing offer and an advance, Thomas had all but given up on the novel. He accepted the money anyway because he needed it, not because he felt he could do it justice. But meeting Sonya's friends at the party had stirred something in him: a familiar itch, a reawakening. These were the people he had wanted to write about, he realized; he had just not met them when he first envisioned it. This was the generation he had wanted to represent; he had just been a little ahead of his time. If he could immerse himself a little, be part of the *scene* for a while, thought Thomas, this might just work. So when Sonya called on the landline (they had a pre-arranged screening process: two single rings, followed by a double) to ask him if he would like to meet her at F Bar, he jumped at the chance. He finished off the last of the vodka bottle he had opened around noon and dabbed hopelessly at his hair a couple of times before setting off on perhaps the tamest gonzo operation to date. 'Standing in front of my mirror, combed my hair a thousand times but came out looking just the same ...' he hummed to himself throughout the cab ride.

Much to Sudhi's consternation, the new arrivals had been granted a free pass to their party and were deep in conversation with Sonya and the General when Thomas joined them. Sonya rose to hug him and introduced the boys, Akshay and Manoj.

'Akshay here,' said the General, 'is an IIT boy, just the way Sonya likes 'em.'

Thomas took a swig of beer and nodded in the general direction of his head.

'And Manoj here,' she continued, 'is a Bang-a*looru* boy, just the way everybody likes them!'

'Chill *maadi*,' said Sonya to loud cheers from Manoj and the General.

Sonya leaned in and whispered, 'Do you mind, baby?'

If Thomas felt uncomfortable, he didn't show it.

'You need to get a mobile, man,' she said. 'My mom will get a heart attack if some strange man answers the phone instead of her Sati Savitri daughter.'

Sudhi perked up: 'Mobile telephony too mainstream for ya?'

'I'm allergic to it,' replied Thomas and Sonya giggled.

'My mom actually makes it a point to call on the landline,' she complained to no one in particular, 'just to make sure I'm home.'

The General brought Thomas up to date on their evening.

'We've managed to establish,' she said grandly, 'with the aid of what is admittedly a small focus group—' She paused to sip her drink. '—that you boys have all been spoilt rotten by your mothers.'

Sonya laughed.

'But Sonya here informs me that you, Senor Thomas, are the first man she's met to never mention his mother. Not even in passing, she says.'

Thomas watched silently as Sonya looked guiltily at Sudhi and mouthed an apology.

'The point is,' continued the General, 'you men have all been brought up to believe that no woman will ever be good enough for you.'

How could men be expected to treat women as equals, she wanted to know, when they thought the sun shone out of their asses? Akshay and Manoj stood up to leave citing an early flight the next day, but the General dismissed their farewell and asked them to stay for another drink. They complied. 'Akshay's only visiting,' she told Thomas. 'He's not from around here.'

Thomas thought he detected an opportunity.

'If it's equality you're after,' said Thomas, 'the problem might be how you phrase it.'

'He speaks!' proclaimed Sudhi.

'I'm just saying,' Thomas ignored Sudhi. 'I think we can all agree that men and women are inherently equal. And I doubt anybody at this table wants to *repress* women, per se.'

The men seemed to be in agreement.

'Women are a little *too* equal, if anything,' muttered Sudhi.

The General picked up on it. 'That's exactly the kind of half-assed attitude that institutionalizes this shit.'

Thomas looked around the table and locked eyes with Akshay. Clean shaven and spectacled, he looked younger than the rest.

'But it's just as hard being a man sometimes,' said Thomas patiently. 'The last thing we want to do is call ourselves feminists simply because it *sounds* too feminine.'

Sonya squeezed the back of Thomas's neck. 'Doesn't stop you from prancing around in my underwear,' she whispered.

'Oh boo! Let's *rebrand* feminism,' said the General. 'A little more originality please, Thomas!'

But Thomas found support from the unlikeliest of quarters. 'The gays are doing it,' said Sudhi, and paused to give the General a meaningful look. 'They're gaying it down because all the flamboyance and the rainbows put them in a box.'

'It's true,' said Akshay. 'What you call feminist media these days often borders on misandry.'

A borrowed term, but his job was done. Thomas leaned back to enjoy the massage.

'Everything modern and *liberal*—films, ads, music videos—they're all either Beyoncé riding big muscular men like horses, or helpless out-of-shape men being babied by confident, attractive women.' Akshay paused from the effort, and Thomas silently cheered him on to the finish line. 'There's no ... *middle* ground anymore,' said Akshay pensively, rolling his thoughts on his tongue before letting them rip. 'If women have a right to be women, men should be allowed to be men too.'

Sudhi thumped the table. 'Bravo,' shouted Manoj.

'That's a very limited reality and you know it,' said Sonya. 'You're talking about a very privileged, upper middle class, quasi-Western media experience. The heartlands ... in fact, screw the heartlands; go to Paradise Cinema in Mahim on a Friday. Half the men in this country still subscribe to the *Bhai* school of exaggerated machismo.'

That took the wind right out of Akshay's sails. He slumped in his seat, defeated, and Manoj slapped him sympathetically on his back, a gesture Thomas recognized from televised football. Akshay may have been substituted just before the final third of the game, Manoj seemed to be implying, but he had taken one for the Team and that deserved appreciation.

'And what if they had chosen the *middle* ground with the Nazis?' started the General.

'Oh come on, not the Nazis again,' Sonya cut in. 'Why must everything end up a Holocaust parallel?'

She stood up. 'I need a smoke,' she said, 'and you boys need to pick your battles. You can call yourselves The League of Extraordinary Gentlemen for all I care. And you're right; there *is* no middle ground. I'm sorry but the truth is if you're not with us, you're pretty much full of shit.'

Outside, Sonya led Thomas to her usual spot. They smoked in silence till Thomas asked, 'So how was your day?' Sonya laughed her no-shit laugh. Thomas thought to himself that she was probably sharper and more cynical than he could ever hope to be; she just didn't feel the need to flaunt it which seemed incredibly sexy and wise in someone so young.

"How was your day?" she mimicked him. 'Oh the bliss of domesticity, Writer-man.' Thomas kissed the side of her head, and smiled. 'I'm sorry I was pulling some strings in there,' he said. 'The Beta Male thing?' inquired Sonya. 'I'm glad you're working on it.'

# 7

# The Girlfriend Chronicles 5: A Revolution That Will Not Be Televised

So the other day, a few of us had an early reprieve from work and were standing around outside, hungrily breathing in daylight like men fresh out of solitary. There was that familiar summer conviction in the air, that feeling that life was starting anew and promising to be phenomenal. In less than a minute however, our band of merry men had diminished to three, the others departing on a slew of errands that appeared to have reared their heads out of nowhere.

I was surprised. I was planning to make the best of our early finish, and get some midweek drinking action going. 'What about you guys?' I asked. 'Got plans too?' Suddenly, pockets were rummaged, hair re-coiffed, sunglasses readjusted. Basically, anything but look me in the eye.

'I'm not really sure,' mumbled KD, after some time. 'I'm waiting for my girlfriend to text back.'

'Me too,' chimed in Leo. 'And mine's in a meeting till six.'

I felt devastated, violated.

'What the fuck, guys,' I said. 'It's only four. Let's go get a beer.'

'Oh come on, dude,' K retorted. 'You do the same thing.'

And that's when it hit me. It was true. Girlfriend was out of town so I had no conflicts of interest that afternoon, but make frantic calls to Girlfriend was the first thing I did on most days after work. She would pick a place for dinner, or assign some kind of grocery responsibility to me, or tell me how many hours I had to myself till we met for dinner. Girlfriend scheduled my non-working hours with an iron fist, and I hadn't even realized it.

I insisted the guys buy some time for themselves and herded them over to the nearest bar. 'Guys,' I said. 'We're adults. We should be able to come up with a plan on a free fucking evening without bringing our women into it.' The guys showed their support by ordering another round of drinks. 'I mean, how did this even happen?' I said. 'When's the last time we picked a movie or a bar? When did we lose all control?' The guys nodded enthusiastically but I could see we weren't making much progress. These guys needed something more raw, more visceral, to shake them out of their slumber. So I called Fatboy.

'The tyranny of the tongue,' declared Fatboy, stroking his double chin. 'Literary emasculation.'

'What the fuck, dude?' That was probably all three of us.

'*Nicknames*,' he explained. 'Drugs don't emasculate men, nicknames emasculate men.'

We looked at each other. None of our girlfriends had given us nicknames. We had all been *called* names, but not ones you'd utter in front of your mom. Fatboy was finally wrong about something.

'This is worse than I thought,' said Fatboy, shaking his head on seeing our blank faces.

'Oh fuck you,' I said. 'Just admit you're wrong.'

'It's not nicknames with you lot,' he said sadly. 'It's just as I suspected. You morons didn't even get the gateway treatment, you just let them stick it right up your asses. Do you realize what you've done?'

'Dude, stop shaking,' I tried to calm him. 'Look, you're upsetting poor Leo here. He's a graphic designer. That's almost like a real artist. He's really sensitive.'

'Eighteen years,' said Fatboy, still shaking his head. 'Eighteen years we fought tooth and nail to get rid of that disgusting, insulting, belittling *label*. A few years of freedom, of independence, of self-respect, and what do you do? You stupid, aspirational-class, Westward-looking idiots. You flushed it all down the toilet and then took a shit on the seat.'

'I want whatever this guy's having,' said KD. In a flash, Fatboy had him by the collar.

'Dude, calm down,' I said. 'You *were* getting a little emotional there.'

'You want to know why your women make all your decisions, bro?' sneered Fatboy. 'You want to know why you don't know what to do with your spare time?' he asked. 'Why every time your women are busy, you feel a bit like a little boy lost in a supermarket?'

Maybe he did know what he was talking about. 'Why?' I humoured his rhetoric.

'Because,' he said, 'you've gone and reclaimed the Label. You've niggerized it, throwing it around, giving it fancy little flourishes, and suddenly you've made it mainstream, blurred the lines. You can't fault the oppressor for calling you a cunt, if you refer to yourselves, *and* them, as cunts.'

'Assuming my girlfriend is who you're delicately referring to as the "oppressor",' Leo started, 'I can assure you she's never called me a ...'

'Not "cunt", you idiot,' I said, and pretended to have followed all along though I'd only just gotten it. 'It's ba ...'

'Don't say it,' said Fatboy, and looked furtively around. 'You'll get us all killed.'

I looked around. We were at Gopalkrishna's, a shady little bar next to Dadar station, a place run strictly for the barely salaried slave to wet his beak before the long commute home. The three of us—writers, artists, struggling all—had never done a day's work compared to these guys. They would eat us alive.

'It's 'baby', you guys,' I whispered. 'They had us at 'baby'. Call someone a baby long enough, and suddenly they're sporting goatees and drinking tofu beer because babies are not fit to make their own decisions.'

'They just respond to breasts,' said Fatboy.

I woke up the next morning, ready for war. The Tyranny of the Tongue had had its time. It was time to restore the natural order of things, re-establish control. Unfortunately, Girlfriend would have to head straight to her office from the airport, so I just texted her saying I'd see her at night. Oh, I'll see her at night all right, I thought. Get ready for Alpha Man, baby.

Girlfriend was already home when I got back at night. The bedroom door was open, there was some French pop star trying to cross over to the more respected Vauxwagen-jingle genre of music, and I thought I smelled Thai chicken curry on the stove. *Tonight we dine in hell*, I thought as I walked in.

Girlfriend was a mess. A blur of mascara and snot and Kleenex and tears and oestrogen, all in a Girlfriend-shaped mess in our bed. I was ambushed.

'What's wrong, baby?' I asked, a little less sure about raising hell.

She looked up. 'I just had a bad day at work,' she said, dabbing at her face. 'Can you give me a hug?'

And suddenly, I realized it had always been a two-way street. The revolution would just have to wait.

---

Tags: Alpha Male, bro, dating, fatboy, girlfriend, manning up, niggerization, the great gatsby

---

# 8

He was hot. More than anything else, he was hot; he had somehow been trapped in some sort of cooking device and he was being roasted alive to feed the fury of some unknown enemy. Somebody was already cutting into his thigh, his buttocks, his cheeks, helping themselves to pieces of his charred flesh, unaware that he was still beating inside. Or maybe that was the point of the whole exercise; they wanted to devour him whole, and alive. He could scream. He had read about similar situations: of a word, a gesture, a tear snapping would-be victims' tormentors back to reality. He needed to conjure up a moment of humanity to give him a fighting chance of survival. He tried. His throat was parched and refused to comply. His limbs wouldn't budge. Humanity, humanity. He tried to think. What was human about him? His eyes. He could open his eyes! There was still light in his eyes!

The discomfort was less sustained than he imagined it would be, like peeling a Band-Aid. Daylight poured in like an army on a rampage, poking at his retinae, hurting his brain.

He blinked and sat up, and suddenly aware of the sun on his face, his naked torso, his legs, he jumped to his feet wondering what he was doing waking up on Sonya's terrace. The last he remembered of their evening at F Bar was the cool night air on his back as they stood outside waiting for a cab. He remembered the two new guys leaving earlier than the rest; he remembered—with some effort—initiating a conversation about something that hadn't gone down too well with the General, but he didn't remember leaving the bar. He hadn't blacked out like this since he had been an amateur, nearly two decades ago.

Sonya wasn't home. Her bed hadn't been made but it didn't look slept in either. He panicked momentarily, only to realize the bedroom still smelled of her perfume. The bathroom was wet, as were her towels—the blue one she wrapped around her body after showering and the white one she reserved for her hair. It was quarter past ten. Chances were she had only just left for work. He called her twice but there was no answer. He rushed to the toilet to vomit and ended up dry-heaving for the better part of an hour, by which time his head was bursting at its seams, threatening to explode in a shower of guilt and regret. Oh what had he done?

Sonya shivered in the back of the cab and hugged herself tighter. She usually took the train to work but she needed to be as far away from Thoma and her flat as quickly as possible, and people, oh there were so many bloody people on those trains, how could she be expected to. Not after. She asked the driver if he could turn the air-conditioning down a little and he looked at her in the mirror as if to say: 'Well, it's *your* money.' Her phone rang and she jumped. Thomas. She silenced the call and closed her eyes to run through the events of the night again.

When Thomas and Sonya had gone back in after the smoke, he had already changed. She could see that now. All night, she had reconstructed the sequence of events in her head, trying to figure out how it had happened, or why. She realized now that it had never been a question of how or why, but when. It had happened because it had happened. It had happened to her, and him, and it was nobody else's business but their own. Nobody need know about this, she told herself, be *strong*. She checked her phone to see if Thomas had called again, then bristled at her own foolishness. That should have been the last of her concerns. Why do we put ourselves in these positions, she wondered, before reminding herself that there was no 'we', that she wasn't part of a disadvantaged collective like the General's girls or their mothers. She was educated, she was independent, and she would get through this just like she had got through everything else that had come before it. She was no victim.

It came back to Thomas in flashes. There had been shouting, and words, and crying. They had had a row, what *The Guardian* might call 'a domestic'. Before the shouting, before they reached home, there had been apologies and embarrassment. He had spilled a drink or dropped a pitcher or *borrowed* a bottle from the bar. There may have been dancing, but he never danced. He may have said something sexist or racist or something equally -ist to the General. What had he done? Why did he feel so guilty?

Sonya wondered if she could have done things differently, more kindly. It was true Thomas had acted silly at the bar. Sudhi had looked on, and at her and through her, but she hadn't cared. Her boyfriend was a little drunk, and he had tried to nick a bottle from the counter after the bartender told them he wouldn't be serving them any more drinks that night but it was all in good fun, in plain sight. Thomas had announced to the table that Sonya was 'up for a good humping' that night and that the General was welcome to join them but they had both laughed it off. The General had seemed in good spirits when she left with Akshay and Manoj even if they looked a little shaken. Sonya had been the perfect girlfriend, understanding and detached, letting Thomas run amok without letting him endanger himself, without ever really taking sides. He was almost sober when they got into the cab, and asleep immediately after.

Sonya remembered giving directions to the Mullah driver who spoke little Hindi or English—out of ignorance or will, she couldn't be sure—and wishing for support. The driver dealt only in patois, some BIMARU lingo that was too localized even for her, a seasoned Hindi speaker unlike Thomas. Sonya had been happy enough playing guide the last few months showing Thomas around her favourite spots and restaurants, but she wondered when he would switch off tourist mode and start dealing with the day-to-day. The vacation was over but Thomas refused to climb out of his swimming trunks. She caught the driver looking at her in the mirror and moved closer to Thomas. She must have nodded off because the next thing she knew, they were speeding towards a traffic signal in an area she recognized vaguely as being beyond Bandra, the stereo blaring distinctly Bhojpuri music.

As they slowed down, Sonya lowered the window and leaned over Thomas to ask two men on a motorbike if they could tell her where they were. They had just passed Santa Cruz East, the pillion rider replied, they would have to go back the same way to get to Bandra. She thanked them and instructed the driver to turn the car around, having decided earlier that it would be futile to argue with him. He muttered something under his breath and made a U-turn, only for Sonya to notice out of the corner of her eye that the men on the bike did the same. She told herself it was happenstance and waited, convinced they would turn into a lane or a byroad at any moment.

A few minutes later, the men were still behind her, maintaining a safe but increasingly threatening distance between their vehicles. The driver had initially been accommodating of Sonya's varied requests—'Bhaisaab, thoda dheere chal lo please'; 'Unko jaane do'; 'Ok *fuck* badao speed, unko peeche chordo!'—but he now looked more annoyed than amused. A grim panic descended upon her as she sought out his stolid eyes in the mirror for comfort, and tried again to wake Thomas up in vain. She wasn't going to break down, she told herself, there was no need to. They were almost home, just past Santa Cruz police station and Three Wise Men; why, they were back on Linking Road already! She knew this stretch like the back of her own hand; there was no need to call a friend or to go to the police. Whatever their intentions, the men would disappear the moment they turned into a residential lane; they wouldn't dare follow her into her own home.

The men didn't disappear. Sonya had stopped turning around to check on them long ago, unnerved by the blank helmeted visage that greeted her when she did, preferring instead to monitor their progress in the rearview. She stopped checking the mirror too after they turned into her lane, past the Malayali cigarette shop and the halal butcher's, and asked the driver to take a left. She called the pothead from downstairs on her phone and requested him to meet her at Muthu's in five minutes. They took another left, and another, and a right after that, and finally came to a halt in front of her neighbourhood Samaritan. Her hand trembled as she reached into her purse to pay the driver, and didn't stop shaking till the men on the bike bid a noisy adieu with a series of honks, each one of which startled her as though it were the first sound to be made on earth. The pothead hugged her and helped her carry Thomas home.

Thomas hadn't craved heroin like this in years, certainly not since Dharamkot. He tried to remember the words that had got him through those months, the *mantra* that had saved his life. He hadn't needed it in so long. What was it she had said, the Bhikkuni who had found him in the throes of a vicious overdose that dark December dawn and bundled him up in her arms and carried him to her monastery and safety? She had thought that he was delirious from fever, sick, till he came to. Spread-eagled on the steps to the What Goes Around café, he had been to hell and back, he explained to her, he had seen the beginning and the end. He wanted to be tied up, chained, so he didn't have to watch it all again. 'Make it stop!' he had pleaded. 'Beat it out of me!' The Bhikkuni listened patiently, wiped his forehead with a damp cloth and whispered: 'If you can imagine it, you can control it.'

Sonya couldn't stop imagining it. Who were those men? What had they wanted? What if the pothead had been asleep, if the driver had stopped and fled? She checked on Thomas, and made coffee while the pothead rolled a joint. He put an arm around her and told her it was going to be okay, that at least they didn't know where she lived. She burst into tears and held him tightly, thanking him again for being there. They stayed that way till she was aware of his mouth on her head, kissing her hair, whispering into it. She almost laughed at the irony of it all, choosing instead to stand up and telling

him he had better leave. She went back to the door thrice to
make sure it was locked and pushed the couch against it after
the last time, wondering why the backs of chairs never quite
fit exactly under the knob like they did in the movies.

When she got back to the bedroom, Thomas was up and
spraying urine all over the contents of her cupboard. He had
miraculously risen from the bed, mistaken the open *almirah*
for the washroom, and decided to piss all over her life. Sonya
broke. She had had enough for a lifetime, let alone one night.
She swore and banged the door on his back, screaming,
cursing. He lurched and fell against the wall, and she leapt
to relative safety from the arc of his attempted ablution. She
had never hated anyone or anything with the severity she felt
for him at that moment, lying face up in a puddle of shame of
his own making. She hoped she wouldn't do anything stupid
and kicked him roundly in the ribs before falling to her knees
to help him up.

Thomas's mother never tired of reminding him that
he had a genuine problem with asking for help. 'Just ask,'
she would say at least once every time he called her during
his lost years, 'and your father will help.' In the manner of
most maternal remonstrations, this was a fallacy designed to
chastise without hurting, to criticize without crushing, and he
had almost believed it: Thomas was a fine boy, if a little proud,
and the biggest of his problems would go away if he were to
rein his ego in a little; it wasn't the drugs, or the aimlessness,
but the pride that needed fixing. As Thomas would find out,
this was not true in the least. He needed help and he didn't
mind asking; it was just a case of realizing he needed it.

The Bhikkuni looked after him like one would a hatchling
that had fallen out of its nest. He had contracted mild
pneumonia from the cold but she refused to call a traditional

doctor. She fed him soup and tea, clothed him and bathed him, held his hand through nightmares and withdrawal. She taught him to meditate and pray and look outwards, not inward. There's a world outside, she told him, full of wonder and joy, and it was his if he would only look its way. She had been the same, she told him, always brooding, always caught up in her own problems, till she finally fled her native Tibet in her thirties, left her family and home, to join the monastery. 'Some things, you have to let go,' she said. Here, she told him, she was safe, as was he. Nobody would trouble them here, not till they wanted to be troubled: *If you can imagine it, you can control it.*

Thomas slipped in and out of stupor as Sonya helped him out of his clothes and into fresh boxers, shouting obscenities and pulling her hair, clawing at her breasts till they hurt. She swatted his hands and contemplated snipping at his groin, singeing his chest. 'You let me down today,' she told his now-closed eyes, 'you screwed me over and I wasn't planning on letting you.' She emptied the cupboard and put her clothes in the washing machine and scrubbed her room clean, all of it. Thomas lay oblivious in her bed, turning one way, then the other, flinging the duvet off him when he felt warm and crawling back under it when he felt cold, the coward, just like any other day. Sonya's anger followed her around like a physical presence, boiling and raging and seething, taunting and calling names and demanding acknowledgement.

'Baby,' she said, and shook him. 'Thoma!' she shouted, and slapped him. There was a gash under his neck from where the door had hit him. If he would just wake up and apologize, she told herself, if he would just hold her and tell her he was sorry, maybe she could forgive him.

'You're supposed to be the man, you bastard,' she wailed. 'You're supposed to have my back, to take care of me'.

Somewhere in the middle of the blows raining down on him, Thomas raised a hand to his face in defence which only served to spur Sonya on.

'Be a man, you asshole,' she screamed. 'Grow the fuck up.'

What was it he had said? What had he said to make her so mad?

'Stop emasculating me,' he had said, Sonya remembered now, before spouting a great deal of nonsense about what was expected of men and how unfair it all was. She had promptly dragged him out of bed with a strength she hadn't known she possessed and propped him up against the parapet on her terrace.

Thomas had only been in Bandra a few months but he knew exactly where he could score. It was like an impulse or an instinct, he thought; he couldn't navigate a ten-minute rickshaw ride home from any of the coffee shops or bars that Sonya and he had frequented but he could guide her to exactly which corner or alleyway they would have to get to if they needed to buy some drugs. He grimaced—not for the first time—at the thought of familiar media portrayals of addiction and junkies that flooded his mind that instant; they were all as helpless as they were hopeless. It was amazing that nobody had got it right as yet, he thought, that nobody had corrected the cliché of the clueless consumer. They were no different from the social worker who forgot his familial responsibilities or the genius who neglected his wife and kids, thought Thomas, they were just wired to a different purpose. A junkie—genius or not—was always aware of just where he could source his next high; always on the lookout for a contingency plan. *Just in case*—that was their motto, the creed that had been ingrained in him by several years of abuse.

Thomas estimated that he had less than a hundred rupees to his name; not nearly enough for what he had planned. Reluctantly, he went downstairs to make a few calls; he didn't want them to have Sonya's number. It was easier than he had thought it would be. Within minutes, he had a number and a name he recognized only too well. In less than half an hour, he found himself in the backseat of a Santro outside the Our Lady of Salvation church in Dadar, already regretting his decision. Thomas let himself be pummelled by the stocky young men who flanked him on either side as Varun drove, looking back only intermittently to check that his old friend didn't bleed on his seats. Thomas caught his eye once and told him he didn't look as pleased as he had expected him to be.

Meanwhile, perched in front of her computer at work, jumping at the slightest intrusion like she had been caught stealing, Sonya was coming to terms with a whole different truth altogether. While she had showered and purged herself, India had woken up to her greatest shame since the days of Sati: a young woman, only a couple of years younger than Sonya, had been brutally beaten and raped by six males— one of whom was suspected to be a minor—while travelling in a private bus in Delhi. She had been accompanied by a male friend who was beaten unconscious with an iron rod which had later been used to penetrate her, resulting in serious injuries to her abdomen, intestines and genitals. The victims were then thrown off the moving bus and found by a passerby who alerted the police. They were both hospitalized and given emergency treatment, after which the woman had been placed on mechanical ventilation. One of the accused men later admitted to having seen a 'rope-like object'—her intestines—being pulled out of the woman by his cohorts. The couple had reportedly been returning home from a screening of *Life of Pi* in South Delhi.

Who was to blame? The Nation wanted to know, just as it wanted to buy the fairness creams and the mid-segment cars that interrupted its investigation. Initially at least, the State seemed most culpable; it was a failure of law and order, of right to life and dignity and equality. The State and its democratically elected custodians responded with questions: What was the couple doing outside at that hour? Why did they willingly board a private bus? There was a whiff of she-asked-for-it that permeated their concerns that did not sit at all well with Sonya's peers—many of them female—in cities and towns across the country. Harried, and in possession of a voice like never before, they took to the internet to protest, to express solidarity and volunteer their own experiences as evidence of a patriarchal system that had long marginalized its women and institutionalized sexual assault, to demand justice. They mobilized hashtags and shared blog posts, stopping only to answer phone calls from horror-struck parents who wanted to know if they were alright and to underline long-held notions of what would and would not be considered appropriate behaviour on the part of their daughters. India's youth vented their disillusionment in real time, on Twitter and Facebook and Tumblr, their collective stream of consciousness quickly disintegrating into theoretical farce. Somebody called out video games, somebody else, Yo Yo Honey Singh. Delhiites pointed at Haryanvi immigrants, and Bihari, and those from UP. Sonya sat numb to it all, wondering how close she had come to becoming news fodder the previous night and just how much she was to blame for putting her safety in the hands of another. It annoyed her to admit that there was a substratum of truth to the rape-apologists' line of questioning: wasn't survival the one unequivocal imperative that history had taught human civilization? She googled self-defence classes in Bandra and signed up for kickboxing with a personal trainer based a couple of kilometres from home.

Thomas had a black eye and what looked like an open wound on his neck which had started bleeding profusely. 'That wasn't us,' claimed one of his assailants as Varun glared at him in the mirror. He pulled over and the two men stepped out without prompting.

'What do you want?' he asked.

Thomas smiled through bloody teeth. 'What do you think I want?'

Varun lit two cigarettes and offered Thomas one. He hadn't changed much by way of appearance, thought Thomas appreciatively, except for a sprinkling of grey on his beard that only lent him an air of respectability.

'I don't work with junkies,' said Varun.

'Not a great idea, as business models go,' said Thomas.

Varun turned around and faced Thomas for the first time.

'What do you want, Thoma?' he asked. 'I should kill you for the shit you pulled but I'm out of that life. I have two kids now.'

Thomas wondered if he was pleading with him. 'With Marlene?'

Varun puffed on his cigarette thoughtfully. No, he replied, Marlene had OD'd a few years ago, as had a few of the others. He was clean now, and married to a Bank of Maharashtra employee who knew and asked nothing about his past.

Thomas hadn't known this was a possibility but he also knew there was no such thing as a one-time junkie. A little push was all it took; a little determination.

'I'm sorry about Marlene,' Thomas told Varun earnestly. 'I'm in a bad way man. I'm getting old.'

He didn't want to get involved, said Varun. Thomas was toxic. Everything he touched turned to shit, including Marlene.

'I'll get you some K,' he told Thomas. 'That's the best I can do. I don't ever want to see you again.'

What about his goons outside, asked Thomas. They didn't seem as legit as Varun claimed to be.

'I don't need *you* to score Ketamine,' said Thomas. 'Come on, we're old friends.'

Varun turned the key in the ignition and set the car to idle. It was his call, he said, he could take it or leave it. Could he at least lend him some money, Thomas wanted to know, maybe there was a job somewhere he could help with? Varun lowered the window and nodded to his colleagues. One hit, he told Thomas, one hit and he had better be gone.

It was her fault, Sonya could see that now. She had been drunk and had fallen asleep in the back of a taxi with a manchild, one she had only known a few months. She could see how that narrative would have played out in her parents' home if *something* had happened to her. She was the victim and she was to blame. She thanked the stars that her mother had called early in the morning, before either of them had had a chance to read the news. Guiltily, she texted the General to make sure she had reached home without incident, and promised to meet in the evening to discuss what she referred to as 'the tragedy'. Not 'the gang rape', or 'the assault', but *the tragedy*. So passive, so incidental. It could have happened to anyone without the right precautions, like neglecting to wear a seatbelt or forgetting to run one's dissertation through the recommended software to check for accidental plagiarism. Things just happened *to* women, not in spite of them.

Thomas and Varun shot up in the car after which one of the goons drove them around town. Thomas vomited a little but felt ready again to face the world. 'Lightweight,' said Varun, and it was like old times again, just about.

'Where do you want to be dropped?' asked Varun after a while, abruptly, and Thomas told him he would like a ride to Lower Parel. He didn't want Varun to know where Sonya worked, much less that she existed. He had a new life—and occupants—to protect too. Varun handed Thomas a sellotaped Nokia box and asked him to hold it for him before thrusting a thickish wad of hundreds in his hand. Thomas didn't think the box contained a phone but also thought better of asking Varun about it; he told him he would call him in a couple of weeks as instructed. They hugged before parting ways outside the train station.

He called Sonya from a phone booth outside India Bulls Centre. He didn't remember much of what had happened, he confessed, but he was sorry. He had never blacked out like that, he told her; whatever he had done, it wasn't him who had made the decisions. He would never harm her knowingly, he told him; she knew that, didn't she?

Yes, she said on auto pilot, she knew.

Had he hurt her, he wanted to know; what had he said?

She told him they would talk later, that he was to meet her at home. He picked up flowers and a bottle of wine on his way back, and made chorizo pasta with sautéed onions, garlic, and mushrooms, careful to use just enough tomatoes to add flavour without overpowering the sauce, just the way Sonya liked it.

She took one look at him and rushed into his arms. She told him what had happened, leaving out—not without considerable deliberation—the part after she had found him urinating in her cupboard. If Thomas was glad that she didn't inquire about his bruises, he didn't mention it just as he didn't mention that her report didn't quite add up, that it didn't explain how he had ended up waking up on the terrace.

'What the fuck happened to your face?' asked the General when she dropped by later.

'He fell down the stairs,' said Sonya and they laughed, and it was like old times again, just about.

# 9

# The Girlfriend Chronicles 7: In Which Fatboy Gives It Those Ones

Fatboy has a spookishly accurate radar for detecting sexual activity and frequency. He once scampered around our old flat for ten whole minutes, scratching at the door, sniffing the air, ears doing a Spock, till he finally put a finger to his lips, mouthed 'follow me' and stealthed his way up the stairs to the roof. I followed him, not entirely thrilled at playing Moneypenny to his Private Dick. But follow him I did and sure enough, in the middle of the terrace stood the unfortunately named Postman Patrick, postman-pants in a puddle around his feet, a hand resting comfortably on the satellite dish, the other gently goading the head of Born Again Mary from flat #10 who was on her knees in front of him offering prayers in distinctively non-Catholic fashion.

When Fatboy came around to watch the game last week, I decided to put him through the paces for old times' sake. I would throw him off the scent, I decided, with some signature Super Sly. He hadn't visited in a while, so I gave the ol' mancave a thorough make-over: binned all my porno, a little air freshener action to clear the masturbatory fug in the living room, not a single paper towel in sight. As customary, I welcomed him with open arms and an open bottle of Kingfisher in each hand. 'Faaatboy!' I said, genuinely excited, as we hugged. He took a sip of his beer, gave my back a friendly pat and pottered over to the couch. It's like taking candy from a big fat baby, I thought.

'So what's happening, broheim? It's been ages!' I said.

'Yeah, real good, man, you gain a little weight?'

'A touch. Haven't been getting a lot of exercise lately. Well, except in the *bedroom*, if you know what I mean.'

'Dude, I always know what you mean.'

'And the couch, too,' I said.

'What?'

'I was just saying. It's not just the bedroom, you know, we do it on the couch, the kitchen; hell I had to defrost Girlfriend's ass once coz the freezer was open.'

'Cool. Hey, game's starting.'

No high five, no 'sweeeeet!', just 'cool'. Something was wrong. Come to think of it, he hadn't even got his Chelsea jersey on.

'Dude,' I said, 'see that ashtray to your right on the floor? Can you pass that to me, please?'

'There's one on your lap,' he said, eyes still on the TV.

'Just get it, ok? New game ritual,' I improvised.

I had opened up a tiny window of opportunity. It would take all my investigative mojo, but it was doable. The moment he bent over to pick up the ashtray, I swung into action. With the lithest of wrists, I lifted his tee-shirt, just a pinch, and there it was: proof—the treacherous flash of white around his waist. Fatboy wasn't wearing his lucky boxers for the game. Something was definitely wrong.

By half-time, I was a wreck. I decided I couldn't wait anymore to find out. But Fatboy could be strangely closed up at times. I would have to play this with some degree of subtlety, lull the poor bastard into a false sense of security before I confronted him. He wouldn't even know what hit him.

'Dude,' I said, 'are you breaking up with me?'

'What?'

'Nothing,' I said as I choked back a tear. 'That was selfish of me. What is it, bro? Cancer?'

'I think it might be the celibacy,' he said, '*your* celibacy.'

'What?'

He leaned forward, sniffed, and breathed in a noseful.

'Two weeks and some,' he said expertly. 'Rough patch?'

'Three,' I admitted. 'I can't believe you caught that. How did you know?'

'Irrelevant,' he said as he stood up. 'I'm here to help.'

'It's just a phase,' I said. 'She's been really busy, and I *have* put on some weight, and …'

'Yeah, loose the promise-paunch,' he interrupted.

'The what?'

'The *promise paunch*,' he repeated. 'It's the adult version of the promise-ring. You get one every time you're comfortable in a relationship. Loose it.'

'That's not a *thing*,' I said, 'and anyway … fuck you, a "promise-paunch" is not a thing.'

He shrugged. 'Porno,' he looked around. 'You told her about your porno, didn't you?'

'How did you know that?'

'Dude, there are some things that are just sacred. One of them is a man's porno. You NEVER tell your girlfriend about your taste in porno. It's not healthy. They figure a man with such *specific* titillatory needs probably knows how to keep himself happy, even if they don't bother.'

'Girls don't care about the quality of their porno?'

'Have you ever heard one admit it?'

'No.'

'Exactly.'

I began to panic. 'What else?' I asked.

'Who tidied up this room?'

'I did.'

'Where'd you pick up the cushions and the ...' he was clearly struggling with the word, 'the soft bedsheet-type thing on the couch?'

'It gets cold in here sometimes and we like to cuddle,' I said, 'and it's a *bolster*, not a cush ... FUCK!'

'Oh, you're in deep, my friend. You've been friend-zoned.'

'She's my girlfriend!'

'I know. That's the worst kind of friend zone.'

'What do I do?'

'Loose all the gay shit. Loose the fucking chocolates in the fridge. What's the straight man's rule of chocolate consumption, bro?'

'Fuck off.'

'What.is.the.straight.man's.rule.of.chocolate.consumption, BRO?'

'*Only* when you get the munchies, and *only* spontaneously. *Never* because you've stocked them at home.'

'Thank you. We don't have a lot of time. Half-time's almost over. Send Girlfriend a text, tell her you're going out with the boys tonight, don't tell her where and switch off your phone.'

'But where are we going?'

He looked away for a second, then turned around.

'Get your tightest leather pants on,' he said. 'We're going to reclaim your balls.'

---

Tags: promise paunch, porn, sex, bromance, bro, fatboy, friend zone

# 10

Thomas and Sonya ushered in the New Year at his alma mater in Kodaikanal with a friend of his named Sanjay. He seemed a nice enough guy to Sonya, not least because he had gone to the trouble of not only booking them a guest cottage at Thomas's and his old school, but also scoring some magic mushrooms which he warned beforehand were likely not as effective as the ones that were available during 'season'. They had been meaning to come earlier, before the rains, apologized Sonya, but they had just not managed to find the time. 'I'm always here,' said Sanjay cheerfully. 'Let me know next year.'

He was some sort of settling-in counsellor at the school, he explained; he had never left. Sonya thought that she may have reservations about a high school cling-on helping her kids adjust to life in boarding school but she dutifully kept her opinions to herself and laughed enthusiastically every time Thomas or Sanjay made a back-in-the-day joke.

The weeks leading up to their trip had been tense, if not downright confrontational. The gang rape and subsequent death of the young physiotherapy intern in Delhi and the exhaustive multi-media post mortem that followed it had affected Thomas, Sonya and the General in ways they could not have foreseen. Though Delhi police, using CCTV footage and sketches of the rapists drawn with the help of the male victim, had arrested some suspects within twenty-four hours, the Nation remained glued to their screens—'perversely enthralled' in Thomas's words—for days on end, watching this most gripping of reality television unravel right in front of their eyes. There were questions aplenty to be answered. Would the minor be tried as an adult, considering the severity of the crime (he was reported to have been the most brutal of the group, and seventeen years of age)? Had the police officers on patrol duty on the bus route that night been negligent? Would the government accept its failure and resign? Would the victim survive? And still more questions to be asked.

Sonya, Thomas and the General struggled to come to a unanimous conclusion as to *how* it had happened, as to who had failed whom. Was it the system or the patriarchy? The law or society? Maybe it was just men in general who were to blame? Or did the girl fail herself, as Thomas regrettably mused out loud, putting herself in such a vulnerable position in a city known as the 'rape capital of the world'? Do we not, as individuals, have a responsibility to ourselves to actively protect ourselves from the very possibility of danger? This was instantly interpreted as being pro-rape or pro-misogyny, Thomas wasn't sure why.

Sonya expounded on the duties of the state to its citizens and the freedoms of the individual, while the General offered personal anecdotes from college: she had once been drinking at a male friend's flat with a group of friends when some local goons burst in, grabbed one of their phones and started recording them on camera, taking special care to get the alcohol and the half-smoked joints on record. One of them threatened to call their parents, another threatened to call the cops and get the girls arrested for immoral *conduct*, possibly prostitution. They had finally let them go with a couple of blows to the boys' heads and a warning to the girls to never be seen in those parts again. Was that her fault too, she asked, and Thomas was at a loss. He would love for women to be able to walk around freely at whatever time of the night, said Thomas miserably, but as long as that wasn't the case, would it hurt to be a little prudent?

Within three days of the *incident*, the young woman who had become the unwitting cynosure of liberals across the length and breadth of India had undergone five surgeries, losing most of her remaining intestine in the process. Committees were set up—judicial, medical and law enforcement. In compliance with Section 228 (A) of the Indian Penal Code, the female victim's name was not initially revealed to the media, resulting in a slew of superhero-like pseudonyms ranging from Amanat to Nirbhaya to Damini (after Meenakshi Sheshadri's character in the 1993 film of the same name'), which helpfully heightened and personalized the sense of drama. Nirbhaya was roundly acknowledged as the most appropriate moniker by popular vote. Demands were made to speed up trial and prosecution, and orders issued by the Delhi High Court for the creation of five fast-track courts to try cases of sexual assault.

Slowly, the debate changed from how to why. The rape was analyzed in degrees of severity. What could have prompted six young men in the world's fastest-growing democracy to behave in such a barbaric manner, to not just force themselves on their victim but to repeatedly rape her using a *jack handle*?

It was the culture of commoditization of women, said the General, citing that analogy often used by men of her age in relation to their views on marriage: 'Why buy a car when you can drive it for free?'

Yes, but how had such an attitude come about, Sonya wanted to know. Did it start with Arjuna, who had unquestioningly agreed to his mother Kunti's unassuming order to share his spoils with his four brothers, though she hadn't known at the time that he was returning home from a *swayamvara* for Draupadi, having won her hand in a sporting competition? Was maternal devotion to blame for how her countrymen treated other women?

Or was it rooted in more recent times, their history of Mughal invasions and empires founded on rape and plunder setting the tone for contemporary notions of masculinity? The General dismissed this as akin to revisionism, singling out Kerala's higher-than-national-average record of crimes against females as evidence, a highly literate state that had never come under any serious threat of Mughal occupation, let alone cultural appropriation. If anything, she felt, it was India's continuing engagement with the caste system and the blind eye the government had historically turned to the mistreatment of religious minorities that promoted violence against women.

If Thomas felt a little out of his depth, he didn't show it. His international school had neglected to educate him about his culture or history, so he concentrated instead on what he called 'the need of the hour', preferring to take a more contemporary approach to their soul-searching, more inclined than ever towards his longstanding theory that consumerism was at fault for everything. Men harassed women because they were promised all sorts of sexual compensation in exchange for shelling out hard-earned money on bigger cars and muskier deodorants, better flats and longer vacations. The ones who spent felt entitled to their pie, and the ones who couldn't attempted to take what they could by any means possible.

The girls didn't respond, so Thomas took it a little further: 'We're a sexually repressed nation. Nobody talks about sex, about *choice*. Teach the kids about sex in school, about mutual respect, and they'll grow up knowing how to treat each other.' Just as he began to worry that his argument would be deemed too simplistic, Sonya jumped up and switched on her laptop. She typed something in and turned around to face them.

'I've been trying to remember what all this reminded me of, where I'd seen it before,' she said triumphantly, and pointed to the screen, 'and I've got it. It maybe the *Mahabharata* or the lack of sex education or whatever, but it's all here. It's the *pornography* that sets the example.'

By Christmas day, Nirbhaya was reported as continuing to be intubated, and 'in critical condition'. Young women all over the country took to the streets to protest, a section of whom were described by a Member of Parliament (who was also the son of the President) as 'dented and painted', which quickly viralled into the ubiquitous soundbyte of the saga. On 27 December, Nirbhaya was flown by air ambulance to Mount Elizabeth Hospital, a multi-organ transplant specialty centre in Singapore, where she finally succumbed to her injuries a couple of days later. She was cremated in Delhi the next day under high level police security, a basic courtesy extended to the bereaved that was curiously criticized by the Bharatiya Janata Party as being 'reminiscent of the Emergency era'.

The plan had been for Thomas and Sonya to fly to Calicut on the same day and cab it to Kodaikanal the next, just in time for New Year's Eve. Though they had booked their flights a month in advance, Sonya felt they ought to postpone their trip in a gesture of solidarity with Nirbhaya and her family after hearing the news of her passing. The 31$^{st}$ was just another day after all, she said; could they not shake themselves free of such capitalist trappings in their country's darkest hour?

They were at Soul Fry with the General, waiting for Anjali and Sudhi. Thomas said he was willing to skip Kodi but reminded her that his ticket was non-refundable. Sonya had only had to trade in her air miles. He wouldn't be able to afford another flight any time soon, he added; they had only chosen to fly rather than take a train to accommodate her crammed work schedule in the first place. 'Work ruins everything,' said Sonya angrily, before coming to the conclusion that Thomas had anticipated with some trepidation for as long as he had known her: 'I'm going to quit, Thoma. I just can't do this anymore. There's so much more to be accomplished than daily meals.'

It had been coming, Thomas knew. Nirbhaya was just the immediate trigger. He had read it in her eyes that first evening in Gokarna, that desire to roam free, to do something bigger, more meaningful, that many mistook to be his own philosophy. The difference, thought Thomas, was that Sonya and her ilk felt it was their *right* to do something grand, that it was in their destinies to do something life-changing. They had grown up in an era of too many overnight-stars, at a time when terms like 'genius' and 'prodigy' were attributed not retrospectively (or even comparatively), but *during*.

'If they couldn't, who could?'—that was the slogan of her self-righteous, head-in-sand generation. They would hammer away too till whatever they were chasing lost its appeal, or burn out before it bored them; their brand of self-serving altruism intimidated and enraged Thomas in equal measure. He, on the other hand, chose to fight smaller battles, to make the personal his agenda rather than the communal, to let his life be the canvas rather than the message. *Come what may*, that was his motto, whereas Sonya was the type who needed to shape what came next, to define and direct, to be in control.

'That's a great idea,' pitched in the General when she heard the news. 'We've been talking about doing all this stuff. Now you'll finally have the time.'

*The General.* How she got on his nerves, the way she went on about *the cause* and the *subaltern*, the need for *this* to change and for *that* to be overcome, turning Sonya's head any which way she pointed. Did the General's father not pay the rent for both her flat and that of her girls'? What made her so different, so *right*? Thomas would have gladly accepted—and applauded—her in the role of a philanthropic wealth manager, a trust fund baby-gone-rogue, redistributing her good fortune to help a few in need. But she was no more a revolutionary than the rest of them—so complacent in their morality, so absolute in their comprehension of the black and the white, so eager to share every passing thought and bowel movement with the world as though it were somehow unique—as entrenched in the system as she regularly claimed not to be. He could forgive the hypocrisy, but the lack of self-awareness he just couldn't stomach.

Thomas reflected that the *stuff* that the General referred to had taken many forms already. First, there was her girls' self-financing art exhibit. Later, on the evening after the news of Nirbhaya's rape first broke, Sonya and the General had wanted to start a website to provide a forum for women ('And men?' Thomas had asked) from all over the world to write about their own experiences with sexual assault.

That idea had died a premature death after the two of them realized that neither of them could operate WordPress with the level of efficiency such an enterprise demanded. Thomas's suggestion to reach out to the General's girls' schools and volunteer to talk to students about what had happened and to help them understand it had quickly been shot down as being too micro. Their intentions were sincere, Thomas knew, but he could also see that they were reactionary, contextual. There had then been talk of organizing a candlelight vigil, and later, a Slut-Walk-of-sorts, both of which turned out to have already been set in motion by various conscientious citizens in different parts of the country. One evening, the General and Sonya went to Toto's to discuss starting up a feminist advertising agency with two 'like-minded individuals' who had contacted them on Twitter, only to discover that they were just college kids hoping to hook up. Their most ambitious proposal yet had been made the previous night by Sonya shortly after she had identified pornography as the culprit.

Sonya's diagnosis had neither been without merit nor sans due diligence. Thomas had excitedly introduced her to a brand new world of depravity a few weeks earlier when she informed him with some embarrassment that she had never actually watched pornography with any real *intent*. Like children, they had cruised the streets and alleyways of the internet's red light districts with abandon, dipping their toes in milder waters initially, steadily stepping it up one, two, three notches, watching and learning, mocking and fantasizing and mimicking. There was so much to learn about human sexuality. 'We're not like animals at all,' Sonya remarked one afternoon. 'It really *is* all in the mind!'

People were so different in their needs; they aspired to such different things: oral and anal, groups and cuckolds, submission and scat and humiliation and domination. Watching pornography with Thomas had seemed a harmless couple-activity to Sonya, more wink-wink than kink, choosing not to dwell on the exploitative nature of the industry and concentrating instead on not judging, on admiring these women's confidence and respecting their right to pursue a line of employment of their choosing. She may even have called it 'empowering', she remembered shamefully. But that had been before life imitated art, before she realized how a lonely man ('or woman,' said Thomas) might mistake fantasy for reality, pretense for permission.

'We need to make sure these things can't just be accessed by *any*one,' she declared. 'Tougher laws,' she said, 'greater regulation.'

But that would infringe on one personal freedom too many, said the General without turning to face her. Sonya reclined in her chair and put her feet up on the bed to think. The first image she conjured in her head was that of her sister. 'No,' she shook her head, 'more parental control. Apps! Psych evaluations!'

The General tore her eyes away from the screen. On it, a blonde woman lay spread-eagled, her limbs akimbo and tethered to poles on each end while three black men inserted assorted household goods in her various orifices. There were metal clamps on her breasts and nose, and insulting names written in felt tip across her stomach and forehead. 'We can't just shut down the internet, sweetie,' she said and snapped the laptop shut.

Thomas thought he detected a helpless lilt in her voice that reminded him of the night of the party. He wondered if his voice was as transparent when he was turned on and shifted his attention to Sonya's feet, the soles of which were a dark coffee-brown from walking around the flat barefoot. He had asked her a hundred times to wear slippers inside the house. 'We should just make more *inclusive* porn,' said Sonya. '*Feminist* porn. That's a thing, isn't it?'

Later that night, Thomas lay in bed watching Sonya make her customary round of the flat, tidying up, mentally taking notes—a speck of dirt on the wall here, a splash of curry behind the microwave there—information that would be relayed to Didi the next day with much clicking of tongue and wagging of finger. These were things Thomas had only noticed recently; there hadn't been time or space or inclination for routine till she started going to work again. In a few minutes, she would close the door behind her and come sit next to him. Must he watch her like that, she would ask wearily; couldn't he read a book or use the computer? It must be exasperating to have someone watch you go about the minutiae of your life, thought Thomas, unable to pick one's nose or fart or talk to oneself without fear of judgment. He tried to picture her making her rounds on her own, in a house bereft of him. Would she dance? Sing? Touch herself in the mirror? They hadn't made love since the morning after the party. It wasn't that she had been cold to him or even unresponsive when he reached for her but something always came up before they could progress further—she had to clean; she was too tired; she was too full; she had an early meeting.

Sonya took off her bra from under her top and smiled at Thomas. The pressure had been mounting on her too but she had kept making excuses to herself for their dry spell. The General had been over almost every night the last week or so, drinking and hanging out with them late into the night. Her period was due anytime now and her body had been feeling sore all over. Thomas and she had skipped courtship and gone straight to living together; maybe he was bored. It was this last possibility that was most prominent in her mind that night.

She straddled Thomas and kissed him. He reached around and positioned her on top of him, already pushing hungrily into her. When she sat up straight to look at him, Thomas followed suit, not an inch between their upper bodies. She lifted her top but Thomas locked her hands behind her.

'I really want to do this,' he said and kissed the corner of her mouth, her cheek, her ear.

'Me too,' she said and struggled to break free.

'But,' he said.

His tongue was in her ear one second, tickling her, running down her neck the next. He let go of her hands.

'Yes?'

His fingers were under her shirt, kneading, squeezing. He bit her neck. She slapped him playfully and reached for him.

'You forgot to wash your feet,' he said.

Sonya lifted herself off the bed without a word. She returned from the bathroom, her wet slippers squelching ominously under her newly clean feet, and climbed in next to him. She turned off the light and within a minute, she was asleep.

Thomas woke to the sound of running water the next morning. Sonya was in the shower, the door open. He thanked her silently for giving him a second chance. He knew he had blown it the previous night and was eager to make amends. Slipping in noiselessly behind Sonya, he watched her: bent over, her hair arched loose and long over her head as she rubbed shampoo into her scalp. Thomas was impatient with desire but he also needed to empty his bladder. He hooked his boxers on the doorknob and aimed a sharp jet of urine at the small of her back, watching it cascade down the crack of her butt and under her in a clear straight line. She jumped and turned around.

'What the *fuck*, Thoma?'

He grinned and readjusted, aiming just above her knee this time.

'Get out,' she screamed.

'What's the big deal?' said Thomas. 'We've done it before.'

He couldn't stop so he turned to face the wall.

'Yes, with my *permission*,' said Sonya, suddenly tired. 'Just get out.'

Thomas shook himself clean with added ceremony for what he considered comic effect and moved towards her again.

'GET OUT!'

Sonya was livid. Thomas didn't know what had hit him.

'But you left the door open,' he started.

'Yes, I left the door open,' said Sonya, 'in *my* fucking house. Now get out!'

They didn't talk again till evening. Thomas had made toast and eggs but Sonya hurried out the door before he could offer her any, still angry or late or both, leaving in her wake the sweetest-scented trail of longing. Thomas tried to write but soon gave up, and fished out the Nokia box Varun had entrusted in his custody. It was heavier than he remembered, its edges taped over maybe four or five times for security. He held it up to his ear and shook it. Nothing. The contents of the box were probably taped in place too. Varun had been clear: Thomas was not to open the box or lose it. He was only to hold the box for Varun, and give him a call in a few more days to hand it back over. But they went back a long way, Varun and him. He wouldn't mind; hell, he would scarcely expect Thomas to not sample a taste of his wares. It wasn't the first time Thomas had fenced a little something for Varun, or transported it from and to. He hoped they were uppers, whatever they were. He knew he had made a mistake the other day, shooting up with Varun. He had been weak. He didn't want to go down that route again, not when he was already doing such a good job of messing up the first good thing to happen to him in years, maybe even a decade. The blackout had shaken him more than he had cared to admit, and—the solitary fix aside—he had been careful since, moderating his drinking and cutting down on cigarettes as much as he could. A man of his limited resources couldn't afford a medical episode.

At work, Sonya was finally introduced to her new team and put in charge of two interns. They opened up to her easily and quickly in that naïve trusting manner of one freshly out of college and still acclimatizing to the real world: one of them played bass in a funk band on the side; the other was hoping to crack the UPSC exam next year. The bassist emailed her a link to his band's Soundcloud, and gifted her a badge that announced them as The Funky Monkeys which she magnanimously pinned to her laptop bag. It would no doubt become the latest inhabitant of a box of assorted gig merchandise as soon she reached home, never to be seen or thought of again just like so many of those bands.

Sonya learned that the Civil Services aspirant had also been born and brought up in 'the *Gelf*' like her (the younger girl had looked her up on Linkedin) and that she was an equally 'fraud Mallu' as she cheerfully—and seemingly without irony—described herself. She wanted to put her managerial training to use in the public sector, she said, she wanted to help 'the poor people'. Sonya almost envied the interns their youth and reminded herself that she had been in their shoes, in their same hopeful greys and pinstripes, not all that long ago. She washed her face and applied lipstick, only to wipe it off with a paper towel before leaving the washroom. 'Damn you, Thomas,' she muttered.

Thomas peered into the box and recoiled in horror. He had seen some things in his time, but nothing like this. Nothing of this—he searched for the right word—*magnitude*. He wrapped a tee-shirt around the box and shoved it under the bed. He lit a cigarette, stubbed it though his hand continued to tremble, and retrieved the box. He couldn't leave it lying around for Didi or Sonya to see. He squeezed it into the leg of a pair of old jeans, tied a *kavi mundu* around it and placed it at the bottom of his rucksack. He locked the door behind him, flew down the stairs only to run back up and check that the door was indeed locked and made a beeline to the phone booth. Varun didn't answer his phone the first few times he tried it, after which it was switched off. Thomas made more calls, getting more agitated with every dead end, till he traced his way back to the Source. The Source confirmed his fears. Varun had had no intention of collecting the 'item' from Thomas. He was well and truly doomed. He ricked it to Anand Wines and spent the last of the money Varun had given him on a bottle of Antiquity Blue and a pint of Old Monk.

Thomas was less of a wreck by the time the General picked him up for their dinner at Soul Fry, but a wreck nonetheless. They ordered a plate of Mutton Suka. Sonya arrived soon after, the badge now occupying pride of place on the strap of her shoulder bag. She had checked out The Funky Monkeys on Soundcloud and decided it was the least she could do for them.

She wanted to *talk*, she said when the General stepped out for a smoke, before they were joined by Anjali and Sudhi. He was sorry about earlier, Thomas said; he was going through some sort of phase. He couldn't seem to do anything right. Sonya took his hand and waited for the waiter to clear the table. No, they didn't want to order anything else till the others got there, she told the waiter. That wasn't it, she said, turning to face Thomas when the waiter had left. She had been dealing with a lot lately, she said; the job, the new team, everything that had happened that fortnight. She didn't think they ought to take off on a vacation just then, all things considered.

The General expectedly offered her support when Sonya told her she wanted to quit her job. Thomas found himself wishing Sudhi would reach sooner. He seemed the type to clip wings, thought Thomas; he would wait to see if Sudhi would play the bad guy before stepping in.

Anjali walked in apologizing for being late. Sudhi was outside paying the cab, she said; what *was* that terrible music they were playing? The friendly waiter materialized miraculously by her side just then, as though on cue. They would be playing Goan-themed music till the place filled up, he informed them cheerfully, but there would be karaoke to look forward to later. Sonya didn't want to discuss her looming unemployment with the group but the General was on a roll. 'We're starting something on our own,' she announced to a confused Sudhi. He turned to Thomas. 'Our man here is contagious,' he chuckled.

Spurred on by alcohol and Sudhi's indifference, Thomas waded bravely into the middle of Sonya's disillusionment.

'I just think you need a plan,' he told her. 'Yes,' she retorted, 'because that's how you operate. With a *plan*.'

She didn't even know what she wanted to do, he said. 'What I want is to find out what I want to do,' said Sonya firmly. 'I would have expected you to understand, of all people.'

Anjali didn't think it was such a bad idea after all. 'You've always wanted to write,' she told Sonya. 'You could start a magazine.'

Sudhi called the waiter over and ordered a pitcher of mixed rum and coke. 'With lemon,' he specified. Sonya caught Thomas rolling his eyes and smiled conspiratorially. They were a team, she realized happily.

The General said that starting a magazine made sense. 'A proper *journal*,' she emphasized, 'quality writing, topical. But it's a lot of legwork if you're thinking paper.' It *had* to be paper, said Anjali; it was more Sonya's style. Thomas wondered about the legitimacy of this statement. Sonya had been quiet for a while. Maybe she had begun to see sense, thought Thomas.

They ordered fried rice, pork vindaloo and beef fry. Sudhi made a joke about the hipster couple in matching fedoras at the next table. Somebody started on the karaoke and Anjali groaned theatrically. 'Law of averages,' said Sudhi. 'You'll never go to a karaoke and not have some idiot singing Bon Jovi.'

Thomas sipped his drink in silence, content to observe. Out of the corner of his eye, he noticed the hipster couple join in and punch their arms in the air when the song chorused and wondered how different life might have been if he had their enthusiasm for anything at all. Sonya asked him if they could step out for a cigarette. 'Let's go to Kodi,' she said. 'It'll give me time to think things through.' Thomas put an arm around her and told her he was there for her, whatever she wanted to do. The trip was going to change a lot of things anyway, she said. She put her head on his shoulder and watched a family step out of the car that had just pulled up. 'I don't know why we keep coming here,' she said. 'Let's go back inside.'

The party shifted to Sonya's flat so she and Thomas could pack. They considered carrying only one suitcase but Thomas reminded her that it wouldn't quite suffice for their *plan*. Anjali looked at Sonya inquiringly. 'I'll tell you later,' she mouthed in response.

Sudhi looked up from his phone and announced that he was leaving. He looked at Thomas. 'Booty call.' Thomas dutifully twisted his face into what he thought was an appropriate approximation of modern male camaraderie. 'Soon you'll be high-fiving each other,' said Anjali snidely after Sudhi had left and the girls laughed. Thomas topped up her drink and shrugged his shoulders in what he thought was an appropriate approximation of modern male self-deprecation.

Sanjay turned out to be a wonderful host and Sonya was relieved to be rid of tour-guide responsibilities for a change. She and Thomas had reached Kodi before noon, and the three of them spent the day drinking ginger-honey tea and trying out the many special pastries at Pot Luck Café. Their cottage was a cosy little hamlet with a kitchen and a fireplace in a far corner of the campus, surrounded by a lovely garden and overlooking the dense deciduous carpet of Palani Hills.

Sonya wanted to see Thomas's old school, so they walked around for a while, coming to a halt in front of the beautiful Lawrie Baker building, all red brick and teenage hormones. It had so much *character*, said Sonya, unlike her old school. Thomas told her it was the newest of the buildings, constructed in the mid-80s. Sanjay waved at the few passing boarders who were spending their holidays in school and kept stopping to chat.

They resumed walking and visited the church and shot some hoops and Sanjay told Sonya that all his memories of the basketball court were soundtracked by *Tupac* and *Biggie*; did she ever listen to rap? She said no and laughed at the idea of a group of rich kids in an international school getting their kicks to *Ghetto Gospel*.

In the evening, they smoked a couple of joints and ate the mushrooms with generous helpings of Nutella. Almost immediately, Thomas ran to the bathroom and threw up. 'You ok?' asked Sonya when he returned. He nodded though he knew there was no doubt about it: his body was warning him—he could give up his ways or it would give up on him.

They decided to go for a stroll. They started tripping when they reached the entrance to Coaker's Walk but it was closed. It was getting dark anyway, said Thomas. 'And chilly,' he added which made Sonya and Sanjay laugh. They rode horses back to their part of town. He knew the perfect spot, Sanjay told them. Sonya thought that she really liked this happy little man after all.

They went to the Carlton Hotel and sat outside. They ordered beers and watched the fireworks, every dazzling trail of light across the sky sending Sonya into renewed bouts of holy rapture. She thought the trees were talking to her, that the river flowed in whispers. Thomas held her tight out of a mixture of affection and freezing cold but she couldn't stay still. This was all new to her, Thomas reminded himself, this view and the psychedelia and the lights. She was a natural, he could see, taking to the trip and running away with it like a child in a toy store. Not for her the sheer physical exhaustion of having played this game too often and for too long.

He let her go and watched as she skipped along the railing, following the river all the way to one end of the courtyard and back. She had never looked more beautiful or contented. At midnight, he kissed her and went inside to warm himself with a bowl of soup and a whisky.

They were still feeling it when they returned to the cottage though the physical energy was fast dissipating. Sleep was neither an option nor a priority. 'I want to come back here during *season*,' giggled Sonya. Sanjay rolled them a joint with some effort, and Thomas helped him lug an old mattress out to the football field. It was on elevated ground, the sky a little closer, the stars like dewdrops waiting to be plucked. Sonya followed, a thick duvet wrapped around her. They lay down and smoked, and watched the moon and the stars melt into dawn.

# 11

Thomas and Sonya took a train from Calicut to Kottayam. Thomas's father had sent a car to pick them up. Sensing her nervousness, Thomas tried to calm Sonya down by telling her that his parents were just people, that she was under no more pressure to be liked by them than she was to like them. Besides, he told her, she should probably save the worrying for the *real* test. She was being so brave, he told her and squeezed her hand; he was proud of her. Sonya was being very brave indeed.

Shortly after finishing school in Riyadh, Sonya had been packed off to her grandparents' home in Thrissur and enrolled in a local coaching centre to prepare for the Kerala state medical entrance exams, which she cleared without trouble. Her parents were ecstatic and flew down to celebrate. To the dismay of her mother however, Sonya declared that she wanted to study Economics instead—and in Bangalore, *sin city*, of all places!—and refused to budge from her stand, albeit with the complicit blessings of her father.

Sonya's mother promptly decided to stay back and supervise the construction of the house they were building in Thrissur. That way, she said, Sonya would still have a home to come to on weekends and holidays. Sonya protested vehemently and in vain; her mother had made up her mind. Consequently, Sonya's sister, seven years her junior, was forced to be uprooted and join her mother in Kerala, much to her chagrin. She ended up attending a girls' school a few kilometres from their home and had only moved the previous year to Chennai for college.

Over the years, their mother seemed to have contracted a severe case of selective memory as to the reasons why she was still in Kerala and not growing old together with her husband; the narrative had somehow shifted to hold Sonya responsible for everything wrong in her life—her loneliness and her intellectual decay and even her arthritis. Her father had tried to be understanding at first and even flown down every few months till he absolutely couldn't make any more excuses to his employers. He had only recently been promoted to Manager at the taxi company where he worked and was still more dispensable than he would have liked despite the many years he had put in as a driver. He continued to ensure that the family spent every Onam and Christmas together for a while but lately, his visits—just like Sonya's—had become more sporadic, less certain, increasingly last-minute, subject to change.

The one thing Thomas knew for certain about his father was that nothing about him was subject to change. He was a rock, a model of permanence. He didn't cling to his youth or make a fool of himself in pursuit of it like so many other men of his age. Even as a young husband and father, he had patiently aspired towards middle age and when it finally came—with some reluctance—it just *settled* on him, forever setting his face in the monkish contentment of one who had finished his journey with time to spare and could now rest while the world caught up with him. His hair was still thick, his shoulders broad, his chest defiant like a soldier's and squaring up to whatever lay ahead. If a lifelong diet of drink and meat had left a mark on his handsome countenance, it was in the form of a permanent flush in his cheeks that only embellished his fair complexion and supposed Syrian heritage: Valiyaveettil Solomon and his family were 'Knanaites', descendants of 400 Christian Jews who had emigrated to India in 345 AD skippered by Knaithomman—the original journeyman to Thomas's serial immigrant.

Thomas could have passed for a younger version of his father if he hadn't let life consume him instead of the other way around, Sonya could see. He already had more lines on his forehead, more loss in his eyes, than his father ever would. Sitting across from him in their living room, Sonya thought that she understood Thomas's despair: this was the image he was chasing, the Alpha to his Beta.

Thomas's parents had been watching a cricket match on television when they arrived. His mother met them at the door, hugging him and ushering Sonya in with a smile. His father turned to face them and nodded in greeting. His mother inquired about their journey and whether Sonya needed anything. She was a pleasant woman, small of stature, more graceful than beautiful, dressed in a simple white cotton saree with blue lilies adorning its borders.

Thomas's first thought when he held her was that his mother had somehow shrunk—an idea that grew clearer in his mind as he watched her touch Sonya on the shoulder, as she guided Sonya by the arm to the washroom. Life was quietly leaving his mother, not in one fell swoop but little by little, while Sonya's was just beginning, on the move and radiant with possibilities.

Sonya, on her part, reflected that Thomas was a true chimera: if he had inherited his father's looks (the low cheekbones, the thick eyebrows), he had also taken after his mother—more mild-mannered and warm (once one got to know him) than likely to own a room, to command its attention (and affection, she thought fondly) by his mere presence like her husband. He bent to embrace his father, taking him by surprise, and ended up draping an awkward arm around his back. Valiyaveettil Thoma was looking good, healthy. When his wife reappeared with glasses of Tang, he gave his watch a customary glance and told Thomas to pour himself and Sonya 'a real drink' if they fancied one.

Sonya couldn't help thinking of Thomas's childhood home as an architectural re-imagining of his father, sprawling but self-contained, imposing without being vulgar. It was surrounded by mango and oak trees on one side and a rubber plantation on the other, between which snaked a long gravel driveway that disappeared round a curve and beyond her line of vision when she looked back at it from the veranda. It was like checking into a retreat or stepping through Immigration.

Sonya could already see how it might have been difficult for Thomas to leave home. The mahogany furniture and the cool marble floor and the muted oil paintings on the wall all echoed his father's candid opulence; they affected a detached sophistication borne not out of Thomas's parents' Catholic education but their immediate ancestry—of generation upon generation not just accumulating wealth but losing it too, of knowing that everything was transient, that time could stand still any second. Even the pair of ornate hunting rifles tacked to the wall in an X formation were majestic and congruent, the nature of their function not in the least at odds with the smells of cardamom and summer rain that seemed to permeate the house. 'Just wait till it's tapping season,' said Thomas's mother, 'the smell of fresh rubber makes me nauseous.'

The four of them watched the game in silence, Thomas's mother nipping in and out of the kitchen every once in a while to replace a plate of fish cutlets with beef *ulathiyathu* or squid roast with fried chicken drumsticks. During advertisements, Thomas's father switched channels to a poker game that was happening in Vegas. His mother snuck in questions about how they knew each other, where they had met. Sonya wished, shamefully, that Thomas would answer less honestly; that he would portray her—and them—in a less dysfunctional light.

The atmosphere changed dramatically when they sat down to dinner. Thomas's father was uninhibited and charming, asking Sonya about her education and work, cinema and politics, as eager to involve her in the conversation as he was to entertain her. She watched out for signs of hostility between father and son and concluded that she had projected it on their relationship out of some preconceived notion; from reading Thomas's novel perhaps, or as a result of her lover's general aversion to hierarchy and order—what Sudhi vaguely referred to as 'the establishment'.

The permanent fifty-year-old worked the table with wit and intelligence, calling on everybody to give an opinion or to be the butt of one of his jokes. Sonya found herself wishing the meal wouldn't end though she had already been full before it began; so taken was she by this gentlemanly patriarch. She supposed she was affected by an element of curiosity; never before had she had the opportunity to look right into a lover's future, to see the man he was going to become. If only

Thomas would learn to wait, she thought, if only he would sit back and let it happen rather than fight for it.

Sonya offered to help with the dishes but Thomas's mother told her the maid would see to them the next day. This was in stark contrast to Sonya's upbringing; in her home, problems—and not just the day's dishes—had to be dealt with as and when they arose. Her parents were always in the process of finishing something or the other, some task they had set themselves months and sometimes even years ago; building their house in Kerala, for example, was a goal that had been set a few years after Sonya was born—it was realized in stages: adding to their ancestral property by purchasing a neighbor's land, demolishing the old house, laying the foundation for the new one, buying stone and wood and cement and raw materials piecemeal, building the ground floor first and adding a second and third floor later.

She tried to imagine her father behind his desk, ticking off one familial obligation after another (he had funded the education of at least three of her aunts while she was still in school; paid for medical procedures and weddings and funerals of a host of other relatives), a list in which she knew her marriage featured prominently and at the top of the table. Though Sonya's father had never let her feel the pinch, she had always known that it was a struggle, that all his energy was expended on a vision of a stable, restful future. He owned his own business now—a taxi company—but she knew that this vision, this restful tomorrow, entailed not just economic security but also unburdening her father from what he euphemistically referred to as his 'primary responsibility'—her. Her sister had somehow escaped from under the radar, perhaps under the assumption that Sonya would shoulder some of his *responsibility* by the time her sibling was of marriageable age. She was suddenly overcome with sadness and sympathy for her father, with guilt that she had inadvertently stolen his youth—a guilt that was tinged with resentment that Thomas's parents had had it so easy, that they had lucked out in the one genetic lottery that truly mattered.

After dinner, Thomas and Sonya sat on the veranda and watched the sky. His parents retired early, warning them to take flashlights and to beware of snakes if they were planning on walking about. 'What's the sleeping situation?' whispered Sonya when she was certain they were out of earshot. 'I really want you right now.' How strange, she thought, that the best advertisement for Thomas was his father! He put a hand on the small of her back—his sweet spot, and hers—and said they could go up in a bit, that he needed a few minutes to imprint the view in his mind. 'It changes every time I come here,' he said, 'not drastically, but I can tell. The texture, the gaps in the leaves, the breeze.' Sonya had never heard him speak of anything with such wonder.

'It's an independent universe, constantly in flux,' said Thomas, 'if you listen carefully, not to the *sounds*, but.' He put a finger to his lips. '*See*? The silence. Listen to the silence and you can hear it too. Always changing, evolving.' Sonya let him be, happy to share in the moment, till her thoughts drifted back to her parents again. 'I'm really glad you're here,' said Thomas. She kissed him back and said, 'Thomacha, I don't know if I'm ready for this. With my parents. They're not like yours.'

Thomas told her it was going to be alright. He sounded distracted and Sonya suppressed a flash of irritation. 'I always thought it was a *you*-thing, your whole calm, let-it-be thing,' she looked at him, 'but it's not. Your parents are just *super*

Zen.' Thomas played with her hair. He touched her cheek, pinched it. She pushed him away. 'They weren't always like this,' he said finally, 'nobody's parents are. But they learnt to be. To accept. It'd be egoistic to think of it as my *gift* to them but I'd like to think I played a part.' Sonya knew what was coming. 'Don't you want that for your parents, for them to put down their load, to stop running and just breathe?'

They had had this conversation before, multiple times. It had started with a phone call when they were having breakfast at South Side Café one day. Her mother was on the line and Sonya turned into her usual panicky alter ego, pacing up and down the corridor of the restaurant with the phone in her ear and a hand cupping the mouthpiece, shushing Thomas, gesturing to the waiter to come back later.

'What's wrong?' she asked Thomas when she had sat back down again.

'Nothing,' he said, 'just wondering who I am this time.'

Sonya smiled. 'You're Anjali,' she said. 'You're always Anjali.'

She sipped her coffee. 'It's not you,' she continued. 'I've told you what it's like. My mother worries at the mere mention of a guy's name.'

Thomas nodded and Sonya hoped he would let it go.

'It's a Saturday morning,' he said. 'I just don't see why you have to lie to your mother about who you're with or what you're doing.'

Sonya sighed.

'Can you honestly tell me,' she said, 'that this isn't about you? Your need to immerse yourself into every part of my existence? You have a *tendency*, you know.'

It wasn't, said Thomas. But where would it end, he wanted to know, when would she stop lying and be herself with her parents? 'You realize you're trying to protect your parents from yourself?' he said. 'And you're doing it out of love, you say, and they're concerned for you out of love, and I hear a lot of talk about love but how do you even know they love you if everything they know about your adult life is a wildly fabricated lie?'

It wasn't all a lie, she started but Thomas stopped her.

'Love is knowing,' he said, 'not guilt.' Maybe she was afraid they couldn't love the real Sonya. 'I respect your need for privacy,' he continued. 'You don't have to tell anybody anything you don't want to about yourself. But what you've got going is an alternate reality, a fictional you. That's just cruel. You're leading them on, and you're doing them a great injustice by not even giving them a shot at the real you.'

The conversation spilled over into the rest of their day, popping up between other conversations and when they were picking out aubergines at Pali Market and watering the potted petunias on her terrace and sharing a beer at Janata.

Later, over coffee back at South Side Café, Sonya said, 'It's scary how easily we let people into our lives, no? Everything we did today, I would have done on my own or with like three different people just a few weeks ago. Now I can't bear the thought of being apart for a moment so I pull you along, holding my hand while we watch a movie, or.' She shook her head. 'Last night,' she said, 'you got up to pee and I woke up and you were gone and I missed you so much I came and talked to you through the door. Do you remember?'

Thomas squeezed her hand.

'I feel the same way,' he said.

'That doesn't make it right,' she said. 'It's psychotic behavior.'

He liked that they dove right in, said Thomas, he liked that they just went for it.

'Full power,' laughed Sonya.

'What I don't get,' he said, 'is how you can keep such an important part of your life from your family. We may not last a month or a year, who knows? But this is you, *now*.'

Sonya said she didn't want to have that conversation, not again, so Thomas changed tack. 'Forget about you,' he said. 'Your parents—*our* parents, all of them—they're the products of a system that taught them this is the way. That everything they do should ultimately be reflected in their kids, *their* success. Their progeny, this ghostly immortalization of their selves. They don't want you to be happy; they want you to be *them* because they've had no time to be themselves.'

Sonya took a deep breath.

'Their wound is geography,' she quoted one of her favourite authors.

'Exactly,' said Thomas. 'Let's face it; this whole thing is about sex. This ... *culture*, this role as guardians of their daughters' chastity. It'll ruin them, rob them of their lives. Always diligent, always protecting them from what? Love? Making mistakes?' Sonya looked around and Thomas lowered his voice. 'You know better. Set them free. Let them live their lives, not vicariously through you.'

The attempts at brainwashing continued for days on end. It seemed to consume Thomas in the manner of one who had just discovered a horrible truth about one's lover. Who had appointed her parents as gatekeepers of her morality, of her *virtue*? Wasn't one's body one's own to do with as one pleased—to fuck and tattoo and pierce and flaunt (or not, he added as an afterthought)? He shouldn't have to teach her Teenage Rebellion 101, he said; it was unhealthy to let parents fetishize their children so. Sonya had no right to talk about equality, about individuality, said Thomas, when she was oppressing herself, changing colours to fit somebody else's ideals of appropriate and inappropriate. She was her own worst enemy, he told her; she was fooling herself.

It occurred to Sonya that Thomas's discomfiture was more about his own ideal of the kind of woman he wanted to be with than about liberation or personal freedoms but she also felt that it wasn't a bad prototype to model herself on.

Sonya couldn't be sure when the *plan* had materialized, but she knew it had been as much her decision as it was Thomas's. It had all made sense, rung true, in their little cocoon in Bandra but it was only while sitting on Thomas's verandah, the wispy rubber trees and their silhouettes playing games with her mind, that she realized the enormity of the task at hand. It had been easy to believe in his rhetoric, to be pulled along by his conviction, when it was just the two of them. But the real world was complicated. The past few weeks had raised some serious questions about where she stood, even in terms of 'them'. *Thomas, who passes out in taxis. Thomas, who lets her run amok in Kodaikanal, high as a kite.* Was this man worth the upheaval? Would they last? Did she want them to? She was underprepared, she decided; she wasn't ready. She was glad that they had agreed to play it by ear.

Thomas and Sonya woke early the next day and drove into Kanjirappally town. They paid their respects at Thomas's grandparents' graves in the Pazhayapalli cemetery and admired the 900-year-old carvings on the pillars of Ganapathyar Kovil. They returned home for a sumptuous breakfast of *appam* and mutton stew followed by pineapple jam rolls they had picked up from Kunju's bakery (which Thomas insisted was the only important cultural landmark in town). Later, they caught a Mohanlal movie at the Grand Opera theatre with his mother. By the time they had to leave, Sonya felt indelibly connected to the town and Thomas's home and his parents. The mushrooms were still kicking about in her system, was Thomas's response when she told him. His father offered to let them keep the car but they declined. He insisted he have them dropped at Sonya's place by his driver at least.

Sonya's house was located just off the main road, near the main bus station. A little before they reached the station Thomas mysteriously took ill, clutching his head and rubbing his chest. He asked the driver to pull over and collapsed helplessly onto the ground. The driver ran to his side and helped him up and fetched a bottle of water from the car which Thomas took a sip of and immediately spewed out. He doubled over and continued vomiting while Sonya looked on anxiously from inside the car. Her mother would never let her hear the end of it if one of their neighbours—or God forbid, relatives—spotted her with this strange man with his long hair and unruly beard.

Passers-by exchanged looks with her, probably assuming that Thomas was drunk or strung out on drugs or both. It was impossible to look at Thomas and imagine he was anything but a slacker. Sonya suddenly realized that that would be the inevitable conclusion her mother would come to as well, whether or not he had his breakfast down the front of his shirt.

He changed in the car and told her that it was probably just something he ate. Sonya wasn't convinced but Thomas refused to go to a hospital or a pharmacy. On her instruction, they drove around in circles, passing her house thrice to make sure he wouldn't need to vomit again.

Sonya's mother welcomed them with a surprising lack of drama and just for a moment, Sonya thought that things might go alright after all before chastising herself for her naiveté. *Nothing* had gone alright where her mother was involved, not in the last few years. It was why the frequency of her visits had dwindled alarmingly of late; she just couldn't deal with her mother anymore without the neutralizing presence of her compassionate, absorbent father. He soaked up her mother's venom and kept Sonya and her sister from suffocating.

Sonya introduced Thomas as the 'friend' she had mentioned might tag along, to remind him of their arrangement as much as to give him a face. Thomas spoke to her mother politely and in Malayalam, Sonya having warned him earlier that having always struggled with English, she had now almost completely unlearned the language thanks to a 24/7 diet of daytime TV and no real necessity or opportunity to apply it in her daily life. This apparent deficiency had never bothered her earlier but meeting Thomas's parents with their textbook turns of phrase and their considered diction had gnawed at some latent middle-class complex that was now making her uncomfortable.

She felt grateful that her father wasn't around; he loved spending time with her friends—the dear man—and getting to know them, but he had a habit of lapsing into a peculiar sort of English in their presence, of enunciating excessively and triggering much behind-her-back mirth in her school days. She knew this was harsh of her; her father had done well to provide her with quality education and the confidence to take her own decisions when it came to matters of professional direction despite his own *vocational* (as he comically referred to his polytechnic qualification) background.

How she might have turned out had her father not immigrated to the Middle East as a young man and chosen instead to pursue a line of employment commensurate with his academic accomplishments, or lack thereof, in Kerala, was a rabbit hole she normally sought to step over; she had always been ahead of her peers intellectually and politically, an anomaly in business school and one of a handful of humanities majors in a sea of engineers and commerce graduates. She would no doubt have reached wherever she was headed, one way or the other. But how unfair that her parents offered such little indication of what she might become; how unfortunate that they projected so little of her!

On his part, Thomas was relieved to finally be able to put a face to the name but his relief was tinged with foreboding. Sonya's mother didn't share many features with her daughter, hadn't contributed her great round eyes or rose bud lips. But there were enough signs pointing to where this beaten middle-aged woman and his own inamorata were headed, enough bodily indicators on display to predict where their paths would intersect. The thickening of shoulders under the neck, the ample bottom almost creaking under the weight of a stacking of waist. So this dumpy woman was Mummy, he thought: Mother, earth to Sonya's eternal bloom.

The phrase that came to him unbeckoned was 'lived in'. Sonya's mother was crumpled, *lived in*. Unlike his mother. His mother still had the slender hips of a child, her face still evoked the waxy impermeability of Mother Mary or Munroe, a semi-formed smile forever playing on her lips that would neither retract nor break out into song and dance. Things— and children—passed through people like his mother, only skimming the surface, urged on by a quiet faith and a quieter indifference. They were vessels, women like his mother, simulations of the real thing.

As a child, the two of them used to visit the hospital where he was born, a Catholic institution in Kottayam town. 'Restraint,' the Mother Superior would tell him as she hunted frantically around her office for chocolates or Shrewsbury biscuits to give him, 'your mother was a model of restraint. Here, have one.' Thomas would look to his mother for approval, for permission. ' "Cry, Susan," I would tell your mother,' the elderly nun would continue. '*Cry*. Let it out. But not her. The hospital wasn't so fancy in those days, you know. Just one big ward for all the expecting mothers, separated by screens. Not just our people, you know, women of all faiths and backgrounds. No men allowed in, of course. And all around your mother, women screaming, cursing husbands and fathers and men, shouting such nasty things that the younger Sisters were advised to close their ears. But not a peep out of your mother, not a single tear.'

And Thomas would look up at his mother and beam proudly. It was a big word for Thomas at the time but also a virtue he learned early on to associate with womanhood: restraint; silent suffering. He suspected that Sonya's mother, with her tired bow-legs and her body giving way on either side as though despite herself, was capable of neither.

Sonya made sure Thomas was comfortable and turned to her mother. 'Where's Su?' Su—short for Sudarshana, Thomas knew—bounded down the stairs as though on cue. They hugged and kissed and fell about like children, exchanging sisterly platitudes about the need to keep more in touch. Though prepared to be surprised, Thomas was taken aback by the contrast between the three generations. Dressed in shorts and a black Bevar Sea tee-shirt, Su was simultaneously

the spitting image of her sister and an improvement on it—
breaking away from it, finding her own feet, becoming her
own person.

Thomas counted off at least three calculated differentiators:
the silver nose ring, the dolphin tattoo on her ankle, the punk-
inspired streak of red in her hair. There were physical differences
too: Su was taller, almost boyish in frame like his mother, her
body still taut from what Thomas could make out from the
flash of midriff he caught when she lifted a hand to wave in his
direction. He smiled back, a little flustered at this unexpected
time warp: standing before him was the past, the present and
the future.

Su's breasts were smaller than her sibling's but her
clothes fit tighter; her ass was higher, legs longer, eyes
the same big orbits as Sonya's that reduced him to animal
instincts. Thomas read into gestures, affectations: Su had
grown into her body while Sonya had grown despite of it; Su
casually and unselfconsciously exhibited signs of an inherent
cosmopolitanism that Sonya's generation had had to fight for.

Thomas tried to remember when he had last been with a
girl of Su's age. She was probably more agile, more responsive,
less set in her ways. In the time he had known Sonya, he had
never once wanted anybody more, never once encountered
a risk worth taking at the expense of losing her; that was the
cornerstone of his fidelity—the certain knowledge that he
wasn't missing anything. He wondered now if that had been
because of the company they kept; the possibility had just
never arisen of a younger, fitter model.

Guiltily, he drafted Sonya into the illicit excursions
of his mind, imagined the three of them together—the
positions, the expressions, the taboo—but it wasn't working.
Watching them now, pitting Sonya in her bland Kerala-proof

kurti-and-denim combo against vibrant, life-affirming Su in the sexual battleground of his mind, Thomas felt cheated. He had been robbed of Sonya in her prime; he had not been offered the best of her—that had been frittered away in the arms of Sudhi and who knew how many others, but not him. He could see that neither of the sisters took after their beady-eyed, world-weary mother in the looks department but that only strengthened the surge of panic: how much longer till Sonya's face took on the same defeated pallor, till she was racked with the legendary (and violent, Sonya had hinted) bouts of depression? She had to get *something* from her mother!

Sonya kept brushing Su's hair, patting her back, touching her face, as she demanded to be introduced to her *friend* though Thomas was right there. It reminded him of a line he had read somewhere, something about the tone of someone's voice 'italicizing the malice' of their reply. This wasn't malice, Thomas knew, more an expression of disbelief as vocalized by a genuinely sarcastic generation that communicated in air-quotes. Sonya pleaded and scolded with her eyes as her mother expressionlessly ordered Su to help her in the kitchen. Sonya turned to check on Thomas and smiled nervously, and just like that, the sum total of Thomas's grievances was nullified. The mixture of anticipation and mild relief her smile conveyed was a timely reminder that there were some things more valuable, less tangible, than the perkier upturn of a younger posterior, and he was glad for the reaffirmation. *We'll be fine*, he mouthed.

Su returned in long pyjamas, a dupatta wrapped carelessly around her neck. She exchanged knowing smiles with Sonya. Thomas thought that her mother could have made Su pull a poncho over her head and she would still have elicited an erection out of him. She was carrying a tray loaded with drinks which she gingerly set down on the teapoy. 'Tang,' she announced and stepped forward. 'I read your book. I want you to sign it for me.'

Thomas had to laugh at the thought that flitted into his head: if they could equip Malayali women during holiday season with one of those wearable devices that mapped one's day in footsteps, no doubt they would find that a major chunk of their perambulatory output was spent navigating that narrow corridor of hospitality between kitchen and living room.

'Sure,' he tried to clear his head. 'I didn't think anybody had heard of it. Thank you.'

'I hadn't,' she smiled. 'Sonya sent me a copy. I'm Su by the way.'

'Sit down,' said Thomas. 'What do you study?'

'English lit,' she said, and paused expectantly.

'You're way too pretty to become a writer,' said Thomas. Su had the same inviting, uninhibited laugh as Sonya. 'Almost as pretty as your sister,' he added quickly.

'Shut up now,' said Sonya and punched him in the arm.

Her mother's reappearance at the door sobered the mood somewhat, and for once, Sonya was glad. She had registered the look in Thomas's eyes and recognized it for what it was. Men were programmed to be fickle, she knew. Thomas could moan all he wanted about how humanity was chasing after quicker and better versions of things they already owned, but he was no different; he was just pushing his cart down a different aisle. She wasn't bitter or insecure; it amused her, if anything, to see Thomas helplessly drawn out of his shell of reticence. He probably thought of it as a kindness, she surmised, some harmless flirting to validate a smitten young girl's affections. He would probably have dropped a compliment or two in her mother's lap if she had seemed a little more accommodating.

Why did men automatically assume centrality in the company of women? They were always placing themselves bang in the middle of imagined sexual *fields*, which Sonya imagined to be a complicated graphic matrix of conversational undercurrents and innuendos of varying degrees of upfrontness, all directed at them. The psychological equivalent of breasts thrust in the face of Man. How did they not tire of constantly decoding gestures and hunting for clues that weren't there? She didn't need to be a psychologist or a mentalist to know how it must have played out in her younger sibling's mind; they were unified by a greater code, a tacit understanding of the world and its ways shaped by being life-long recipients of unwanted attention. Sonya only hoped Thomas wouldn't embarrass himself any further, the old fool.

Thomas was distracted, even unresponsive, during dinner. Twice, Sonya had to rouse him from his ruminations; once, to answer a question her mother had asked him and a second time to heed Sudarshana's request to pass the chappatis down the table. He finished his meal quickly and went back to his room, citing exhaustion. She hoped he wasn't feeling sick again.

Thomas had looked disturbed since he came down after his shower, asking inane questions to her mother about the house ('Did you buy it?') and its occupants ('Did you know the earlier occupants?') and even the road it was situated on. No, her mother had answered in her matter-of-fact way, they had built the house from the ground up except for the bit in the front. Her family had owned the land for generations but they had had to demolish most of her ancestral home to build it. The road was newly widened—a later development and a windfall in terms of property appreciation. There had been hardly a streetlight in their vicinity when they started building the house except the big sign in front of the bus stand next to them. Sonya hoped her mother hadn't noticed. She didn't have the strength tonight for one of Thomas's breakdowns. Or her mother's, she thought wearily.

Thomas stood on the balcony of the room he had been allotted, an unlit cigarette in his hand. It was not yet a city skyline but it looked out over and across the bus depot, modern apartment buildings taller than any he had seen in Bandra looming in the background. The lights in their windows didn't go out one by one as they did back in Bombay but in an abrupt descent of darkness at the stroke of ten, as though taken by surprise. Soon this town would be like any other in Kerala: a convenient marriage of the rural and the international; young professionals and dreamers immigrating *en masse* from the villages to rent from the NRIs the town was made over for, trading open skies and impressionable minds for a slice of the urban pie.

A dog wailed mournfully in the distance, out of loneliness or boredom or both. A BAR sign flickered nervously in the horizon, a beacon of uncertainty in a sea of *nouveau riche* predictability and gentrified permanence. He thought he had noticed it hanging from the roof of a hotel they had passed when they drove around the house earlier, a place with a name that ended in Garden or World or something along those lines. Below him, buses moved in tired sequences, mechanical beasts obligingly backing in and out of garage doors to be looked in the mouth, under the belly, inside the brain. From a backlit hoarding advertising a newly opened jewellery showroom, a toothy Maradona beamed glibly at

Thomas, fingers clenched and thumb raised in incongruent certification of the quality of the shiny wares he was peddling. The house had gone quiet too; no more the whimsical clatter of the sisters' laughter floating up and around him, no more the sounds of television or the grinder or the telephone. The dog couldn't be heard anymore either; maybe it had found a companion for the night.

Thomas cautiously navigated the stairs in the dark and glided across the hall, a ghost with a conscience. The bolt slid noiselessly in its frame and finally he was out, the door shut securely behind him. He had been willing himself to go without all evening but something in Sonya's house had shone a light on a long-neglected alcove of his mind, laid bare a gaping void that could only be filled by drink or death. All evening, he had felt its walls sigh and ache, shiver and shake, bursting to tell a story that was older and wiser than their years. There was a light in the ground-floor window that stood between him and the gate. He suspected the gate was locked, in any case. He crossed the courtyard and hunted by moonlight for a gap in the rose hedge that lined the walls of the compound. Finding one, he gently placed the palms of his hands on the wall, gauging its stability, before launching himself over it in one quick motion—an exercise that, to the casual observer, would have been over in a few seconds.

But Time. Time can be so relative. To Thomas, the up-and-over motion that was scaling the wall took place in phases and entailed the following: first, the delicious freedom of lift-off, of legs suspended in mid-air; second, as his body floated timelessly over the wall, the fear and ecstasy of having left behind the point of no-return, of having committed a deed that cannot be undone. Phase 3 was longer, darker—on the downswing, as his legs treaded air for the first time and he instinctively arched his feet for minimum impact: *panic*. He had been here before, in another life and form. He knew it before his feet touched the ground, before he collapsed for a second time that day by the roadside, delirious and out of breath. He cowered where he landed, folding into himself. He wished fervently to be smaller, lesser. He told himself it was in his head, that his body was convulsing as much from the need for alcohol as from paranoia. *If you can imagine it, you can control it.* But his limbs were made of stone, heavy and lifeless. His breath was struggle, his heart a traffic jam. He sat rooted to the spot till the sun came up, his body immobile while an epic war played itself out inside his head, one with dragons and missiles and aliens armed with axes.

# 12

Their trip to meet their (respective) parents was a success, by most standards. Not a bad word had been uttered about either of their partners, though Thomas had only—albeit transparently—been introduced as a friend. When they were about to leave, Thomas's mother had simply inserted a wad of 500 rupee notes in his shirt pocket and whispered, 'She seems nicer than the last one.' Sonya's mother had been detached and self-contained, almost at peace with the world (though they did have a shouting match at night that Sonya hoped Thomas hadn't heard). Sonya felt happy that her mother seemed to have at last found her niche, even if it was only daytime TV. They both returned to Bombay chastened by their own conventionality and a little ashamed at how much they cared for parental approval.

Sonya plunged herself into work straightaway, and Thomas let himself believe for a while that they had ridden out the storm, that Sonya would have no more epiphanies or attempts at self-realization. The General continued to drop in every few days with pamphlets and pot; they had the flat to themselves otherwise, Sonya usually too exhausted to do anything even on weekends after the long hours she put in day in, day out. But tragedy soon arrived in the form of the Torso, that long-standing bastion of Indian masculinity. He had just starred in *Missed Call 2*, the much-awaited sequel to his superhit of 2010 about a fun-loving womanizer who liked to leak video footage of his sexual conquests on the internet—all done in fun of course, all in search of the one impenetrable fortress of a *Bharatiya nari* who wouldn't succumb to his charms. The story arc of the sequel was rumoured to run along similar lines, with the Torso expected to continue womanizing using the same modus operandi—a missed call to initiate contact followed by the inexplicable catapultation of his prey into his bulging arms. He had had his time in the sun, thought Thomas, but it looked like it was about to rain on the Torso.

It was not the General but Anjali who first brought the item number in *Missed Call 2* to Sonya's attention. It was a catchy, suggestive song somewhat unimaginatively titled 'Booty Call' that featured a scantily clad former Miss India—much like the Torso's recently deceased former lover—dancing rambunctiously in the rain, spurred on by a group of clearly titillated men, presumably in some ritualistic exercise to will the giant butt-shaped telephone in the background to ring. The video was causing a furore in the media, with commentators questioning its propriety on the back of recent revelations that the Torso had inundated his ex-girlfriend's mobile phone with hundreds of calls and text messages 'of a threatening nature' in the days leading up to her murder. They invoked censorship and bans, rape statistics and Nirbhaya.

The song had its defendants too, who argued that it was facile to criticize a 'mindless entertainer', 'a masala movie in the Bollywood tradition', on the basis of the personal life of its star. In any case, they argued, there had been no evidence to suggest that the Torso had acted on his threats in any way.

Watching the video on YouTube again with Thomas and the General, simultaneously translating the lyrics into English for his benefit, she felt the decisions she had made over the holidays unravel. The 'item number' itself was a cinematic device that Sonya had long struggled to come to terms with. An ardent fan of Bollywood, she had grown up singing along with and dancing to those trademark hypnotic beats. She could still remember the illicit thrill of running around her house as a child, humming 'Choli ke peeche kya hain?' under her breath. She remembered mimicking Malaika Arora in the mirror, practising for hours on end to get the shake of her midriff just right; the seamless juxtaposition of the sounds of the train Malaika danced on top of with that rousing rendition of 'Chaiyya Chaiyya' still gave her goosebumps. 'Chaiyya Chaiyya' was a *concept*, she thought; she could write an entire essay on how that song had enriched her life. But she hadn't known as a child that she was pouting for a collective gaze, that the invitations her body was sending out in mimicking those moves were more than just vibrations set to music. They weren't, she corrected herself, but they *could* be taken as such. Whose fault did that make it, she wondered; was it the artist or the audience that was at fault?

She remembered the numerous times her mother had asked her and Sudarshana to 'cover up' when they were expecting guests at home. What had she been protecting them from? What had she been teaching them to be ashamed of? Sonya wondered for a moment if the much-maligned item number had in fact been waging a righteous war all along. Was it possible that the item number was the lone medium in Indian pop culture that consistently portrayed strong, independent women who knew what they wanted and pursued it uninhibitedly and vocally? That it liberated not just heaving bosoms and comely buttocks but also a traditionally oppressed gender, gave it wings and an imagination? So what if there was a touch of the performing monkey to the sight of (usually) one woman dancing for a roomful of drunken gangsters and leering Lotharios? Weren't they all performing monkeys in one way or the other? So what if the item girl was never the heroine, never the virtuous love interest of the hero, never 'girlfriend material'? So what if it was targeted at a male audience? It was a cynical gimmick calculated to put bums on seats, no doubt, but maybe she had been going about things all wrong.

'No', declared the General when Sonya broached the subject, 'just *no.*' Thomas was just as aghast. 'It's blatant objectification of women,' he said. 'They're *called* 'item' girls.' Sonya felt the nuances of the item number were lost on Thomas and the General. They didn't understand Bollywood like she did; they didn't appreciate the drama or the colour, didn't understand the idiom. They were too elitist in their preferences; too hung up on the 'parallel' and the 'alternative'. The same amount of suggestion, she argued, would have passed for art in a Sofia Coppola movie, would have been lauded as ironic or quirky in a Wes Anderson production.

'Possibly,' said Thomas, 'but they're made for a *knowing* audience. They're in on the joke. There's a difference.' This, Sonya found patronizing: 'So it's ok if *you're* watching it?'

The General said she thought she could explain better. 'The men who pay to watch this stuff in theatres multiple

times, the men who set the cash register ringing,' she said,
'I'm sorry but theirs is a different reality. It just is. They believe
it when their matinee idol tells them that women who wear
tight clothes like being harassed, that they're just gagging to
be approached.'

Sonya felt a familiar rage seething, rising up to the
surface. Being in a relationship had somehow rendered her
complacent; she had forgotten about the Eternal Battle.

'I just don't think you can justify any content without
analyzing the market it's catered to,' said the General. 'No
science without fancy,' said Sonya, 'no art without facts.'

Sonya fired the first salvo the next morning before the
General or Thomas had even left their beds: an email to
everybody in her contact list to join the trio in their 'protest'.
She reread the email, made a few changes and forwarded it to
her boss. By noon, she had arranged for all her colleagues to
be exempted from work for two hours to participate in what
was now being referred to as 'the Action'.

HR was quick to warn her that she wasn't to involve
the firm's name in any way, that the firm was for or against
Nothing. 'Participation *must* be voluntary,' said HR. 'The
Action will be deemed purely personal, not representative of
the firm's leanings in any way.' Sonya agreed wholeheartedly.
'This *is* personal,' she assured HR. For every woman who's
been catcalled or groped or threatened, she added to herself.

Sonya's friends were quick to express their appreciation
though many of them wouldn't be able to make it—they had
a *thing*, they were sorry. One of the guys from Marketing laid
out a picture of The Torso on Photoshop and slapped on a
line: 'STOP BHAIFICATION!' Sonya thanked him and rid
the poster of exclamation. Anjali emailed the poster to her
flatmate and soon it was doing the rounds on the internet,

attracting much attention from both the liberal brigade and the right wing.

The Action was accused of being sensationalistic, duplicitous, even communal. There was vociferous support for The Action too, thanks in no small part to its endorsement by a popular Bandraiite chick lit novelist who liked to blog about one-night stands and her love of cats. Everybody had something to say about The Action; some piggybacked on it. The Funky Monkeys promised to eulogize The Action in song. A representative from a luxury taxi company that had only recently started operations in India wanted to know if they could get 'involved'. This was quickly followed by an email from higher management explaining why the taxi company couldn't be involved and how it was regrettable that one of their employees—a recent hire, a fresher—had initiated the correspondence without consulting the company handbook. Sudhi pitched in with a bullet-pointed POA to increase audience engagement in an email addressed to Sonya and the General, titled 'LET'S BLACKHAT THIS BITCH UP!' She fired off a preemptive reply, dryly pointing out the irony of his *faux pas* before the General could do so in her inimitable style and Sonya ended up an unwitting participant in the electronic warfare that would undoubtedly ensue.

By evening, the talk had turned to logistics: should they arrange transport for the activists? F&B? Umbrellas? The gang had assembled at Three Wise Men for some drinks and discussion. Thomas was of the opinion that they should wait before entering into any financial commitments; Anjali said no, couldn't he see the overwhelming response on social media? It was time to act, agreed the General, to channel the *energy*. They could afford to spend a couple of thousand to make the Action as comfortable and hassle-free as possible for the hundreds of kindred souls who had already agreed to take part in it.

Sonya and Sudhi were willing to sponsor 500 mineral water bottles; Anjali and the General would pay for the banners and promotional literature. They looked at Thomas. He would pitch in with first-aid equipment, he said. 'In case things turn rough,' he explained. And, said Sonya pointedly, he would help with the literature.

'Why would things turn rough?' asked the General. Thomas thought she was joking for a moment but the bewilderment on her face was unmistakable. Anjali looked at him expectantly. Sonya scratched her chin, going over this new development in her head.

'You read the comments,' said Thomas. 'People take offence at the slightest.' Sudhi stood up and stretched meaningfully. 'Nobody's going to get hurt.'

His words were meant to placate and instil confidence but they did the opposite; they gave the possibility of violence flesh and blood, made it real, palpable. The General was the first to react. 'It's a peaceful protest!'

Thomas watched Sonya jot something down on a paper napkin. She didn't seem as affected as the others; Thomas wondered if she wasn't just a little happy that the Action had developed an edge. 'We're organizing a sit-in outside the cinema to censor a superhit movie,' said Thomas. 'We're taking on the country's biggest movie star in his home ground.'

This much was undeniably true. The actor had famously put in an appearance at the first screening of all his recent films at the historic single-screen theatre. The choice of venue was as much a nod to his populist predisposition as it was to the notoriously hardcore demographic that accounted for the majority of his fan base. 'Somebody's bound to play the Muslim card.'

Thomas felt Sonya stir in her seat next to him. She crossed and uncrossed her legs and slipped her hand into his. 'We'll play it by ear,' she said, a phrase she used often. 'If somebody incites violence. Well.' She looked around. 'Our side or theirs, that's just a risk we'll have to take.'

Later in bed, Thomas wanted to ask Sonya if she was secretly pleased by the prospect of danger. She didn't seem the type, he thought, but maybe that added to the excitement. Sonya had other things on her mind. She put a hand over Thomas's mouth and broke from his embrace. 'Do you think of what we're doing as censorship?'

Thomas had been mulling over this for over a day. 'I don't think it's fair to expect everybody to be able to detach art from life,' he said, 'especially the ones for whom movies are the only escape. I wouldn't be surprised if they internalized what's onscreen in real life.'

Sonya sat up and switched on the light. Thomas blinked and wrapped an arm around her waist. 'You're advocating a nanny state,' said Sonya. 'Does the artist have no responsibility?' Thomas considered himself familiar with the way her mind worked. He knew she was just thinking out loud, that she wouldn't be satisfied till she had arrived at her own conclusions.

It had been complicated at first, judging when she wanted definitive answers and when she didn't but it was a role he had quickly grown into. Or so he thought. He had come to look forward to these nightly exchanges; he liked playing sounding board to her innate curiosity about good and bad, right and wrong. He had caught himself wishing fervently on numerous occasions lately that he would be around for the end of her journey. 'You're taking a stand,' he assured her, 'you're doing a good thing.' Humour me, she said.

He got up and leaned by the window. 'Do you mind?' Sonya passed him the lighter. 'I don't think the artist has a responsibility to anyone but himself,' he said. Sonya didn't reply. Thomas took a long drag on his cigarette and blew the last of the smoke out the window. In the sky, a crescent moon was being gently eased out of its cloud prison. He turned around and shrugged. 'I wish there were a better way.'

Sonya returned early from work the next day carrying four big bags of banners and flyers. She had translated the literature Thomas and she had prepared the previous night into Hindi. She worried now that she had taken too simplistic a tone with the language; maybe she should have sought the services of a native speaker. It didn't help that Anjali had declared it fitting in such a distasteful manner. What was it she had said?

'LCD-appropriate,' she had called it. Meaning lowbrow. Meaning less-than-middle-class. Meaning manual labourers and goons and clerical staff and those who hadn't gone to a fancy college or university and couldn't speak the language of privilege without an accent, all bunched into one convenient category. 'Low Est Co Mmon De No Mi Na Tor,' Anjali had added, slowly, as though speaking to someone with learning disabilities.

Anjali had done that for as long as Sonya could remember; it was a running joke between the two of them and she had always found it adorable. It had never affected her till today. How had the game come about, she wondered, who had assigned them their respective roles? How had she been slotted in to play the dunce to Anjali's benevolent *Babu*?

She remembered the first time she had visited Anjali's home in Riyadh. They had only started school a couple of months ago and they were already gaining a reputation for being inseparable. Their teachers and parents alike had been talking about it: they swapped lunches; they talked in class; they bullied the overweight kids; they spoke on the phone all evening. One fateful night, Sonya's father had abruptly announced that he and her mother were urgently required to go to Kerala to visit her grandmother; she had slipped in the bathroom and was hospitalized with a broken hip. None of his colleagues (the less-than-middle-class had no friends) had children of Sonya's age. Would she mind spending the weekend at Anjali's?

Sonya nearly fell off her chair in excitement. She was delirious with joy by the time the phone call had been made and Anjali's parents had confirmed that yes, they would in fact be happy to finally meet this diabolical little creature that their offspring couldn't seem to stop talking about and take her in for as long as necessary. It was always Sonya this, Sonya that, they had informed her father. It was the same in their household, Sonya's mother had exclaimed in response, on the extension. It was too bad they hadn't yet had the opportunity to get acquainted, agreed both sets of parents. 'After we're back,' promised Sonya's father.

'They sound like nice people,' remarked Sonya's mother when they had finally disconnected the call. 'Rich people,' said her father. 'They live down Belmont Ave.' It was the only time Sonya had heard her father mention money—or more accurately, allude to a paucity of it in their household—in any context.

The ride to Anjali's house was spent assuring her parents that she would be alright, careful, well-mannered. They had said: 'Don't fuss about meals.'; 'Shower twice, daily.'; 'Sleep on time.'; 'Obey the rules of the house.' The emphasis was on *behaving*, on putting up a dignified front. As though she were some sort of animal. But she had kept her adolescent indignation in check and promised them that she would make them proud; that she wouldn't 'disgrace' them, as her mother had been concerned she would.

As her father walked her to the apartment from the car, she had pulled on his hand till he stopped and bent down like she knew he would so she could inquire softly in his ear: 'Are we not rich, daddy?' Her father had smiled and pecked her on the cheek. He handed her her things, rung the bell, and stepped back. 'Don't let anybody tell you you're anything less than perfect,' he said and before she could truly imbibe his words, the door had been flung open and hands were being shaken and her cheeks were being pinched and Anjali appeared in the hallway and she had run inside, whooping like just the kind of animals children are.

First impressions of Anjali's house: posh; the rooms were all dimly lit, except the study (this surprised Sonya no end, that rich people lived in so much darkness); her parents were both doctors; Anjali's room had a cupboard just to store the toys she didn't like playing with anymore; English, *so much English*, though both their sets of parents hailed from the same land; yellow, lots of yellow; all meals were to be eaten using a spoon or a fork, no hands.

'What's this?' Sonya had asked while Anjali kept her company in the bathroom later that night. It was a question she would repeat over and over again in the next couple of days, her tiny hand pointing at one curio or the other. 'Are you done?' Anjali separated her ring and middle fingers to crack open a window in the hand that covered her eyes. Sonya wondered why Anjali was the more embarrassed of them both though Sonya was arguably the one in a compromising position. She pulled up her pyjamas and stood up.

'That's a bidet,' said Anjali. Sonya had laughed, then stared at Anjali incredulously. She refused to believe that anything of import could have a name so silly. Anjali jumped off her perch on the edge of the bathtub and landed with a soft thump on the balls of her feet. She pointed a finger in the air, like their teacher did in class. 'A bidet. *Bi. Deyy.*' And so it had begun.

Thomas relieved Sonya of her bags and asked her if she was nervous about the big day. There were less than twenty-four hours to the Action. 'It's not a celebration,' she snapped. The flyers look good, said Thomas. He watched her march to the bed, shrugging off her pantsuit in bits and pieces on the way, and climb under the covers, all in one fluid motion. In the middle of all that, she had somehow also managed to deposit all her clothes in a neat-ish pile on the chair.

Not for the first time, Thomas was amazed by just how much he had learnt from Sonya about the human condition at its rawest; not once had he caught her make a clearly practised gesture or a calculated movement. She took her cues from some greater power, some natural force above and beyond— or perhaps it was deep inside her—and it manifested itself in her physicality. How much effort, how many hours of practice, would it take the greatest of thespians to recreate the same sequence of movements? How many years of *tapas* and unlearning would it take a man to clean his slate so, to rid himself off all worldly accoutrements, of external stimuli?

Sonya unfolded herself from the foetal position and looked up. 'Come here. Hold me.' Thomas wanted nothing more. As he slipped in next to her, she changed her mind. 'No, let me hold you.'

Lying in her arms, his ear to her heart, his hand around and under her, he wondered if this was it. Was this the Meaning, the antidote to his ridiculous despair? *Ridiculous*. It was one of Sonya's words; not his style at all. But it did seem ridiculous right then—impossible, almost—the idea of misery. Had he never really loved before? Was this even love? It felt like so much more. *Love* sounded simple, trivial, with its watered down monosyllable clang; a made-up word for a dressed-up nicety. What do you call being so invested in another person that you feel what they feel, see through their eyes, hear the music in their dreams? Empathy? Or maybe this *was* love, this sensation of having gone where no one has gone before, of sharing the world's happiest secret.

Sonya looked down at the head she was cradling in her arms and kissed it. She recognized the smell of dust from the construction site two lanes away, cigarette smoke, the slightest hint of shampoo. She rubbed his back, traced his spine with the tips of her fingers, applied pressure at the bottom. 'Is your back still giving you trouble, baby?'

Thomas was distracted, his mouth working on her breast, a hand boldly reaching for her deepest-darkest. She wondered how they had moved from A to B without her knowing, when her legs had separated for him without offering or being asked, when she had gotten so wet without thinking. She cupped her breasts together and took in the accusatory stance of her nipples; two righteous parties at a duel. Thomas's head was just a blob under the covers now, somewhere in the region of her waist. Maybe his taste buds had had enough of her breasts and craved a change.

Sonya shuddered helplessly at first contact. Was that a tongue between her thighs, a finger, a spoon? She knew Anjali liked this, this pose, that of the faceless lover servicing you under the sheets. It was empowering, she had once told Sonya, because it could be *any*one. 'Plus men make the funniest faces,' she had added, 'doesn't matter what age they are. See a pair of breasts, and they all become caricatures of the star of the last porno they watched.'

Sonya had laughed and agreed at the time, but she reflected now that Thomas didn't fit this mould. There may have been a gradual increment in their comfort levels as Thomas and she got to know each better—why just last night, she had dropped to her knees on impulse and taken him in her mouth while he was brushing his teeth, making a mockery of her freshly-applied mud mask as it cracked and tumbled from her face like so much debris—but she had never once suspected that he was putting on a show.

She held down his head with her hand—there, don't move, *there!*—and realized that he could never be just *any*one, not to her, headscarf or not. She whisked off the covers and pulled him up and kissed him. 'Did I look silly with the mud pack last night?'

In under a couple of hours, Thomas and Sudhi were seated by the bar at The Bend, watching Sonya and the General tack posters for the Action to the wall. It wasn't a particularly-anything place, but they had deals on drinks practically every day of the week and they served freshly made food from the organic café next door which made Sonya feel less guilty about her lack of exercise. Thomas had a folder of music saved on their system which they allowed him to play from more often than not. He and Sonya ended up going to The Bend quite often.

'So how's the writing going?' Sudhi was in a conversational mood.

'Good, how's work?'

Sonya clambered onto a chair to press an errant tack in place. Her shorts showed off the shiny calves of her legs, the soft hollows of her knees, the steady climb of flesh up her thighs, the apple of her hips. Thomas caught a waiter looking, who averted his eyes reluctantly. Sonya twisted and turned on the chair, oblivious.

'You're a lucky son of a bitch, you know that?' Thomas turned around. 'I realize it's all casual and fashionable now, but I don't like that word very much,' he replied. Sudhi made a face and appeared to be reigning in an outburst. 'She told you about the email,' he said finally. 'I still don't know why they made such a fuss about it. I was on *their* side.'

The girls ambled over, their work done. 'They've agreed to host the girls' exhibition for an entry fee!' The General hugged Sonya and promised to get the next round. 'What have you guys been up to?' she asked Thomas.

'Oh I was just telling our man here,' said Sudhi, 'that he's no Gentleman Jack either after a few drinks.' He looked pleased about the reference. 'Remember the night at F Bar?'

The General laughed. Sonya took Thomas's hand in hers and squeezed it. He responded in kind and abruptly looked away. What would alcoholics do with their regret if they weren't alcoholics, thought Thomas. Had drinking come about as an evolutionary mechanism for the perpetually guilty, for bad sons and unkind fathers? He had come round to accepting that he had a problem: he had swapped one dependency for another and it was now threatening to engulf him, to pull him under and into the darkness again.

He had been studying his drinking graph like a scientist, mentally making notes of when he tipped over and into the realm of the haunted. There was no discernible pattern to it, no set rules as to how many drinks caused how much damage, but this much was clear: his tolerance levels were plummeting. The hangovers were longer, darker. He remembered less and less of the previous night, sometimes hours. He was maybe a step away from clinical addiction. Out of the corner of his eye, he caught Anjali stepping out of a cab through the glass doors of The Bend. He went over to the bar to help the General with her round.

Sobbing into her pillow, Sonya wondered later that night if she could have done things differently, done something to prevent what had transpired. Had she not seen it coming, heard it announce itself loudly and clearly in the first discordant note of the evening? She had ignored it at first out of embarrassment. When things got worse, when the lack of propriety had made way for bitterness and meanness, she had insisted they go home. That had only served to provoke; viciousness poured out of Thomas like a bat out of hell. It was the most difficult thing she had ever had to do, to watch the face of her lover disfigure and morph into an impenetrable wall of resentment, to not recognize the voice or the words that came out of the mouth she had kissed a thousand times.

The man she had dragged back home—the one who had smashed her phone into the wall, the one who had ranted and careened wildly in the hallway like a drunken windmill— that wasn't the man she loved, that hadn't been Thoma anymore; that much she knew. Thomas had never said a harsh word to her, never made her feel anything less than perfect. Was it her he resented, was it her that nourished and teased out this monster inside him? Or had it been inside him all the time, lurking? She cried for herself, for Thomas and for all humanity, for everybody who had ever had to come in contact with this terrible affliction, whatever it was. She went over and over the night in her head like an obsessed scholar, convinced she had missed something, determined to break the code, to narrow it all down to one crucial moment, a *turning point*.

She had first noticed the stirrings of the change in him fairly early into the evening. She referred to it as *the change* in her head now. She had already disassociated herself from it, an isolated incident that had happened to somebody else, not to her or Thomas, something she could rerun in her mind with the same detachment she reserved for watching films about werewolves or zombies. The General, no, *Anjali* had just said something, something harmless. She pictured her impish smile, the General's lackadaisical approval, Sudhi's obvious discomfort. And Thomas? Thomas sat beside her, his arm around her as he had taken to doing of late even when they had company. Had his face made a sign, given a signal of things to come?

A few minutes earlier, Sonya had been scanning The Bend in an inexplicable panic, overcome by a feeling of having lost one's moorings for no reason she could think of, till her eyes landed on Thomas, joining the line at the bar, and she was becalmed. It was as though her heart learned to be still again, quietly falling back in step with the rest of the world. Overwhelmed, she had left their table without a word and stood behind him. She spotted a long grey hair in the back of his head; the bottom of his white shirt was crumpled at the back and bore a wet handprint. Someday, she thought, I'll have time to just watch him be, to notice the little things that make people people. She inched closer and smelled the cologne he had dabbed under his ears, brushed the palm of her hand against his butt. Thomas turned around and smiled.

'Just stop looking so happy, will you?' Anjali had said when they returned to the table. 'I hate how you guys look like you've been doing this all your life.'

The stream of conversation immediately after was a blur in Sonya's mind but there had been something about living together and commitment and. *The magazine!* Anjali had brought up the magazine. Sonya had been intending to talk to Thomas about it but she had somehow never found the right time. They rarely managed five waking minutes together before she left for work and she was usually too drained after. It had only been an idea anyway, something she and Anjali had been discussing hopelessly at lunch since the turn of the year, like convicts dreaming of escape. It usually lost its sheen the moment they left the building and disappeared completely into the background by the time they reached home, coming up again only the next morning, revved into life by the doorbell or the phone alarm, much like the sun.

Thomas had seemed interested initially, if a little patronly, as Anjali filled him in. They had wanted to do something on their own for the longest time, said Anjali, purveyor of preambles like no other. See, they had both been—Anjali and Sonya, she meant—editors of the school magazine, regular contributors of poems and stories to this journal and that. They had what she called a literary *streak*, and it made sense to mine it, to see where it could take them.

Sonya clearly had a gift, said Thomas loyally, judging from what little she had shown him of her writing.

'Yes!' said Anjali, and she was good at organizing, running an operation. 'We've decided to start a magazine,' said Sonya, 'a literary journal. Something niche but quality, with a different academic on the editorial board every issue. Feminist. And *topical*.'

They wouldn't make a profit initially, said Anjali, but she was certain she could get advertisers on board once they had established a reputation. Sudhi sucked on his straw loudly and said something about alternate revenue models. Anjali and Sonya had thought of that too. 'We're looking into online subscription,' said Anjali. But the paper journal would be the flagship product, said Sonya firmly.

The General clapped the girls on their backs. Thomas stared intently into his drink while they waited. When he looked up, he murmured something non-committal about being happy for them that Sonya didn't catch, but it was his eyes that gave him away. Sonya knew straightaway that Thomas had already left the building. She got him a glass of water and ordered a plate of fries, the only thing Thomas ever ate at The Bend. She had thought that he would come around, that she could use one more drink, that they deserved a big night before The Action. Online interest in it had fallen drastically. She was concerned that they had, as Sudhi had put it, 'peaked too early'.

Sonya paused the movie in her head to think; what confounded her about the chronology of Thomas's descent into madness was that it was intermittent: veering between Thomas and The Other frequently at first, then less frequently, till all of him was wiped out without trace. There was no *trigger*, she decided, just an unending, inevitable build-up. Thomas hadn't stopped drinking or passed out. They had danced in between, discussed God and free will. But he had also tried to grope her in full view of her friends, called Sudhi a number-crunching peasant.

It was almost as if every sip after a point raised The Other a little from the ashes, slowly making him real, drawing him out, till he was an all-consuming force in their midst, a vindictive deity threatening to take back everything it had blessed them with. If only Thomas had stood up for them, she thought. If only he had fought a little harder.

The movie continued playing, unwinding in flashes. They were talking about The Action now, about how many people were likely to show up. The setting changed without warning and they were smoking a joint outside the bar and making jokes about the musical preferences of the occupants of a car that had just driven by. They were back in the bar again, Thomas and Sudhi embroiled in a heated argument about governance and corruption. Thomas and she were making out in the dark, he was picking fights with strangers, he was antagonizing Anjali. She had said something about his book, asked him if love would figure more prominently in the next one.

Sonya struggled to recollect his exact words. 'I believe in chemistry,' he had replied pompously, 'not love.' Anjali asked him to elaborate. 'I think certain bodies click, and minds fit, and sometimes they create beautiful-looking compounds.' Sonya hoped he wouldn't go on. 'But everything has an expiry date,' he continued. 'I believe in the finiteness of things, and in not wanting more. And some chemicals, no matter how lovely the hallucinations, should just never be mixed. Some chemicals spell doom for each other by their mere existence.' And he had looked at Sonya with so much hatred that she feared for herself.

When she suggested that they go home, Thomas accused her of being ashamed of him, of wanting to castrate him and putting him in a box. Sudhi tried to intervene but Thomas angrily brushed him off. At the General's insistence, Sudhi and Anjali left for SoBo. Sonya said they would stay a little longer, till Thomas felt better. He said she was turning him into a consumerist, a cog. He was too used to it now, he said, he felt trapped. He owned too many things, slept too comfortably and for too long in the same bed, with the same person.

Sonya flared up. Nobody was forcing him to, she said. He was free to do as he pleased, if that was what he wanted. She would expect the same liberties, she said; could he stomach that, Mr Free Love? Monogamy was a misogynist institution, he said, he was only trying to help her, to educate her. He hadn't even finished college, she retorted. And so it went on.

Thomas sobered up without warning in the rickshaw on the way home and apologized unreservedly. She said they would talk the next day, that he could sleep in the hall. They reached home and Thomas departed meekly to the quarters assigned to him. Sudhi called just as she was getting ready for bed. Despite the torrid time she had been through, she had been dreading the thought of sleeping alone and had left her door unlocked. She now felt foolish about her sentimentality. Yes, she was alright, she told Sudhi; Thomas was fine now. They talked for a while about nothing in particular, The Action and college days and about how maybe it would rain soon.

Thomas had come barging in just as she was hanging up, and she recoiled instinctively. He wanted to know who she had been talking to, what they had been talking about.

'I detest your boundary-less generation,' he screamed. 'WhatsApping and texting at four in the morning,' he ranted. 'While I'm lying next to you. You think I don't know?' He threw her phone against the wall and she broke down in tears. She was trapped in somebody else's nightmare and she couldn't get out.

They couldn't look at each other the next morning, but there was work to be done. The Action was scheduled for 11, thirty minutes before the first screening of the day. She had been reading and replying to emails all morning, borrowed strength steadily draining from her body as she came to terms with one cancellation after the other, seeing through thinly veiled excuses and outright works of fiction.

Thomas hovered in the hallway—a wounded dog or a sleeping beast, Sonya couldn't be sure. The General arrived soon, displacing the tension between them if not lightening it. They took separate taxis to the cinema, the girls in one and Thomas and the things in another.

Sudhi and a small group of Sonya's colleagues were already assembled outside the cinema. They had found a corner partially hidden from the sun, and were awaiting instructions. Sudhi informed Sonya and the General that Anjali would not be able to make it to The Action apropos of a resounding hangover.

Sonya and the General set to work without delay, setting up a desk and putting up posters on electric posts, garbage bins, just about any surface they could find. Thomas shook hands with Sudhi and slapped him on the back in apparent apology. How easy it was for men, thought Sonya, how easy to live by the law of the sword. The brotherhood of men.

A few curious onlookers gathered around the desk but backed away when asked if they would like to get involved. The security guard stood his ground behind the gate to the cinema, uninterested, even when they started accosting the first of the film-goers. Some of them accepted the literature and marched right in; others stared at them in bewilderment. The General checked her phone regularly and confirmed Sonya's biggest fear: nobody, absolutely nobody, was talking about The Action on the internet either.

One of Sudhi's friends started a chant that was slowly taken up by the rest of them. As they stood in unison across the entrance of the cinema for the next three hours, drenched in sweat and hoarse of throat, Sonya contemplated the modern retelling of the tree in the forest: if something that happened does not get covered on social media, if the peanut gallery 2.0 doesn't 'like' and 'tweet' its appreciation, did it really happen? Inside the cinema, shreds of carefully crafted action literature rained down like confetti every time The Torso flexed his muscles or delivered a punchline.

# 13

Out of the many lies that Thomas and Sonya told themselves about the nature of their relationship, the most prevalent one was perhaps that of the Squatter Without Rights. They both subscribed to the fiction that Thomas didn't actually live with Sonya. That they weren't really flatmates. He did this by not accepting the spare key as his own but leaving it under the mat every time he locked up after himself, by asking her days in advance if he could have somebody over even after several months of cohabitation.

Though these exercises in the seeking (and granting) of permission (Thomas's invitations however never seemed to bear fruit—his friends either cancelled at the last minute, or he did) may have appeared—to the untrained eye—to be the careful consideration of a compassionate partner, they were made with all the self-serving humility of a house guest. It was contemporary domestic drama at its finest, and vital to the longevity of the show they put on for themselves day after day, night after night. They laboured diligently and corroboratively to maintain the status quo of the long-term visitor: Thomas was staying at hers for a few days, though how long he would stay, or where he was going, they neither seemed to know nor wanted to acknowledge.

This should not be taken to mean that Sonya was a reluctant housemate, or worse, that Thomas was an indifferent one. Within a few weeks of his arrival (and subsequent moving in to her apartment the very same night), Thomas and Sonya had worked out a living arrangement of such utilitarian pragmatism that it could only have been the fruit of Mutual Convenience: an old couple that the universe just hadn't gotten round to putting in a room together. Thomas fit Sonya like the flared grey denims she favoured on down-days; as for him, he had never known a greater intoxicant than the smell of her when he was between her legs.

From the onset, it was clear that Thomas was a nester, a beast too introspective to be sent out hunting (but a beast nonetheless). She had never met a man so averse to the outdoors, so affected by the sun and the rain and the dust (he carried a bottle of hand sanitizer with him whenever he was forced to take the local train), so content to circle her lair, haunted by some inner fury that only seemed to abate when she offered him to her. She, on her part, was both unaccustomed and receptive to the joys of being tamed; of being sniffed at and sized up like prey, of being backed into corners and overpowered and turned over and feasted on; of being nudged, pawed at, shaken awake, only to be gorged on again.

Like children in a dark room, they played their game of cat-and-mouse for as long as they could keep out the real world, till work and bills and ambition came barging in. Thanks to the ability of technology to render one omnipresent, they had kept it up longer than most, she from behind her

Blackberry or laptop, he from behind her, atop her. Clothing felt increasingly restrictive; their bodies felt seamless, meaningless. They owned neither nook nor cranny the other didn't feel entitled to poking around in, upheld no personal law or preference that couldn't be broken or changed. Their only interactions with the outside world those first few months had been with: (a) delivery boys who stood shyly by the door, careful to keep their eyes averted from an exposed leg or the swell of a breast under a hastily wrapped bed sheet, while one checked their order for a pesky piece of garlic bread that had snuck its way in or a truant mutton bhuna roll which had given its transporter the slip, and the other hunted for change; and (b) Didi, her maid, who would drop in every morning with cigarettes and provisions and stories of strangers and smells of cleaning agents and called Thomas 'bhaiya'. In their little game with no rules (or rules that could change on a whim), they may not both have always played cat (and one may have donned the mantle more frequently than the other) but they were always king *and* queen.

It was this fiction, this *foundation*, that was now being threatened with obliteration. Thomas listened grimly as Anjali callously bulldozed her way through the life Thomas and Sonya had built for themselves, through what he had come to think of as home. They wanted to start a magazine, she said. They wanted Thomas to help, said Sonya; hadn't he worked with one before?

Thomas had only a vague recollection of telling Sonya this but it was true: Thomas had spent a summer in Delhi many years ago as a stringer for one of India's first indie music magazines. The magazine wasn't making enough to pay him but they had let him cover local bands and gigs of his choosing, review the works of obscure international artists old and new, and he had never had to 'go in to work' at a specific time or date. He had done it for the romance, for the ambivalence of being part of a fledgling publication run by three ageing metalheads who couldn't distinguish "alternate revenue models" from their behinds, but could tell the difference between a great riff from a merely good one in their sleep.

He supposed Sonya and Anjali could claim to be driven by the same redundant concept as the metalheads: "passion". Millennials were always talking about *passion*; about wanting to do something they were *passionate* about. As though there were any other reason to do anything; as though *passion* were a genie they could unbottle at their convenience. Still, he thought, it was possible that he had overstated his role in the subsequent rise of the magazine as a respected curator of the gig scene, as a whistleblower of mediocrity.

But Anjali had sped past aspirational territory and was now dealing in body blows. She was talking about Sonya and her quitting their jobs, about doing this 'full time'. She would have to move out of Bandra, objected Sonya, get a place in the boondocks.

Or not, said Anjali excitedly, maybe Thomas and she could just accept what they had going and start living together, formally. They could split rent, and grow their own vegetables, and split bills, and do whatever it was functional couples did when they lived together.

There was a lot of *splitting* to be done, from what Thomas could gather. He bowed his head and concentrated on his drink. How had he let this happen, he wondered. He had been so careful, all these years, to never grow roots, to be one backpack ahead of everybody else. How had he ended up on the verge of eviction from his own home, *again*?

'Oh I couldn't,' Sonya was saying. 'Thoma's not that type.' She squeezed his hand under the table. He looked up and said that he was happy for them, happy that they had found *direction*. But what was this "type" Sonya was talking about? Was it better than him? What type was he?

As far as Thomas knew, he possessed only one distinguishing characteristic: he was a nomad, a wanderer. He grew bored of people and places quickly. Or as an old lover had put it, he didn't feel at home anywhere because home to him would always be *his* home, the house where he was born and raised, soundtracked by the trees growing and brooks babbling and the patter of his own tiny feet chasing shadows. He had been running away all his adult life because he was still trying to find his way back in.

Thomas had always accepted that there was an element of truth to this analysis. He had made a virtue of one of the earliest lessons he had been taught: that nothing was permanent. But he liked to think there was more to it than that. The way Thomas saw it, he had been robbed of his bearings as a child in the most brutal manner because his father had decided early on that his land, his resources, were his to do with as he wished. He hadn't even been offered the dignity that was extended to *kudikidappukar* by the Kerala government in the sixties which his father still held responsible for his own downfall and the usurping of what was *rightfully his*. Thomas resented the innate feudalism of his father's school of thought; as he grew older, he rejected outright the idea that anybody should profit from something as fortuitous as ancestry or as selfish as the aggressive pursuit of wealth. This was the battle he had been fighting all his life: that of ownership and mortgages, of rent.

Thomas wondered now about the price he had paid
for what was essentially childhood noumena, if it had been
worth it. He thought back to squatting in an unoccupied flat
in the State Bank of India residential quarters in Delhi, to
weeks and months of holing out in buildings that were under
construction in Chennai. He remembered the tangible fear
of being caught that followed him around like a stray dog
he just couldn't shake, always nipping at his heels, barking,
threatening to expose. He remembered being chased away
by builders, thrown out by the scruff of his neck by security
guards.

He hadn't been alone either: there were plenty like him,
young and old, men and women, homeless by day and
haunting the abandoned or burnt down or waterlogged
edifices of newly urban India by night. Rooftops were their
only consistent ally: they waited all day for the sun to go down,
for the lights to be turned off, before moving in single file up
rickety stairways or shimmying up trees or electric posts to
congregate on rooftops, to rest aching backs and exchange
tired tales of belonging and loss. Not all of them were poor
or aimless or lost. There were artists and intellectuals, junkies
and criminals on the run, beggars and pimps, all desperate
to put their loads down for a while, to slip into their parallel
lives, to rest and partake of some semblance of community.
On the rooftops, they were dervishes, sharing what they had
and offering more than they could spare. They taught Thomas
a great many skills, not least picking locks and making chairs
and cutlery out of nothing. They taught him to read a city by
its lights, to find love and compassion in the dark.

But that had been in the beginning, when he was young,
when he was still *searching*. Once he realized there was
no greater purpose, no Other, that *this was it*, he started

preferring the solitude of water, the stoicism of the hills, to the illuminated poignancy of city skylines. Over the years, he had steered clear of cities altogether, making his way through the coastlines and the Ghats, Hampi and the Himalayas, staying through 'season' and moving again. There was always work to be done in exchange for lodging in these tourist havens: cooking, plumbing, DJ-ing, drug dealing.

Sometimes, he was propositioned by lonely travellers; at times for sex but more often for company. Some of his longest relationships had been with recent divorcees and elderly widows, jilted lovers and career professionals on sabbaticals, broken beings all, all looking for the 'boyfriend experience'. He had made love to the scarred and the ugly, the wicked and the unlovable. They stayed for three months, some for four or six, and he held them and helped them heal, nursed them back to life. Some made demeaning demands; some demanded to be demeaned. Some he fell in love with, and some with him; some came back, some didn't. The only constant was parting.

It was Varun who had introduced him to the business. They had only recently been acquainted at the time, at a poker game, and Thomas had made enough losses to cost him, literally, an arm and a leg. He had slipped out of the casino that night knowing fully well that there was no corner of the world he could hide out in for too long before the house came to collect.

Varun told him the next time they bumped into each other that he knew a lady who may be willing to help, a nice British woman who was in Panjim to celebrate her retirement. All she wanted in return was some intelligent conversation, some considerate companionship while she shot up, and a body beside her to keep her warm at night.

Varun and Thomas quickly grew thick as thieves, preying on the alone and the needy. His new friend taught Thomas to look for tells, to identify prospective *hosts* (Thomas didn't like referring to them as customers because he never took money from them), to let them approach him and not the other way around. Varun would step in to 'help' them procure heroin or acid after Thomas had them already hooked on the biggest placebo of them all: companionship. They were hustlers and it was a scam but it was also an honest living; they weren't selling anything their victims didn't want. No, Thomas decided, he had no regrets.

That hadn't always been the case. Initially, Thomas had felt the need to justify, to contextualize. He was a writer, a creative person. He needed Hemingway-esque *experiences*, and more importantly, a roof over his head, to do anything useful with his gift. It was a line of thought that Varun encouraged; some might even say 'coaxed out'. The struggling writer in search of his muse: it was a narrative tailored for his clientele—it gave them hope to hope for Thomas, filled them with a sense of purpose and meaning to fend for him and— dare they say it—possibly even inspire him. The longer they hoped, the longer they stayed.

It was an exercise that paid dividends in the form of *Kill Them All*, Thomas's first book, which had materialized out of thin air, in one urgently typed flurry on Marlene's laptop over the course of three sleepless heroin-infested weeks in Gokarna. But it didn't last. Even before the irrefutable failure of his novel to capture the imagination of a mass market audience that had recently discovered—and was revelling in—the hundred-rupee paperback, and his consequent downward spiral into depression, Thomas had arrived at the conclusion that writing, like cooking or plumbing, was just

another trade, a means to get by. He didn't think anymore
that he did it particularly well but he was objective enough
to know there was nothing else he could do better. Armed
with the realization that he was neither special nor different,
he had stolen away one night without so much as saying
goodbye to Varun or Marlene, five kilograms of Varun's
heroin safely tucked away in the back of his Cielo.

Thomas woke up on the day of The Action with little
memory of the previous night. It was becoming a regular thing,
these blackouts. He had been making a conscious attempt at
moderation but there was always something to mourn or
celebrate to warrant more drinking, more consumption. He
left the couch and peeked in on Sonya, which was when it
hit him. Not a clearer picture of his last waking hours, but a
wave of guilt, terrifying and real. What had he done? He had
visions, partial and visceral, like images on a flickering reel.
Had he thrown things, yelled, said hurtful things? He was
overcome by the alcoholic's need to apologize, to put right
and make amends, but Sonya sat calmly behind her desk,
checking emails. If only she would throw a hint his way.
So he hovered uncomfortably, lingered outside her door,
waiting for a bone.

The turnout for The Action was dismal, if unsurprising.
Thomas had been dubious about the enterprise from the onset,
staunch in his view that electronic emotional contagion would
not carry over into real life, that 'likes' and 'shares' were just
that—online manifestations of idealized alternate selves that
were too rewarding on their own to inspire any significant
spill-over. There were sixteen of them in all, seventeen if you
counted the pothead from downstairs who had breezed in
about ten minutes before the end. Thomas wanted to comfort
Sonya, to congratulate her on having fought a good fight,

but she was aloof, distant. When they finally got a minute
to themselves, she informed him that she would be staying
at the General's for a couple of days. He said he understood
though he didn't; he said he was sorry though he didn't know
what for. He wanted to offer to leave, to let her have her home
to herself, but he didn't know where he could go. Her place
was their place after all.

# 14

Thomas went straight to Sonya's flat from The Action and retrieved Varun's Nokia box from his backpack. He opened it gingerly, stared at what was inside it for a few seconds—willing it to life, daring it to make the first move—before closing the box again and placing it in the middle of the bed.

The contents of his backpack lay strewn all over the floor, which he swept to a corner of the room with the inside of his foot. Jeans, books, a set of three plain tee-shirts from Globus that hadn't even been removed from their packaging. A pair of Lennon sunglasses Sonya had picked up for him as a joke in Colaba, a bottle of Chivas he had been saving for an occasion. Army-issue trekking boots he had purchased for a steal in Dharamshala and never used, leather jacket, binoculars. These were the things that would identify him when he was no more, separate him from every other washed-up junkie. He would probably be given a Catholic funeral though he hadn't set foot in a church since he was a child. Everybody gets a complimentary makeover at the end.

He cleared a space on the floor and sat down cross-legged, his back upright, and concentrated on his breathing. He recited out loud the list of *kleshas* as he had been taught to and focused on their attenuation, on the all-healing stillness. He found it difficult to let go at first, to not interpret his being in terms of his body and what it was doing, but it soon came back to him, that familiar calm. *If you can imagine it, you can control it.*

Sonya spent the evening with the General's girls, catching up on their lives and playing Parcheesi. The General was distracted, edgy. It had been apparent within a few minutes of their arrival that she was more uncomfortable than usual with playing host but it was more than that: a shift in their dynamic, a change in their *equation*. She seemed unsure about how to treat Sonya, about which topics were off limits and which were not.

It reminded Sonya of her mother in the months after what they only referred to as The Tragedy in their household, presumably in a bid to protect Sudarshana from the shame. The boy was never so much as mentioned in these retellings, as though he had somehow not been involved at all. It had started out as sympathy for Sonya, as grief for the horrible fate that had befallen their family, but it had quickly changed complexion from kindness to a kind of caustic evasion of reality, a wordless laying of blame solely and surely at her feet: *she* had tempted fate, she had lured in *tragedy*. *She* should have known better; her father and mother had taught *her* better.

Her parents had consulted a jyothishan, an astrologer, who confirmed the worst: the fault lay not in the stars but with Sonya herself. Pujas were done, fasts observed. On his advice, her name was changed from 'Soniya' to 'Sonya', ostensibly to appease some higher power that handed out good fortune by syllable. Her uncle and aunt had stopped speaking to her altogether, and—she suspected—her mother would have done the same if it hadn't been for her approaching medical entrance tests. Over the years, The Tragedy had changed shape from recent calamity to a sort of dark abstraction, an infinite vagueness, something too terrible to have happened to anybody as God-fearing and morally upstanding as her parents, but an uncomfortable truth nonetheless. A moral science lesson for the non-vigilant girl child; a shining example of how not to be. It had lurked and leered in the background ever since, always threatening, always warning, rearing its head at the slightest provocation.

It had come up when Sonya visited her mother at New Year's too, after Thomas had gone to bed. They were seated on Sudarshana's bed, playing Rummy. All evening, Sonya had been waiting to be interrogated about Thomas, about his intentions and hers. Her mother had maintained an admirable detachment, a resolute peace, in Thomas's presence, but the calm was slowly unravelling, prejudices seeping through.

'I didn't want to say anything,' she started. Sonya braced herself against what was inevitably coming. 'But I can't let you set a bad example for your sister.' Sonya tried to be casual, sporting. 'She's big girl, Mummy. She can make her own decisions.' Sudarshana clapped her hands theatrically. 'Hear, hear.'

Perhaps it was the mock-applause that had rankled their mother. 'Like *you* did, you mean. We all know how that turned out.' Sudarshana wrinkled her face in apology.

'As long as she lives under my roof, I will expect her to maintain a certain—' Sonya smiled sadly at Sudarshana as her mother searched for the right word. '*Decorum*?' she offered. 'Don't you dare talk down to me, Sonya!'

There it was, the infamous maternal mood swing, the voice-raising, the whiplash of anger. 'I'll stop when you stop treating me like some ruined woman,' said Sonya. 'How do you think I feel? You bring it up every time we talk, you changed my name like I'm some bad omen, like you're sorry I was born!' Sonya took a deep breath and gathered herself. 'You mutilated me,' she said. 'I was seventeen, a *child*. Just let it go, Mummy.'

It was over in a flash: the deck of cards flying through the air, her mother's pronounced grip on the bun of her hair, pulling her head back, hurting. 'Tell *God* to let it go! Tell the people of this town to let it go!' She released her grip on Sonya's hair and burst into tears. 'They still talk about it behind my back. I'm a prisoner in my own house because I'm ashamed to step out, I'm scared of their condescension!'

Sudarshana moved to hold her mother, to rub her back, but she spread out on the bed. The sisters spent the rest of the night comforting their mother, one apologizing for her very existence, another promising not to turn into the other. The price of desire, of one teenage aberration. Sonya wondered now, all those years later, if Thomas's behaviour would have a similar impact on her new life, if the incident would colour her friends' perception of her just as cruelly.

Thomas leaned back from the computer and closed his eyes. He had been writing all night, furiously and relentlessly. He wrote because it was the only way he knew to cope, to shut out the voices and ignore the demands his body was making. It was turning into a black hole, his body, threatening to consume anything in sight, to reach for the nearest intoxicant and swallow it—and him—whole.

He turned around and looked at the trash bag he had deposited all the bottles in. He hadn't had the heart to empty them over the sink like they did in the movies, and he knew that would turn out to be his undoing, if not that very night then the next. Or the one after that. He collected the bag and went downstairs to the pothead's. The pothead opened his door a crack and peered out suspiciously. 'I heard a lot of shouting last night,' he said. Thomas silently handed over the bag and returned to the flat.

He wondered if Sonya had called and considered trying her number again. It was still switched off. He went back to the computer to resume writing but he couldn't sit still. He lit a cigarette and left it to smoulder between his lips, suddenly weary of words.

Sonya and the General put the girls to bed. Or rather, that's how Sonya thought about it in her head though all they had really done was put away the now empty pizza boxes and switch off the television. *Put the girls to bed.* With a start, she realized that was how she approached life with Thomas too, checking the door was locked before they went to bed ever since the night of the *incident* and placing a bottle of water by the bed.

It seemed to have no *filter* (one of Thomas's words; not her style at all), it didn't seem to discriminate by age or gender, this yearning; this void that called out to be filled up. How easy it was to fall into the trap of caring, of looking after; how manipulative the right combination of words could be. Was there an element of free will, of choice, to these combinations or did they just get handed down generation after generation, transmitted through the body and not the mind? Was that what it was, who *she* was—a mere automation of her body? How sad that all her education and the unending quest for the self had culminated in what her mother could have told her from day one: she was her body. Everything she was and would ever be lay nestled in the bulge of her hips, announced itself to the world in the protrusion of her breasts, in the modest sweep of her feet.

The General reappeared at the door, a robe hanging loosely from her slender frame, like a shirt on a coat hanger. Her hair had grown longer, fuller. Sonya watched her hunt for the remote control with the sense of inquiry one reserves for lab animals. Her subject was almost boyish in figure, almost adolescent in gait and manners. How had this sprite of a girl managed to do so much, to provide a home for the homeless, hope for the hopeless?

Without the earrings and make-up—as she was now— she could almost pass for a teenager, the *zebibah* the lone blemish on an otherwise spotless face. She was Sonya's only religious friend, though none of them were atheists or non-believers. But their prayers were responses to things, silent pleas for divine intervention when faced with a late period or a daunting deadline. They were even audacious enough to give it a name, this tendency to only remember at times of crisis: *spirituality*. They were all spiritual, not religious, because religion this-that. Religion was opium, propaganda, control. Though they all prayed to Gods they grew up with. Though they all cried out to Jesus or Krishna or Allah when they needed a little help. Familiar Gods, familiar faiths, familiar solace. The General was not like them; she was a believer in the truest sense of the word, a practising Muslim who held herself accountable to—and *only* to—God.

'The first rule of Remote Control,' Sonya reminded her friend playfully. The General slapped her forehead in self-retribution. 'You can lose it anywhere you want but you will only find it behind the couch.'

Sonya opened a bottle of wine and plopped down next to the General. She was too sad for TV, too introspective for conversation, but she decided she didn't mind watching the General. How did the General channel her yearning? Sonya chose to ignore the obvious answer and tried to identify instead a pattern, a cosmic clue. The dainty frame, the silent flame. Maybe the General was her body too, just like Sonya was hers. Did that explain it? But that would be too easy, too blinkered.

They had never discussed her sexual inclination in so many words but the General had come close to letting Sonya in on the secret one drunken night not dissimilar to this one, on this very couch. Sonya was getting over a fling that had spilled over into *other* territory without warning and the General was—. The General was just *there*. Sonya had been selfish, she knew, but she had wanted to be held, to be comforted. She had wanted a body against her body and she wasn't ready for another man. She had let herself be caressed, let her forehead be peppered with spidery, brave little kisses, and pulled away. She could see the hurt in the General's eyes for weeks after. She wondered now if she was willing to risk losing her friend again.

Thomas paced the tiny corridor in front of the pothead's door like a giant in a cage. This would be the third time he had come down and returned home without acting on his craving. One drink won't hurt, he told himself, one drink won't change anything. But could he be trusted with a bottle? Maybe he could have a drink with the pothead and leave the alcohol in his custody. One drink won't kill you, one drink won't hurt. But this was about more than the physical or the literal, this abstinence. It was about symbolism, about *meaningful expression of remorse*. It was to be his apology, his white flag, his way back in. He sat down on the stairs and tried to clear his head. 'If you can imagine it, you can control it,' he repeated under his breath. Familiar demons, familiar faith, familiar solace.

# 15

## The Girlfriend Chronicles 8: The Forbidden Gadget

There are few sights more beautiful on a lazy morning than sleeping Girlfriend's visage. Aah who am I kidding, it's my favourite sight of all time: those few minutes of bliss before Girlfriend wakes up and becomes ... well, *herself*, again. A vision so tranquil that I regularly douse her morning coffee with whisky just to see those curtains come down again, however temporarily. Not that I'm some kind of compulsive coffee-spiking psychopath. Sometimes, I just pepper her pasta with finely powdered Paracetamol. One particularly lovelorn afternoon, I knocked her out with a rolling pin. Those tightly shut eyes, those gently cascading eyelashes, are the promises, the visions, all relationships are built on—the promise of calm and quiet, the hope that those sleep-gooey lips will not always chastise or criticize or order you to stop smoking during meals.

Since we started seeing each other regularly, I have always made sure I wake up a good five minutes before she does just to get a glimpse of those non-judgmental eyes. It wasn't easy in the beginning, what with my predilection for sleeping in, and Girlfriend's demanding job that requires her to don pinstripes and create PDFs or pour through Excel sheets or whatever it is real adults do for a living as early as 9 in the AM. But when you want something strongly enough, you're all sorts of resourceful. The solution to my little conundrum, I discovered, was fairly simple: I'd just have to wait for Girlfriend to fall asleep at night, and reset her alarm to a later time. Must be love.

Imagine my surprise then, when a few days ago, I woke up to find Girlfriend not just awake, but not even in sight. I shut my eyes, telling myself it was just a dream, that I'd wake up any second now. I was jolted back to reality by the sound of the bathroom door opening, and out peeped Girlfriend's head. It banged shut again almost immediately, Girlfriend's head retreating like that of a startled turtle the moment she caught my eye.

'Girlfriend,' I call out, 'you ok?'

'Yes,' comes her voice, cautious but steady.

'Did you forget to flush again?' I ask.

'I told you that was the cat!' she shouts back.

'I forgot. So what's wrong, baby?'

The door opens again, and out steps suddenly nonchalant Girlfriend, clad in boxers and tee, laptop in hand. 'Nothing.' she says, defiantly. She places the laptop on the dresser, and busies herself in front of the mirror. 'Baby,' I say, 'were you using your laptop in the loo?'

'What if I was?'

'It's a little ... *weird*, no?'

'There's an entire stack of your magazines by the pot.'

'I know, but they're *paper*. A dump is not traditionally a technology-friendly activity.'

'A tech-friendly *activity*? Why is everything so complicated with you?'

'It's a slippery slope, that's all. Next thing you know, you'll be texting at the cinema, and playing fruit-chucker on your tablet.'

'It's called "Fruit *Ninja*".'

'Oh my god.'

'What?'

'How do you know that? You don't know any sixteen-year-olds.'

Aah, the calm before the storm. The lull before Techocalypse. That guilty-flirty look Eve gave Adam while biting into Apple.

'I got an iPad, ok?'

'What? But we're against mass-produced consumer goods.'

'No, *you* are.'

'But they cut off the poor little Chinese kids' fingers after they assemble those things.'

'They build computers, not the Taj Mahal.'

'But ... when did you get it?'

'Two weeks ago.'

*Modern life is rubbish.*

'Where is it? How have I not seen it yet?'

'Coz I knew how you'd react. I keep it at work. And in the car, sometimes.'

'You've never brought it home?'

'Only ... just on that night you were out with Fatboy.'

'Is it bigger than me?'

'What?'

'Sorry, I anthropomorphized my fear of being displaced by technology. It's a guy thing.'

'No it's not. It's a *you* thing.'

'How would you know?'

'There's an app for it.'

---

Tags: Apple, fatboy, fruit ninja, girlfriend, iPad, music recco, smoking

# 16

The office was a beehive, not of activity but of worker bees and drones alike slumped despondently over their workstations battling 'Montag Fatigue' as Intern 1 put it with obvious relish. He was clearly still a little drunk from the previous night and Sonya found his enthusiasm heartwarming, if not contagious. She let him twaddle on about what a great set the Funky Monkeys had played the previous night, about the chicks and the drugs and the perks of being a musician (or 'rockstar', in his words).

She needed the distraction, the white noise, to work her way back into the state she had arrived at work in. She had been so certain, so determined, but the clarity she had woken up with had been chipped away at all morning by emails and phone calls, internet memes and courtesies, and it was beginning to feel distant, dream-like. It wasn't Monday, but information that had fatigued her. Just a couple of hours in front of her computer, and she already knew what her friends had been up to all weekend, who had said what, had had the most to drink, nursed a hangover, eaten grilled cheese for breakfast, had become an uncle, had turned a year older.

And not just her friends but also friends of friends, complete strangers, celebrities. Somebody had set a world record for something despite a debilitating condition, Madhura Honey was rumoured to be considering writing a book, the Aadhaar card continued to polarize opinion, the Maruti 800 was a national treasure, The Torso was looking increasingly guilty, cupcakes, lolcats, sale, Obamacare, the stock market was crashing no soaring no crashing, Google-this, Google-that. She remembered something Thomas once told her about the 'filter-loop': she was being recommended 'related' news by every single social media platform she was on, effectively entrapping her in a prescribed information circle jerk. She needed to shut out the voices, to hear herself think.

Intern 1 was asking her something, something about a new something in Colaba, did she want to check it out with him and someone else but she would have to something something. She excused herself to go to the washroom but stepped out for a cigarette instead. The smoking corner was populated almost entirely by people she had no interest in speaking to so she pulled out her phone and pretended to be busy, manically refreshing Thomas's blog as though the right number of clicks would reward her with a new entry, a reason to smile. She had only bought the phone the previous night and switched it on this morning; she could still feel the disappointment at finding that it wasn't inundated with frantic texts professing undying love and meaningful expressions of remorse. But Thomas was no Torso. She had told him she wanted to be alone for a couple of days and he had agreed respectfully, obliged unconditionally, the bastard.

Sonya felt incensed by the *lack of initiative*, the lack of effort on his part. She stubbed out her Marlboro Clove and marched back into the office, filled with a new resoluteness.

Thomas looked again in the mirror, *at* it, making sure he hadn't mistaken it for a painting or a TV screen. He hadn't eaten or slept in two nights. His bowels had shut shop. Everything in his body ached or felt broken or unhinged. Yet here he was, fresh as morning dew, the very picture of health in the mirror. He threw a towel over it and went back to writing, and wishing, and wanting.

Sonya marched all the way across the office and up to Anjali and told her it was go-time. About that, said Anjali. Maybe they should give it some more thought, come up with a plan.

'I already emailed my resignation. What are you talking about?' Sonya was due at HR in less than an hour to discuss her decision.

'It's just that I don't know if we can't do both,' said Anjali guiltily.

They would talk later, replied Sonya. She was confident Anjali would come around, she said, she was just getting cold feet. 'It's perfectly understandable.'

Everything was understandable, unfortunate, unforeseen, in the modern workplace. There was no emotion that couldn't be masked with a lazy euphemism.

The meeting with HR was not predictable, to say the least. They wanted neither explanation nor excuses from Sonya, just her signature at the bottom of a document that stated in sterile language that she was leaving of her own volition and that she had no misgivings about (a) the firm, (b) her colleagues and the work culture and (c) recommending the firm to prospective employees. They didn't want her to stay and serve the obligatory 30-day notice period either. She had only just started on a new project anyway, and Sonya had no work pending. She was free to leave that afternoon if she felt like it.

Sonya wasn't expecting to be caught on the other foot one bit. She had already allotted space in her life for a weaning phase, already planned the various activities she would entertain herself with while she *should have been working*. To her great credit, she smiled and informed HR that she would, in fact, like to leave straightaway.

Her knees trembled all the way back to her desk, nervous the way only limbs can be when required to perform something as simple as walking after everything she had just accomplished. She reached into her bag and pulled out a bottle of Teacher's she had picked up the previous evening. She had meant to stash it under her desk, to save it for the right moment, but she wouldn't need to wait after all. She poured herself a 90 and set about putting her things together. She was done in five minutes and walked out without uttering a word of goodbye.

Thomas skimmed over the last few paragraphs he had written and sighed. It was a short story that owed its inspiration to Sonya. She and Thomas had gone camping one night in Lonavala not too long ago, where they had met a man who claimed to have lived in the valley all his life. He wasn't *backward* or tribal, just a resident of the jungle. He had appeared out of the darkness, startling both of them, as they sat outside their tent watching the sky.

Sonya apologized for being spooked and invited the man to join them. They had some whisky and some aloo parathas—would he like some? Perhaps he'd prefer some *charas*? She made space for him to sit but he squatted by the fire instead.

Within moments, he had transformed their flickering flame into a roaring fire, using much the same resources as Thomas. He was clearly a creature of the wild, tall and lean and sculpted by nature. Thomas studied the man with instinctive suspicion, the presence of Sonya and the otherness of strangers triggering some reptilian impulse for caution. Their guest spoke little English and stared intently at Sonya throughout the duration of his visit. Thomas felt increasingly ostracized as the two of them felt around for conversational touchpoints and finally discovered a comfortable rhythm, in a language he barely understood. Their friend from the jungle appeared to be struggling with Hindi too, though Sonya was trying her hardest to speak slowly, clearly.

Thomas felt intruded upon by the man, and betrayed by Sonya. She was being inconsiderate, and foolish. They lived in a world where the possibility of violence, and specifically violence against women, was a daily reality. They were in the middle of nowhere, and blindsided by night. He didn't think she would have invited the man to stay if she had been alone, or with girlfriends. But what difference did Thomas make? He had no delusions that he posed any kind of threat to the man, that he could overpower him in a physical confrontation. Thomas had never felt more helpless or enraged all his life. He felt cursed by his manhood, by society, by gender norms. He was a man who couldn't protect his woman, couldn't do a thing to defend her honour if this stranger turned on them, yet it was his mere presence, the presence of *a man*, that had encouraged Sonya to take a risk, to invite danger in.

Thomas had turned his inadequacy into a story over the course of the weekend in an attempt at addressing his eternal shame. The words had practically shown themselves to him at the time, peeping over the brow of his mind like the sun over the hills in a child's drawing. It had felt clever, right, important, even good (they had never felt good before).

But the words had lost formation somehow; perhaps they had waited like naughty children till he was out of sight to rearrange themselves. They peered back at him nonchalantly now, daring him to try putting them back together again.

How did writers manage to keep their sanity, he wondered; how does one deal with the constant self-doubt, the tyranny of the blank page? He had been hoping it was the start of something real—a book, a novel—but they were just words. Words that lacked meaning or coherence or depth. It was nothing more than the whine of a man who had never really *owned* his manhood. He was reminded of something Varun used to say about driving: 'You've got to feel the car as an extension of your body. It's your brain, your foot, your dick. You don't drive a car, you *own* it.'

He poured himself a whisky, his third of the day. His resolve had died a premature death many hours ago but it had been replaced by a new resilience, a wilful reluctance to accept defeat. He had been careful instead of cowardly, refusing to fear the bottle, rationing his input, never more than a peg an hour. Everything in moderation, including moderation.

On the train to Bandra, Sonya went over what she was going to say to Thomas. There could never be a repeat of that night; that much was obvious. This was his last chance. She had already forgiven Thomas because she knew he had not been himself, had turned into the Other. But could she forget what had happened as easily? How much of the venom he spewed was based on reality, embedded in his subconscious? She remembered Thomas's pontifications about one's responsibility to the self, to avoid potentially dangerous situations. Wasn't this exactly the kind of behaviour that prompted such draconian responses: putting her faith—and safety—in the hands of a clearly unbalanced man?

She stood up and made space for a visibly pregnant woman not much older than her. The woman was accompanied by a loquacious child, maybe six years old, who sat down and thanked Sonya profusely. The woman smiled helplessly and remained standing.

The problem was, thought Sonya, that she was inclined towards imbalance, attracted to chaos, but she had never had the opportunity to act on it earlier. She had learned so much about herself in their time together that she often thought of their relationship as an apprenticeship, a gestation period that would release her inner gadfly. She believed in Thomas, in his philosophy (though he blatantly denied being in possession of one), and she wanted to see his journey through to what she considered its logical end. The problem was, as ever, this: how does one, in the inherently skewed mathematics of mating, account for something as unpredictable, as unquantifiable, as Potential?

Thomas flipped through one of Sonya's magazines in a bid to rouse himself from his melancholy. Yoga for the soul. Food groups guaranteed to make you sweat less and taste better. A picture of David and Victoria Beckham in their underwear, in black and white, looking unreasonably angry. The offside rule explained, for women (How had they not cracked this yet?). The Torso, shirtless, a hand through his hair, his eyes fixed on something peripheral, absorbed.

Thomas turned the pages back to the Beckhams to inspect the image again. He had a vague memory of Victoria's Posh Spice avatar, from a poster in someone's room at school, sticking her tongue out, middle and index fingers split in a

V in the universal gesture for rebellion, atop a blue London bus. She had had three or four children since but she looked smaller than he remembered, thinner, like a petite Ziggy Stardust. David glowered for the camera from behind her, face set in a gladiatorial grimace, tattoos like freight trains running across his body, every vein visible, not a hair out of place. Thomas turned back to the Torso. More veins, more muscles, more man. When had this come about?

Thomas unveiled the mirror again and looked at himself. He was bare-chested too, naked from the waist up. His nipples weren't set at right angles to his pectorals; they didn't stare out at him accusingly. His stomach didn't triangulate in a V over his groin. He googled it. It was called an 'inguinal crease', the V-shaped furrow. It was a ligament, he learned, not a muscle. He typed 'how to' next to the phrase in the search bar. Turned out you didn't exercise it, you starved yourself till you were the proud owner of less than 5% body fat.

He exhaled and pinched a roll of stomach between his fingers and pulled on it till it hurt. It wasn't much but it was unquestionably ugly. It was ugly in the sly way anything less than perfect was ugly; it was an ugliness that crept up on you unawares, bit by bit, day by day, apparent to everybody but you, till one day you looked in the mirror and jumped back in horror.

Thomas estimated that he had at least a few more hours till Sonya finished work. If she intended to show up at all. The sun was still up but he decided to go for a run.

Sonya ran up the stairs with a vengeance, pounding the steps with her feet to prevent her from dithering. She had made up her mind, and it was final. She paused at the door, out of breath and riddled with doubt again. A variety of unpleasant scenarios presented themselves to her: Thomas was a journeyman, a wanderer; what if he had left? Or worse, what if he was in there with another woman? Or worst of all, what if he was inside, wasted and inhuman like the monster he was capable of turning into?

She rang the bell and waited, a visitor in her own home. This was *her* house, she told herself, her *domain*. When it became clear that nobody was coming to the door, she let herself in with her key and stepped gingerly past the shoe rack and the trash can, the kitchen and the hallway. She almost collapsed with relief when she had confirmed that Thomas wasn't home, a relief that quickly turned to joy when she saw what was on her bed: a Nokia box. He had remembered! He was trying to make amends, in his own screwed up way.

The computer blinked, temporarily jostling for—and winning—her attention. She ran to it to see if he had been writing. Yes! Yes, he had! She sat down and excitedly ran her eyes over the open document, scanning it for signs of atonement, of repentance. The story wasn't what she was expecting but she was undoubtedly the muse. 'If a writer falls in love with you, you can never die.' So true, so true! Heart racing, her body light as a feather, she reached for the box and flipped it open.

In any other life, at any other time in this life previously, Sonya would have laughed. She would have assumed it to be a toy, a prank. But so much had happened these past few months, so much darkness had come uninvited into her life, that she knew straightaway that it was the real deal. She wasn't terrified or angry as one might expect to be in these situations, just numb. Just a thoughtless, emotionless, acceptance of reality. She carefully placed the box back on the bed and stared, unable to take her eyes off it. From between the unassuming walls of the cardboard box stared back at her the cold metallic barrel of a handgun.

Sonya undressed in the mirror and carefully rid her face of the last vestiges of make-up. To her surprise, she discovered that she had put on significant weight recently and inspected the damage with a detached curiosity, a poke here, a tired squeeze there. She found herself thinking about Justine, the Sadean heroine, the very embodiment of virtue, forever drawn to tragedy, to exploitation, in her relentless quest for goodness, though it wasn't Justine who had left an impression on her in her repeated readings of the book, but Madame de Lorsagne.

Justine lacked imagination, lacked wonder, ending up a depth-less, passive plaything of the novelist's own libertine fantasies, much like the female protagonists of modern male-centric pornography. Human blowjob machines. Glory holes. They were all variations on the same theme, of women who were done *to*, helpless participants in a man's game, enslaved, overpowered by vice. The Madame on the other hand had made a virtue of vice, albeit temporarily, thereby freeing herself of oppression and suffering, of the misfortunes of virtue. But the Madame had ended up undercooked—Justine's inadvertent vanishing twin—in the Marquis's narrative. Sonya had always wondered how Jane Austen would have treated a Madame de Lorsagne— or better yet, one of the Brontë sisters—but she had never asked herself what she could have done with the same character. She wondered now if there was something there and determined not to let it languish under her overflowing to-do list.

Leaning in, Sonya uncapped her stick of Colossal Kajal and applied it in two thick lines under her eyes. Slipping on her robe, she wondered what was missing. She was just short of the desired effect, one finishing touch away from being stage-ready. Shoes? No. Those silver hoops Anjali had gifted her on her birthday? No. I bet Thomas doesn't know my—. That bast—. No, just *no*. Something statement-like, less feminine. She had envisioned this mimesis a thousand times already and she wasn't about to dial it down now, to compromise. What should have been the startling discovery of a handgun on her bed, in her home, had only served to underline the need for change, to accessorize it.

It came to her just as she heard the inimitable shuffle of Thomas's feet outside the door: her hair. It was too long, too soft, too *softening*. She contemplated chopping it all off for a second, shaving her head, but that would have been too easy. She was not going to be disfigured or dismembered for a token metamorphosis; she was going to stand straight and breathe fire. She hunted frantically in the bottom of her cupboard for something she could use and discovered a bandana, a relic from college days. It was navy blue and paisley, one a biker roommate used to wear under her helmet. It would have to do. She tied it around her head and *assumed position* just in time for Thomas to walk in, severely out of breath.

Her first words: 'You look ridiculous.'

Thomas was dressed in a sweat-drenched tee-shirt and running shoes, Sonya's khaki shorts clumped in an ungainly mess under his belt. He stood speechless for a long dangling moment, then lurched forward. 'Darling, I'm *so*—'.

Sonya shifted in her chair so she was fully facing him now. Thomas stopped and took in the view: the bandana, the warpaint, the robe and the view it afforded him of her legs—the legs! How he had longed to be between them the past forty-eight hours! And here his blood turned cold: the handgun, Varun's parting gift, protruding snugly out of her clenched fist, her fingers wrapped surely around the butt. 'I can expl—'.

Sonya put the gun to her lips. 'On your knees.'

Thomas complied, his thoughts suddenly turning to whether or not Sonya knew the gun wasn't loaded. It was absurd to even consider that she intended to use it, he knew, but on the off-chance that he was wrong, he didn't want to subject her to one more indignity. He moved forward on his knees, hands impulsively up in surrender. Sonya stood up and let her robe fall open. Thomas took a deep breath and stayed kneeling in front of her, his eyes dancing with hers, pleading with her to hit him, punish him, liberate him. He couldn't read her, could detect neither sorrow nor anger. She traced a circle around his mouth with the muzzle of the gun and slowly inserted it between his lips. 'I'm beginning to get the appeal of putting things in girls' mouths.'

Thomas opened his mouth as wide as he could as she pushed the barrel further in but he couldn't help choking. Sonya withdrew it almost immediately and drew his head to her, pressed his face against her stomach. He kissed her passionately, under her navel, on her hipbone, inside her thigh. He felt her body wrack in preparation before he heard the first sob, an anguished guttural cry that sent a shiver down his spine. He wanted to tell her he would fix them, that nothing was irreparably broken, but her hand pushed down hard on the back of his head, holding him still. When she finally spoke, it was as though the words came crashing down on him from a great height: 'Don't ever pull that shit on me again.'

# 17

# The Girlfriend Chronicles 9: My Anarchist Valentine

Girlfriend and I had the Conversation a few weeks after we started going steady.

'Christmas?' I said.

'No,' she said.

'Me neither. New Year's?'

'Passé.'

'Ok good; birthdays?' I asked.

'Remember to wish me. No gifts, maybe dinner, nothing fancy,' she said.

'Same. Valentine's Day?'

'Bleuuurrgghhh.'

The consensus was clear: neither of us were big on Days. We were united by our common disillusionment with the consumerist practice of hyping up dates into 'days', and were destined to live happily—if frugally—ever after. Except I was lying through my teeth. It was one of those white lies you say when you're still trying to get into someone's pants ('Birthdays? Oh, who gives a fuck, right?'), but it had somehow snowballed into a philosophy.  Besides how many men readily accept they're suckers for romance?

Which is why this conversation with my boss would be especially difficult. After fretting for weeks about how to bring up the topic of doing something special for Valentine's Day, I found out a few hours before Cinderella-time that Girlfriend was in fact on suspension for the next couple of days for picketing her employer's annual ball. The placard she held up outside the venue seemed to indicate that she thought a 25th anniversary bash for a multi-million-dollar company was a tad bourgeois. Or as she worded it, succinctly as always: 'DIE, CAPITALIST CUNTS!'

'So why do you want leave the next couple of days again?' asks my boss.

'Well my girlfriend's some sort of political ninja, and it's Valentine's Day and...'

'I see,' he says. 'So?'

I look at him for signs of smugness, of bastardry, but he appears genuinely puzzled. Fuck, I realize with a shock, Boss-man is a true-blue alpha male. He really doesn't get Valentine's Day! He's who I pretend to be to get laid! I man up and try to explain.

'See Boss-man,' I say, 'when a man loves a woman...'

'Yes?'

'Well, sometimes when a man loves a woman, you pick up ... infections.'

'Like an STD?' he grimaces.

'Yeah. It's Girlfriend. I think she's cheating on me.'

'Wow,' he says, 'what a bitch.'

HEY! Enough is enough. *Nobody* calls Girlfriend a bitch.
'No, no,' I say, 'it's not her fault. I think I might suck a little in bed.'
'Well that makes sense,' he says. 'She didn't seem the type.'
'Yeah,' I say, and take in the scene again.

'Boss-man,' I say, 'why's your finger on the intercom?'
Guffaws and laughter and hoots from across the office erupt through the intercom and fill Boss-man's cubicle as he says, smugly, bastardly,

'There are two things you never admit to as a man: not making your woman happy in bed, and ...'—the smug bastard is laughing so hard he can't even complete the sentence—'... celebrating Valentine's Day.'

Two days' paid leave in hand, I go to Girlfriend's place to lick my wounds and die a slow, unmanly death. But Girlfriend is in no mood for inactivity. 'Come on to the terrace,' she says. 'Let's fire up a joint and chill.' I slip into my sickday pajamas and trundle over to the terrace. I'm shocked and awed. Girlfriend has strung up the Christmas lights we never used. There's a table and two chairs in the middle, candlelight, a bottle of wine and what looks suspiciously like the tub of mango ice cream she had had delivered home last week to help me get over *Crazy, Stupid, Love*. Damn Ryan Gosling and his bedroom eyes.

'You thought I forgot, didn't you?' she says quietly.

'Forgot what?' I say.

'Today's Valentine's Day, silly,' she says and nuzzles me under my chin.

I'm touched. I'm loved up and mushy and ... try as I might, just can't seem to stop myself from bursting her bubble.

'Baby,' I say, 'this is very sweet but Valentine's Day is tomorrow. The 14th of February.'

'Fuck you, baby' she says. 'It's today, the 13th. That's why it's an unlucky number.'

'You think Valentine's Day falls on the 13th coz it's traditionally an unlucky number?'

'Doh,' she says, 'the "number of the beast" and all.'

I'm speechless. The number of the beast?

'You don't like?' she says, dipping a spoon into the ice cream.

I can't bear to break this to her. I decide Dates don't matter after all.

'I love it,' I say earnestly. 'I love you. This is the best Valentine's Day ever.'

---

Tags: Alpha Male, birthday, dating, girlfriend, manning up, ryan gosling, valentine's day

# 18

They say women can smell it on you almost as quickly as cities can. It should come as no surprise that the last of the great survivors have a nose for these things but men have had it too easy for too long to appreciate instinct. You can't truly understand mortality if you've never experienced birth pangs. Women know, just like cities know, because they've been bracing themselves against loss all along. Death was always an inevitability, centuries and civilizations before we learnt to fear it.

Take Sonya and Thomas. It happened overnight, though Sonya would look back and wonder if she ought to have known better, and earlier. Any woman would. Sonya would wonder if she should have told Thomas first, but she had to be sure. Death, unlike a difficult in-law or judgmental acquaintance, is not the kind of house guest you announce without absolute certainty. The proof, usually, is in the brooding.

A better man, a manlier man, would perhaps have diagnosed it himself. But Thomas, poor Thomas. Thomas, who had never picked a fight or kicked a ball in his life. Thomas, who had never killed a bear for warmth or shot a deer for sustenance. Thomas, his own worst self-fulfilling prophecy. Thomas: every mother's recurring nightmare. Thomas, who sank deeper and deeper into a cesspit of irrelevance of his own making by his very existence. Every waking moment of Thomas's was an exercise in self-sabotage; every breath an apology for some imagined masculinity. Sonya had to be sure because Thomas would never be.

It happened on a Wednesday, or a 'humpday' as Thomas had taken to calling it. That was one of the first tells—his regression into a second childhood of sorts, rung in by the most twenty-first century of symptoms ranging from social media angst to the un-ironic adoption of internet-speak. This sort of behaviour would have passed for the generic societal disillusionment of an intellectual if he had expressed it with the vicious condemnation of a Franzen or at least the carefully cultivated flippancy of a Lena Dunham. But Thomas had too much heart to be flippant about anything.

This particular Wednesday morning—a sexless one, unlike the mornings of earlier times—Sonya woke up with a shudder. As Thomas never tired of describing fondly (and to Sonya's great embarrassment), she breathed like an asthmatic in the last hours of her sleep, taking in huge lungfuls of air with her mouth open, the sound of her breath a recurring tentative drone. She sat up and looked at Thomas, her thoughts temporarily suspended to rejoice in the sight of his return. She had fallen asleep before he had got back from a weekend trip with his 'support group' or whatever he was calling it this week. Long gone were the days when she would wake up to Thomas's mouth mimicking her breathing patterns on her, down under. She put a hand on his forehead, and wondered what the stink was. She hoped he hadn't shat himself.

Not wanting to wake him up, she got dressed as noiselessly as she could and made her way to the kitchen. Didi had come and gone, and had cleaned up the flat, though they owed her at least a couple of months' wages. She hadn't made coffee or breakfast because—as had lately become routine—there was nothing in the house to cook with. A rummage in the fridge no longer rewarded one with sausages and cold cuts and at least three different varieties of cheese, all handpicked by Thomas from Nature's Basket. Sonya had initially enforced austerity as a precaution, insisting they shop at the grocer's instead of the supermarket, take the train instead of a cab, but it had quickly become a necessity. Between Thomas's inability to contribute more than a pittance towards rent and the magazine not quite taking off (but generating 'significant interest' nonetheless, if her one and only employee was to be believed) as she had hoped, the money she had put away for her entrepreneurial excursion had quickly dwindled.

Sonya reflected on the peculiar nature of her poverty. It was an intrinsic part of startup culture, if the many conferences and networking events she had attended were any indication. They were everywhere, young people like her who had left well-paying jobs to *do something on their own*, trading on the illusory asset of anytime-employability. Jobs were there for the taking if they wanted it—that was the assumption. 'If you're doing it for the money, you're doing it wrong.' That was the refrain, the credence dished out by the ones who had got it right, the ones who had converted ideas to currency. The longer the struggle, the greater the rewards, the better success would taste in the end. Like everything else in the startup universe, her poverty was liminal; it was flux.

Picking up a dozen eggs and a loaf of Modern bread, she promised the Malayalee boy who ran the shop that she would clear her tab next week. He and his brother had done well to grow their business so quickly, the once-*pettikkada* now a tarmac-covered walk-in closet of sorts that housed everything the young couples and single professionals who lived in the immediate apartment complexes might need. Families were few and far between in that lane. She had long suspected the boy of harbouring a crush on her, and self-consciously tucked a stray strand of hair behind her ear as she caught her reflection in the display window behind him. Returning his smile, she made a last-minute addition to her pickings: a bar of Cadbury Silk. An impulse buy she regretted the moment she stepped away from the counter.

'Thoma!' she cried as soon as she entered the flat. 'God, it smells like something died in here.' She let herself be amused for a moment, having ticked off one more phrase that she had never expected to use in real life. But the memory of that first whiff, the one that had crept in uninvited and woken her up with a shudder in the morning, wouldn't lend itself to distraction. 'Thoma,' she called again, and set about inspecting the flat. Maybe a cat had dragged in something, a dead bird or a rodent. It didn't seem to be coming from the kitchen or the living room. Armed with a broom and a dustpan, she switched off the fan and circled the bedroom. Behind the curtains, maybe. Under the bed. Nothing. Thomas stirred in his sleep and flung the covers off his body, swatted at some irritant or the other. Still on all fours, Sonya crawled closer and held her face over his. And sniffed: ashes, and the tomb.

They had discussed death before, she and Thomas. Or more accurately, they had discussed immortality. It had started as one of those silly games lovers play: invisibility or the ability to fly? Breasts or ass? Fame or money? Fame, Thomas had replied resolutely.

He had been surprisingly candid about his desire for fame, his *rasion d'etre*. It was all he wanted in royalties from his work: recognition. He would consider it a failure, he had said, to die when nobody was looking. He looked forward to making a spectacle of his last act, to setting himself a stage and self-destructing in full public view. It had sounded heroic at the time; they were only just getting to know each other.

'I can't wait to save you from yourself,' she had replied. How naïve, she thought now, how downright unintelligent, the words that came out of lovers' mouths sometimes. Death was neither romantic nor performance art; real death was decay, intellectual and personal.

Sonya sat on her haunches and considered the contours of her somnolent lover's face. The sunken cheeks, the crooked nose. It had lost its alcoholic's flush. Those blackened lips. Long eyelashes like a girl's. The hair, the salt and pepper in his sideburns. When had this happened? She touched his forehead. Warm. She put a hand on his heart. Sentient. She unbuttoned his shirt to let him breathe. They had turned into people who slept in their clothes. Thomas lifted an arm and relocated it under his head. She buried her face in his armpit, suddenly nostalgic for the smells of their bodies in the morning.

After a breakfast of scrambled eggs and toast, Sonya set about rearranging the living room. Not because it needed rearranging but because it was something to do. She felt uncomfortable moving around the bedroom while Thomas was sleeping. A childhood quirk resurrected; some cautionary tale her grandmother had told her about the perils of waking up one who was blissfully asleep. And in any case, the living room doubled up during the day as the editorial/ administrative office of Colour Purple, 'a webzine about everything'.

They had looked into traditional publishing initially but it was too costly, too labour-intensive, with hardly any returns. Maybe after the webzine had established a *presence*. She looked at her watch. Mikey would arrive any minute now. Sonya brightened up instantly at the thought. Sweet, innocent Mikey. There would be laughter.

Mikey had become the first (and only) employee of Colour Purple simply by virtue of being the first to apply. They hadn't even advertised any vacancies. He had responded to a mutual friend's rhetorical inquiry on Twitter about web developers on behalf of an internet magazine a couple of people he knew were *planning* to found.

Turned out Mikey had read *Kill Them All*. Turned out Mikey was a huge fan. He was a fan in the way only young people could be, rereading and recommending and referencing without inhibition. The product as identifier, as brand name. Thomas had been reluctant at first, seeing perhaps in Mikey an unwanted reminder of the one demographic his book had managed to reach out to: youthful, privileged, male.

Fresh out of college, Mikey was writing a novel that *could* be a movie (as though these media interchanged form without warning); teaching himself to play the harp or the cello or some other ironically unsexy musical instrument; saving up (presumably in a naturally self-replenishing account at the Bank of Parents) to travel. The Holy Grail of douchebaggery.

But Sonya had been adamant that they not turn down a clearly enthusiastic young man without giving him a chance, especially one who didn't require to be remunerated for his services. Besides, she argued, it would be good to have some *diversity* across the board; she expected to hire more women as the webzine caught on.

Thomas slowly warmed to Mikey, grudgingly growing into the role of mentor that Mikey had assigned to him without doubt or hesitation. He dutifully read the stories and poems, articles and plays, that Mikey inundated his email with. They all centred on death or the afterlife or somebody's fascination with either. The boy wrote prolifically, if pretentiously, and though Thomas was of the opinion that any constructive criticism could only be made by the casual reader ('yes' or 'no') and did not wish to contribute to what he called the age of comparison they lived in, he started believing that he could help open Mikey up a little. So he persevered quietly, convinced there was more to the boy than the endless parade of polka-dotted shirts and geeky glasses and brightly coloured chinos, prompting Sonya to jokingly complain that Thomas didn't show her an iota of the same consideration when she went to him for an opinion. Everybody was a writer in the era of free publishing.

Sonya now leaned over a polka-dotted shoulder to stare intently at a graphical representation of how Colour Purple was performing. Mikey smelled strongly of cologne, something citrusy today. As had been the case for a while, their webzine continued to attract more hits from the US and Europe than India, and she vowed again to create more localized content. As they had discovered early on, the internet had no dearth of writers. It was quality content that was lacking (exposure), unique voices that were being drowned by the onslaught of text tailored for transient attention spans.

Sonya had originally been ecstatic about the number of submissions they received daily but that was soon soured by the realization that everybody held the same opinions, perceived everything the same way, and sounded exactly like everybody else (and by the General's repeated requests to publish some of her girls' work). Thomas had been right about that much: writing, as a profession, was dead in the water, bloated beyond recognition with media mercenaries and celebrity crusaders the new thinkers and philosophers. Every popular article on the internet was a means to another end (to promote an event or a brand or a charity, to monger hate or fear); every word clickbait. Some were not even written but *aggregated*; not researched but *compiled*. Her generation had pulled the plug on not just the longform, but also the author.

A note on the transformation of an infinite, owner-less resource into virtual real estate: early adaptors felt compelled to reference the original DIY ethic of the medium to such an extent that all online advertising took the form of ten-second meditations on self-improvement, irrespective of the product being peddled. A face cream had just as much capability to change your life (and lives—of the girl child, the indie artist, the African lion, a never-ending supply chain of disenfranchised misfits and have-nots whose lives needed saving) as a refrigerator or a vacation in Peru. And you knew your life needed a facelift, because Facebook.

In the space of the three months in which Colour Purple had been operational, the webzine had changed tone and complexion drastically from overtly intellectual to aggressively middlebrow, save for the odd apercu. Low. Est. Co. Mmon. De. No. Mi. Na. Tor. A result of both supply and demand. Thomas and Sonya had initially gone after the big guns with gusto—the academics and the activists— but they were irresponsive or otherwise committed or disinterested or apprehensive or had too much on their plates already.

So they downed gears to the second tier—the aspiring academics and research scholars and fledgling organizations and those in need of 'publications' to their names—to put out a debut issue that addressed some of the questions and upheld many of the values Colour Purple had set out to discuss. They may as well not have tried at all. Soon they were scraping the bottom of the electronic barrel, approaching social media 'influencers' and self-proclaimed 'thought leaders' for prose or plug.

Sticking to Sonya's vision of topical analysis, the debut issue of Colour Purple had focused broadly on the theme of 'Technology and Gender', drawing on contributions from social scientists as well as working professionals and consumers of technology and new media. The editorial was an intensive study of income disparity between men and women in the technology sector in India, co-authored by Sonya and a professor of hers from B-school. Sonya was uncharacteristically proud of her thesis: though the figures were shocking and conducive to sensationalism, she had diligently maintained objectivity, hacking away at causative factors and steering clear of hyperbole.

Her professor had managed to procure enough data to conclusively establish that women received significantly smaller remunerations in both supervisory and non-supervisory roles in the technology industry; Sonya made what she thought were convincing arguments to show why this was the case: practical considerations like preference for men over women in roles that required them to work in night shifts, socio-cultural factors like men expressing reluctance to report to women in superior roles. She didn't want to write a flash-in-the-pan news story; she wanted to offer coherent insights to employers to help them address the problem.

Not only did the issue sink without trace in the main, but it also elicited some vitriol from the virtuous far right. It wasn't her piece or the interview with the popular YouTube comedienne or the photo essay on the Mumbai local commuter's experience sourced exclusively from user-generated Instagram uploads that attracted their ire but a story on the phenomenon of 'revenge porn': the practice of sharing nude photographs and videos online of former girlfriends and wives by men in an attempt to 'shame' them, often to get back at them for perceived wrongs. What was essentially a liberating, technology-aided exercise in exploring sexuality, the article argued, was being exploited by jilted lovers to gain a twisted sort of closure in a criminal and immoral betrayal of their former partners' trust, many of them underage.

The tragedy was that the only people to respond to the article were also the people most likely to condone this sort of behaviour. 'They deserved it,' was the overwhelming theme of their outraged modesty; permitting someone to film oneself naked was indicative of character, of an innate corruption and perversity that warranted worse punishment. The fact that there was a response at all would have been encouraging for Colour Purple had anybody sprung to their defence but Thomas and Sonya (and to be fair, Anjali and Sudhi and the General and a few of their friends) soon found out that the only rational response to right-wing trolls was radio silence. A word against one of their kind and the rest of them came crawling out of the woodwork, causing the website to crash twice in three weeks.

The solution was obvious: ~~take out the Comments section~~ build Colour Purple's 'own kind'. Content, said all the experts Sonya turned to, was key to building a following. Not just content, but Regular Content. A bi-monthly just wouldn't do, not on the internet. Greater, much greater frequency of publication. SEO. Adwords. Crowdsource. Virality. User Engagement. Sonya returned home every evening with acronyms and aphorisms for the digital age ringing in her ears. She assumed they were true because everybody else seemed to think so. Thomas refused to attend these events on grounds of principle, as did the General: she had thought Sonya was in this for the long haul, said the General. It was typical of people of their age, said Thomas, the unwillingness to wait, to nurture.

Instant gratification. Meretricious millennials. The Age of Right Now. Kitsch culture. Everybody called names and spoke in catchphrases. There was no getting away from their voices in her head. Sonya wanted to be heard too. Did they think this was easy for her? 'Let's all just sit around waiting for *inspiration* instead,' she said. 'Money doesn't grow on trees.' She turned to Thomas. 'Oh wait, you're *above* money. You don't need money because you consume people. You suck in everything in sight. You're a fucking black hole!' He hadn't meant to criticize, said Thomas; couldn't they wait—. 'We're a month due on rent alone.' Yes, but—. NO MORE BUTS! And round and round they went.

*Tattanatattataattana tattanatattataattana tattanatattataattana tana tana tana tana*

Strains of one of the greatest guitar licks of all time, now escaping from under the door of the editorial/administrative office of Colour Purple to rouse Thomas from his slumber. Unlike most patrons of the old school, he had no qualms attributing the phrase 'of all time' when discussing contemporary music, but he took care to ensure it was always preceded by the qualifier 'one of the'. But this particular band he considered truly worthy of the title, believed they had done enough to join the pantheon of great musical innovators already. Thomas would recognize their sound anywhere. He mulled over the band's name: My Sleeping Karma. He wondered if that was how Sonya felt about him. The song was called 'Brahama'. The God of creation; male. The son of Vishnu, born out of his navel. The track changed to 'Parvati'. The feminine energy of the universe. The Goddess of all power who was so ashamed of her dark complexion that she had entreated Brahma to colour her gold.

Thomas instinctively dug around in his pockets before remembering that he had smoked his last cigarette with the chaiwala outside KFC on Linking Road the previous night. He slunk out of the house in a pathetic bid to avoid Sonya, an intruder in his own home. She had probably already smelled the alcohol on him this morning, no matter how much gum he had chewed, irrespective of the tasteless pakoras he had gulped down. He had never had to conceal his indiscretions before, had always burnt brightest in full public view. But they had arrived—via the occasional slip-up—at an arrangement, a *modus vivendi* of sorts, since Sonya's self-proclaimed mimesis: Thomas on a classic merry-go-round of denial, Sonya wilfully oblivious to anything she couldn't see or touch. A whiff of alcohol could be anything from mouthwash to paint thinner from the construction site next door (How he hoped they would never finish building that thing!) as long as she hadn't seen him raise glass to mouth or take a sip. The tacit agreement between two polar powers that a war without collateral damage wasn't war at all, that dark skin painted gold was the colour it appeared to be.

At the cornershop, Thomas picked up fifteen chota Gold Flakes, a couple of Marlboro Cloves, Rizlas, a pack of extra-ribbed, delay-lubricated condoms, and a bar of Cadbury Silk. He understood the science of atonement better than most. The Malayalee boy behind the counter shook his head in warning. Thomas grudgingly parted with some money and cleared their tab. He had won a reasonable amount at the table the previous night but most of it had gone the way of clearing pre-existing debts. The house always won, even when it didn't. On his way out, he knocked over a stack of Lays by the entrance and waved an apologetic hand in the air.

Poking his head through the front door, Thomas's ears were treated to a series of monotonous, low-pitched, barely musical squeals from the office. Mikey and his artistic endeavours. Why did young people these days presume to be able to do everything? Why couldn't they just pick something—preferably something noiseless—and stick with it? Maybe it was the schools; maybe it was something they put in the water. The squeals were followed by prolonged and enthusiastic applause, no doubt from Sonya. The General hardly dropped in anymore—not since she had found a lover, a scene kid with all the personality of Mikey's literary meditations on death, still wet behind his ears—though Sonya said they talked often. Thomas pictured the two of them in his head: Sonya estimating an expression of appreciation and Mikey bowing theatrically, blushing. The hopelessly talentless artisan and his obliging patron. Shrugging off his jeans and depositing them in the laundry hamper, Thomas quietly made his way to the bathroom.

They were out of toilet paper—one of the healthier habits he had picked up in boarding school that had stayed with him. *Once you go white*. It had been the object of much good-natured ribbing when Sonya and Thomas started living together—'such a *sayippu*'—but in the manner of all domestic warfare, the unassuming household item had turned into a bone of contention in recent months: 'Do you EAT the stuff?' The embargo on the humble toilet roll was Sonya's personal revolution, her line in the sand, one Thomas adhered to by making do with newspaper on occasions like these when he had neglected to pick some up himself. He would have preferred the glossier texture of one of Sonya's magazines but as he had found out five ripped pages later one fateful evening, she liked her publications in full: 'DO YOU HAVE NO SHAME?' Cursing, he stood up and retrieved his boxers, stubbing the cigarette out on the window sill.

He stepped into the hallway and hesitated outside the office: he had neglected to flush. Music, musical music this time, seeping through its walls: *Samsara Blues Experiment*. His music. He would be back in a second; he could get away with it. Mind made up, he hurried to the bedroom and looked frantically around for the paper. Alt-J, Arctic Monkeys, The Black Keys, Manu Chao. They were all her bands, her musicians, *her* music. Pavement, Mogwai, The Machine, Causa Sui. They were his. No generation was immune to the charms of pop cultural signposting. It didn't stop at music either. Futurama, Black Books, Louie, Top Gear; all his shows. The Thick Of It, Game Of Thrones, Borgen, Deadwood—hers. He didn't trust sitcoms with laugh tracks; she liked continuity and preferred the sequential to the episodic. Just *where was the damn paper?*

It was a game they played proudly and often—this proprietorship of other people's art by virtue of being the first to sample it. And if one of them managed to *convert* the other, bring one over to the other side: gloating, victory. Hobbling to the kitchen, Thomas was painfully aware of a spreading stickiness, a pulpy wetness no longer contained between his buttocks but oozing, making its way out. Damn pakoras. The music was lowered, then stopped abruptly. Thomas hovered uncertainly in the doorway, ready to leap across the corridor, to protect the dignity of his castle if necessary. He breathed a sigh of relief and deposited a spoonful of scrambled egg in his mouth; Sonya was on the phone. 'Yes, but. No, of course. Is this a *joke*?' He would find out soon, no doubt.

Grabbing a handful from the stack of old newspapers by the fridge, he made his way back to his throne and collapsed onto it. He lit what was left of the cigarette and tried to drown out Sonya's incredulous voice. 'Of *course* I'd like to meet. Yes.' He fished out a Mumbai Metro from his newly acquired possessions and settled in. An old issue, about a week behind. An 'intelligent' actress—a rare species, judging by the repetition of the word one, two, four times—responded to criticism about a fashion line she had walked the ramp for recently, one whose designer claimed to have been inspired by Draupadi, the 'embodiment of the empowered woman'. This was deemed decidedly ignorant or misogynistic or both. A handsome young man, the scion of the country's most famous liquor baron, was in the news for posing handsomely—and in the nude from the waist up— with equally handsome cricketers and actors for next year's calendar. This was progressive, feminist. Everything was either pro or anti woman post-Nirbhaya. The Torso was in trouble again for some ill-advised comment or the other, this time about army wives. His PR agency spun this as: this was The Torso being the Torso—provocative but fun; this was normal. Nothing had changed; nothing would.

Two doors across from Thomas on his porcelain throne, Sonya sat down and whistled. Opening her call list, she saved the last received number as 'Tammy Bhattacharya'. This was by far the most momentous thing to happen to her in her professional—what did that word even mean anymore?—life and she needed a moment before she could share the news with Mikey or Thomas. Or the General! How would the General react? She scratched at a spot under her bandana, then pulled off her headgear altogether. There was so much to be considered, so much to be sorted out, but it was an achievement nevertheless. Colour Purple, her conceptual mouthpiece for the disenfranchised and the discerning, had finally reached some ears. Diamond-studded, Ray Ban-propping ears, but ears nonetheless. Mikey arched his eyebrows from behind his Mac. Sonya smiled and quietly closed her eyes.

# 19

Sonya had subjected herself to much soul-searching in the weeks leading up to the online launch of Colour Purple. Most of these contemplations were devoted to the topic of tangible returns. What, she wondered, had her education equipped her to do best? She tried to analyze it objectively, as she had been trained to: she had slogged and secured admission to one of the top B-schools in the country, arguably one of the best in Asia. This in itself was a form of capital that granted her the security of 'anytime employability'. She had admittedly been a bottom feeder through first year at school, just about keeping her head above average waters on the back of borrowed notes and last-minute cramming sessions, not to mention the charms of the Relative Grading system. Sonya wasn't the only one in her batch to see this RG-*giri* as a glitch in the system just waiting to be exploited: with close to a fifth of the students gaining admission through reserved quotas for minorities and OBCs, it was only natural that a significant proportion of them performed poorly in comparison to those who had made their way in by scoring in the highest percentile of probably the most difficult competitive entrance examination in the world.

Second year saw her blossoming into a different—but resplendent—creature altogether, thanks in no small part to her discovery of a life hack. Unlike in first year, she now had the freedom of choosing her subjects, of determining her own syllabus. Sonya played it fast and loose with academic compatibility or coherence, focusing instead on shoring up her average. Already turned on to what they referred to as the 'human angle' by the General, she exploited in full a recent philosophical—if tangential—expansion of the school's curriculum (or as Sudhi helpfully described it, 'a PMS moment') to include subjects as foreign to established Indian managerial education as Behavioral Science and Confucian Ethics in Management. The coursework for some of these papers was so abstract and stoner-friendly that she often caught herself wondering if she had understood the assignment correctly; once, all she had to do to clear a term paper was write a five-page account of the story of her life. The professor, an accomplished scholar with an anthropological bend, not only awarded marks generously but also gave all her students remarkably inaccurate breakdowns of their personality traits based on their answers. The hack had worked; her average shot up, thanks to which she could now reasonably expect to abandon her entrepreneurial enterprise at any moment and find employment at a Slot Zero firm—a finance or consultancy company—of equal standing in a matter of weeks.

The obvious advantage of attending her school had become demonstrably apparent during placement season. Sudhi made a call on behalf of Anjali and Sonya to a partner at the firm that would eventually hire them and when the time finally came, both the girls found themselves shortlisted for five-figure glory at adjacent desks. An alumnus of their school and their senior by a year, the partner had developed a close friendship with Sudhi in their time together on the football team. It wasn't overly optimistic to think that they would probably have been placed at similarly reputable firms anyway but this kind of favouritism was not unheard of in B-school circles. It was why undergraduates across the country sacrificed going to parties and keeping up with the latest movies and impromptu road trips and devoted all their waking hours in preparation for cracking the common entrance test: to get into an institution like hers, to become part of the *network*. Of course Sonya had had the luxury of taking a year off after her degree to study for it but she had put in the hours, had grafted twice as hard as anybody to compensate for her Humanties background, and she felt entitled to her rewards. There were no shortcuts to a school like hers, not even for those on quotas, and the truth was that those who passed out of the institution with a grade like hers or Anjali's or Sudhi's were quite simply the cream of the lot, one way or the other.

But Sonya was quickly realizing that a heightened analytical aptitude and being trained to manage a business did not necessarily equate to being qualified to start and grow one. Since school, she had been consulted on four multinational mergers, had helped floundering companies streamline their operations and turn around loss-making ventures, but none of this had provided any real insight into building a small business. The popular joke wasn't entirely off-base after all: business consultants did borrow your watch to tell you the time. If she had only stuck with it, she could have kept the damn watch too.

The General on the other hand appeared to have gained more on this front from running her NGO than Sonya had from two years of dedicated corporate consultancy: she had mastered the hardest trick of all, that of patience. To her great frustration, even Thomas seemed to bring more to the table conceptually than she did, though his contributions usually began and ended with conceptualization. She had somehow delegated to herself the logistics—making phone calls and drafting emails, meeting with potential investors and advertisers, data entry; she was reduced to being the workhorse while Thomas and the General sat back and discussed the political direction Colour Purple would take.

She genuinely cared for the cause, she wanted to put out a quality publication, but she was handicapped by her inability to see beyond the immediate: she wanted to bring in advertisers and funding straightaway because she spent sleepless nights worrying about cash flow. She was well-versed in the theory: the audience was the product, she knew, the audience was what she would eventually sell to the market, the advertisers; but she didn't have the time to build one. She had spent a chunk of her money on a MacBook for Mikey, she paid the rent, she bought the fucking *bhindi* and the detergent. She couldn't wait for Colour Purple to find an audience because she didn't know how long her savings would hold out.

A grudging respect. That was how she thought about it. She had developed a *grudging respect* for Thomas's professional aimlessness because it had taught him to embrace uncertainty without fear, to welcome it with open arms and throw his house open to its whims. It was this stoicism she had mistaken for heroism at first. Thomas didn't shiver or shake at the prospect of chaos or brave it head on like a warrior might a mighty foe but sat numbly by, content to let it happen, to batter and mould him into any shape or form it chose to. In the words of one of Thomas's own idols, what a hell of a way to not live. She couldn't imagine spending her youth the way Thomas had, doing odd jobs and depending on the kindness of strangers, barely hand-to-mouth, unsure where his next meal would come from. But his way of life had also necessitated a steely selfishness, nurtured in him a self-centred, self-absorbed core she had long given up on attempting to remedy.

It was a recurring theme in the narrative of their growing disengagement, the stony earth at the root of their problems: his lack of empathy, his positioning of self over all else. He was an animal, a survivor, a parasite—materially and emotionally. Sonya could either pet and pamper him for the indescribably delightful reward of his attentions, or kick him to the curb and spend the rest of eternity dragging her loss around like a phantom limb. She had abandoned all fanciful notions of herself as muse, as inspiration, and replaced them with reality: he preyed on her for story, for pith, because he had none of his own. He sucked the life blood out of her and splashed it blindly on a cynical canvas and hoped for immortality. Unfortunately for her, her own vanity she could let go of, but not hope. Not her faith in Potential. What lovely pictures Thomas painted sometimes; how deeply his words moved her when he tried! She was helplessly taken, consumed with him, and how. Some days she loved him, some days she didn't, but she always, always, wanted him.

Sonya now looked up from her computer and smiled at Thomas. He strode in, freshly showered, his tee-shirt damp in spots he had neglected to dry, a bowl of scrambled egg in one hand and a mug of coffee in the other, a Cadbury Silk held precariously between his teeth. 'Slept well?' Letting him drop the bar of chocolate in her lap, she hastily opened a new tab and rubbed his neck. She had been in the middle of making her monthly remittance in her mother's account. She would have to start again but it was worth postponing the predictable discord that would occur if Thomas found out.

It had been the source of considerable friction between them in the last few months, the allowance she provided her mother with. He was of the opinion that her mother had no right to such magnanimity on Sonya's part, especially now that she wasn't earning anymore: didn't she have a husband to provide for her? Sonya couldn't expect Thomas to sympathize with the oppressive dependency of a Malayalee housewife, the overbearing shame of relying on an absentee husband's handouts for the smallest of indulgences. He fathomed neither shame nor pride; words like self-reliance and dignity were hollow concepts to him, capitalist creations, nurture over nature.

It used to anger her at first but she had lately been introspecting about this along different lines: was it at all possible that Sonya's own dissatisfaction with Thomas arose from a misplaced pride, a reversed projection of how she perceived her parental dynamic? She considered their established roles: Sonya the provider, the giver, versus Thomas the provided for, the taker. That was their understanding; their unwritten, unspoken, contract. How many instances had she read about, of men suffering from low self-esteem in the event of prolonged unemployment, of being unable to provide for their wives and children? Often, this plunge in confidence manifested itself as infidelity and crime, as abuse directed towards their families, physical and mental. Besides, Sonya had another reason for wanting to ensure that her mother continued to receive her allowance: she hadn't had the nerve to tell her parents about her new venture, about resigning from stability and security. Who was being selfish, and to whom?

Taking a bite of chocolate, she watched Thomas peek over Mikey's shoulder at his screen and frown. The poor boy was struggling to shake off a blush that had crept up his neck. He was still unnerved in the presence of his hero, routinely stuttering and stammering when Thomas asked him a question. She knew he was working on the layout for an article, a ten-point list of something or the other that a feisty young girl had submitted: 'Ten Feminist Moments From Nineties Bollywood' or 'Ten Unwittingly Progressive Bollywood Dads' or something like that. Bollywood and Nineties Nostalgia: a match made in internet heaven. And lists. How the internet loved lists! Exactly the kind of thing Thomas would point to in his sleep as editorial compromise.

But there was simply no money to be made from a *Manushi* or a *Pratilipi*, as they both knew. The only choices they had been left with were to publish or perish. Thomas, as though aware of her eyes on him, suddenly looked up and smiled. That moment, that moment when their eyes met unexpectedly, and taking in the scene—Sonya biting into his offering, his gift, watching him—the frazzled corners of his mouth turned up to break into a smile (how proud he seemed to have her partake of his humble gift, how boyishly vain he clearly felt about his thoughtful gesture!) was the stuff their relationship sustained itself on, the glue that held them together. It was only a moment, and it was momentary and finite and transient and a hundred other impossibly tragic things Thomas regularly warned her about, but how weightless it made her feel, how overcome with joy!

It was only a moment, and these moments were becoming increasingly few and far between, but she knew that if pressed, they would both confess that it was probably enough.

A few minutes later, under the quickly descending ceiling of their bedroom, Thomas climbed off Sonya and looked away defeated, turned his back to her. Age. Diet. Exhaustion. Health. Cigarettes. Mood. Stress. There were so many things he could blame it on. The many markers of his approaching mortality. 'You should get back to work.' She put her hand in his hair, whispered meaningless consolations in his ears. 'Hey!' Thomas brushed off her hand and sat up in bed, readjusting the pillows to support his back. It had started aching again. He pulled a blanket over him, ashamed of his nudity. Another failed congress, another afternoon tryst with disappointment.

'Are you not attracted to me anymore?' Typical. She had to make it about her. It was always her this, her that. Her dreams, her expectations. But how could he tell her she was right, that something had eroded his appetite for her, diminished his desire, repressed his once insatiable longing for her? He knew what it was, the *something*. Weeks and months of conflict, of haranguing, of flaws being pointed out and held up to be scrutinized and detailed. How had she turned into this hypercritical hag, he into this ghost of a man who had accomplished nothing, could do nothing right? He was a fool to fear mortality. Death had come and gone; it had already claimed its prize. It was in him, eating away at him, one indignity after the other.

He watched Sonya leave their bed, beads of sweat shimmering in the dimples on her back as she looked at him in the mirror. He could only read accusations in Sonya's face now; his own inadequacies stared back at him, mocking, laughing, when he looked into her eyes. He had tried to change, to be more *involved*. He had been writing, had started exercising. His body was in better shape than it had been in years, externally. Except for the rare lapse, he was sober, lucid. But it had come at a price, this clarity. He was no longer shielded from the naked truth, from the shambles of his life; he was *permeable*, vulnerable to doubt and self-reproach. His bones rubbed dryly against each other, his ribs poked painfully at his lungs; his heart pumped hot air, no longer lubricated, cushioned by drink. He wondered again if they wouldn't be better off without each other, if they ought not to return to their old lives and selves. But he couldn't leave her, or be left. Hers was the only love he had ever been offered without asking, without demanding something in return. It was a love he had accepted hungrily, reciprocated lavishly, and yet he had been caught lacking, repeatedly. And therein lay the crux of his problem, his indecision: Some days he wanted her, some days he didn't, but he always, always, loved her.

There had often been times while working for the firm when Sonya questioned the decisions she had taken, the choices she had made, especially after she met Thomas. The youth and hours and air miles she offered in prayer at the feet of the Bitch Goddess. She had envied the time and leisure at the disposal of less ambitious 9-5ers, the engineers and mid-level managers and cogs in the companies she was called upon to help streamline or expand; craved the money and the independence of more assiduous peers from B-school who had been placed in I-banks and brokerages. Crossing the floor of the editorial/administrative office of Colour Purple now, one more unsuccessful coupling behind her, averting her eyes from Mikey's meaningful gaze, she was filled with an unprecedented clarity, a sense of destiny: this was what it had all been leading up to. Quickly transferring the money to her mother, she reached for her phone and hit Call. 'Tammy? Yes, Sonya. Yes, I'd love to meet. Does five o' clock work for you? Seven? OK. See you then.'

Legs. Her legs wouldn't stop shaking, her toes anchored to the floor, the heels of her feet in the air dancing to a desperate, silent beat. What does one do with restless legs? Reclining in her chair, she put her feet up on the desk. Too forced, uncomfortable. She sat up straight and crossed her legs, uncrossed them, crossed them again, tightly. Mikey's eyes, still on her. She was tired of turning away, of *averting*. Putting away the ball pen she had been chewing on, she glared at Mikey. He looked down, cowed. Poor boy. His was a fanatic curiosity that almost bordered on jealousy, she knew. She could have been anybody or a flower vase or a bowl of water; Mikey's obsession was with Thomas and the ink he dipped his pen in, not with her. 'Hold off on publishing that list piece, okay?' Going back to her screen, she googled Tammy Bhattacharya again.

A legend in B-school circles, an alumnus of her very alma mater. A topper and seven years Sonya's senior, Tammy had famously opted out of placement services (or 'OOPS-ed it,' as they used to say in school) to start up her own image consultancy. This, at a time when both the industry and startup culture 2.0 were at their infancy in India. Sonya clicked through the agency's website: Tammy speaking at a conference in LA. Tammy inaugurating a startup incubator in Cochin. Awards and accolades, clients ranging from MNCs to A-list celebrities, a blog on entrepreneurship, recommendations, testimonials, services, glitter and gold. This was the tangible return Sonya had been trying to identify, this was how attending B-school would finally pay off. The accessibility, the *network*.

It was true that Tammy had come across Colour Purple thanks to paid promotion on social media, true that the stars had aligned in Sonya's favour in most fortunate fashion, but it was the brand name that had brought them together, the school connection that had made the older woman pick up the phone and call. If the General had completed B-school, if she had stayed just a couple of months longer, it was entirely likely that Tammy would have by-passed the middle-woman and approached the General directly instead. Sonya flipped through the many entrepreneurial success stories she had bookmarked, young people like her who had turned overnight millionaires. She knew hers was not a big-money property but she hadn't known she was interested in the big money either. With the right mentor and long-term investment, there were no limits to how far Colour Purple could go.

Woken from her reverie by the slam of the front door, Sonya stood up and checked the time. A little over three hours till the meeting. She hardly smoked cigarettes during the day anymore, but she could use one right now. Helping herself to a Marlboro Clove from her bedside stash, she wondered where Thomas had gone. She wouldn't be surprised if he was sneaking a drink somewhere, probably at The Bend. It had become a vicious cycle, the disappointment and the consequent numbing of hurt. He had struck up an unlikely friendship with the manager there, DJ-ing on weeknights in exchange for snacks and drinks. He didn't do tricks on the turntable or play especially customer-friendly music; she suspected the manager, Shaun, just wanted to help him out. Thomas had that quality about him: people wanted to help him, protect him from the world. He inspired a helpless loyalty in adults once they got to know him, an almost-guilt at how easily they fitted in to real life. Or perhaps they were subconsciously cheering him on, hoping he would last the eternal race to the finish without compromising, without growing up. She would find out soon enough. If the meeting went well, she would have to go to The Bend herself later that night.

Turning her thoughts to the task at hand, she wondered if she ought to prepare a presentation of some sort. It was too early to involve the General, even if she had a right to be involved. As for Thomas, Sonya wanted *real world* perspective, a second opinion. She considered calling Anjali but they had grown apart since her resignation. It was a temporary rift, an unacknowledged chasm that could be fixed over dinner and a bottle of wine at any time but neither of them had managed the energy or the humility to initiate it and now was not the time. Sudhi was out of town on an assignment and Mikey was, well, Mikey. She had always prided herself on her support group, the family she had gotten to choose, but for the first time in her life, at possibly the most crucial juncture in her life so far, she had nobody to turn to. How had she ended up without a friend, a shoulder?

Damn traffic. Tammy's office was only a few kilometres away, in BKC, but it took her nearly forty minutes in the cab. Thank God they were headed *towards* the city, and not the other way round. Suburban exodus, this time of day. Sonya thought in short bursts, breathed in and out. She was asked to wait by a receptionist who towered over her from behind a desk adorned by the letters TB in ornate purple and gold. Looking around the lounge, Sonya wondered if the unusually tall receptionist was an aspiring model or an actress, temping her way through uncertainty till her big break, like so many others in Bombay. They were all temps in a way in this city, all aspiring towards the unattainable, all waiting for the right moment.

Glass ceiling, glass walls, the opaque kind. Heels. She should have worn heels. She should have drawn up a business plan or at least brought along her laptop to keep up appearances. But she had wanted to keep it informal, to affect only a casual interest: the game of who-needs-whom? Besides, she was still uncertain about the moral implications of what Tammy was suggesting though there was no doubt in her mind about the fillip it would give Colour Purple, both in terms of exposure and money. And what a gift it would make for the General's girls, what a victory to give their work (and their plight) the stage Tammy was offering. In any case, she was not in a position to make decisions, Sonya reminded herself; she shouldn't get ahead of herself. She was going to look, but not touch.

She had tried on a pantsuit at home and changed into denims and a polo tee at the last minute, not wanting to be overdressed. She had a compact case in her bag, lipstick; she could—. But the multistorey receptionist was already showing her to the conference room, holding the door open, pointing at this and that. Sonya hoped she wasn't sweating and craned her neck to the side to see past her guide. Projector, chairs, oval desk, a dais. A room like any of the scores of rooms she had attended meetings in, made presentations and conducted performance reviews in. 'This is home turf,' she told herself as she followed the receptionist in. The room was empty. Oh thank God! There would be waiting. She could wait. She wanted to wait as long as possible. Her anxiety must have been palpable. The receptionist gently touched Sonya's arm, catching her by surprise, smiled, and left the room.

Tammy Bhatt *swept* in (there was no other word for it; Sonya thought she had felt her approaching minutes before she actually appeared at the door, as one might an earthquake or a plane crash) trailed by two smartly dressed women of Sonya's age—secretarial, judging by their demeanour. The legend herself was impeccably attired in a sharply cut navy blue skirt suit and suede leather pumps that matched the thin belt around her waist. She was taller than she had appeared to be in the photographs, and of darker complexion, her face framed by a medium bob.

'Thank you for coming in.'

Shaking Sonya's hand warmly, she introduced her team and indicated that they sit down. Sonya only caught one of the other women's names but she found herself relaxing, almost becalmed by Tammy's pleasant manner. Holding out a hand, on which the nameless secretary promptly deposited a folder, Tammy turned to face Sonya. Behind her, a projector screen lowered itself from the ceiling, slowly covering the breadth of the room from wall to wall. 'I've always felt there's a special place in hell for women who don't help other women.' That attentive smile again. Sonya wondered how many times Tammy had used that line before. She recognized the quote but couldn't place it. From the screen behind Tammy, The Torso peered back at Sonya, just as attentively, over his Ray Bans.

# 20

A young Torso, twenty-four years younger, collar turned up in defiance, shirt unbuttoned, hairs springing like tiny coils from his chest. It was still the decade of the mullet, and of unrequited love. *Click!* A slightly bulkier Torso, a couple of years later, signature lopsided smile spreading cheekily across one side of his face making light of the index finger pointed accusingly at Sonya, either feet planted surely on the seats of two motorcycles driven by enthusiastic extras immortalized in one evergreen frame. The dawn of a new decade, heralded by the resurrection of the roadside Romeo. *Click!* The Torso, suited and booted, a baseball cap perched back-to-front on his head in impish irrelevance, a diamond stud gracing one of his ears. The exorcism of the angry young man of the eighties was complete. *Click!* A shirtless, sensitive Torso, hands cradling a guitar and eyes primed for compassion, nary a hair on his expansive chest. The turn of the century and the grand awakening of the metrosexual. *Click!* More of the Torso, and more torso this time, in a vest stretched to its limits to contain his broad frame, totemic tattoos on arms as big as pillars, blood dripping from a gash above one eyebrow. The birth of the *Bhai*.

Tammy swivelled around in her chair and let out a shudder. 'I'm so hard right now. Tell me you don't feel hard right now.' The secretaries noised agreement as Sonya battled desperately to contain a giggle. 'This is what we're dealing with, Sonya. A handsome man, a Bollywood legend, a *star* like one we won't see again in our lifetimes.'

Sonya couldn't argue with that. For all his perceived failings, she doubted the Hindi film industry would produce another matinee idol with the sheer pulling power of the Torso in a long long time, maybe ever again. The era of the star-driven blockbuster was already winding up in the West thanks to greater accessibility of production technology and electronic distribution models; India would inevitably follow. 'The industry still has at least two other male stars in the same pay packet bracket, if not higher. They've all been around as long as each other. You're a smart girl, Sonya. Tell me what's different about how I would have showcased their life story compared to our man here.' *Life story*. Were people's lives really encapsulated in the work they had done, the posters they had been on?

Sonya sensed that she was being tested. Instinctively rising to the occasion, she tried to think objectively, clearly. She knew the stars Tammy was referring to. She had watched every Bollywood blockbuster ever made since the early nineties, including those of the Torso. How would she have presented those movies, reminded her audience of their essence without robbing their stars of credit? 'He flies solo,' she said finally. 'He's the USP, the essence of his movies.'

Tammy orchestrated a slow clap that quickly reverberated around the room. 'He's the *essence* of his movies.' Shifting in her seat, she gestured to the nameless secretary. 'Take that down.' Sonya decided conclusively that she was lowest in the pecking order. 'And if you were to pitch me one of the other stars, what would have been a significant component of your presentation? Visually.' Sonya had known this was coming. But what about the inherent sexism of the Torso's movies? What of the misogynistic stains on his widely publicized personal life, and his links with the underworld? Realizing Tammy was waiting, she answered grudgingly: 'The co-stars. They both play off their female leads.' Tammy thumped the desk with passion. 'You're going to be bigger than me some day.'

'He's made close to a hundred films so far. Highest grossing films in the country in Ten. Different. Years. Seven of them grossed over a billion dollars worldwide. Not one of them,' Tammy lowered her voice, 'opposite a superstar heroine.' She paused to let this information sink in. 'He *carries* his films. He works hard, looks great. So why this animosity? He's not even a full-blooded Mozzie, *saala*.'

Flinching from Tammy's hand on hers, Sonya reflected on her statement. It was true that the Torso's parents were of different religious backgrounds but he had somehow become synonymous with the faith of his paternal lineage. It was true that a lot of the opprobrium aimed at him was—at least in part—elitist playing up of the perceived failings of the religion towards women, of cultural inferiority. While the rest of the Bollywood superstar triumvirate (both of whom were, ironically, Muslims, born and bred) had slowly and diligently distanced themselves from their religion in the public sphere as they grew older and chosen to act in movies that catered to more urbane, multiplex and NRI audiences, the Torso had stuck to a tested formula and continued increasingly to peddle zero-plot, *dishum-dishum* fare that worked best—and assuredly—in the marginalized heartlands and suburban ghettoes.

Was it possible that much of the criticism aimed at the Torso was thinly veiled religious bigotry? Come to think of it, it wasn't just their religions that the other two had watered down, neutered. The Torso was a man in a way neither of them had ever been, not on screen at any rate, and could never hope to be. They had both married early, coincidentally to Hindu women, and wore their fatherhood on their sleeves. The Torso on the other hand, flew solo in real life too, still partying hard and getting into fights and crashing cars, still as wild and rambunctious in his late forties as he was in his womanizing heyday. Was the post-millennial backlash against the nineties' poster boy just the disaffected rumblings of a dickless generation of men like Thomas who had conveniently found a voice behind the anonymity of their computer screens? 'The guy has seven sisters,' Tammy was saying. 'He gives more to charity than both the other *super*stars combined.' But she had lost Sonya's attention, having already won her sympathy.

Closer to home, Thomas was quickly exhausting his supplies of sympathy at The Bend. 'I'll have another one.' The bartender helplessly scoured the room again for Shaun, the manager. Thomas had been at it since evening, right from the moment he and Shaun had stumbled in, blitzed out of their heads on some locally sourced Ketamine. He had refused to play but Shaun had waved him through, instructing the bartender to keep the tab running till it hit two grand. Not only did Thomas now owe the bar close to four thousand on top of his waiver, but Shaun was nowhere to be seen. 'Don't tell my girlfriend,' cautioned Thomas as he gulped down the last of his drink. 'What are you waiting for? One more!'

Turning to one of the regulars beside him, a 'freelance writer' who worked out of the organic café next door by day and spent her nights getting wasted on her self-designated barstool, he wondered if he was capable of infidelity towards Sonya. The girl's name was Diane or Devika or something else entirely that started with a D. They had become friendly in the past few weeks though Thomas had never found her attractive. Taller and bigger than him, bespectacled, pale, she was not pretty in any conventional sense but Thomas had always found convention boring. He weighed her up, as one might cattle or a second-hand car, and decided that he was faced with a mountain that was not altogether insurmountable if it was willing. 'How old are you?'

She looked him up and down, and smiled. 'What's it to you?' Target engaged. 'I'm going to play you a song,' he said. As he made his way to the console, he only hoped that she would have the good sense to look in the mirror and liberate the piece of lettuce wedged between her teeth before they got down to business.

'Robert Johnson,' he replied in answer to her query when he got back. 'Blues maestro?' The Mountain nodded noncommittally. Sonya would have wanted to find out more, asked questions about the singer's nationality, contemporaries, era, influences. 'Legend has it,' he continued determinedly, 'that he sold his soul to the devil in exchange for his guitar. Not his guitar literally, but technique. He was transformed overnight.' Taking a sip of her beer, she looked back at him without blinking. 'Founded the 27 club, more or less. How old are you again?' She wasn't even listening; she was checking her phone, the silly cow. 'Clearly I missed the boat by a few years.' He was just talking to the top of her head now. 'What do you guys have on these *smart*phones that's so much more interesting than real life?' He reached for her phone, a friendly gesture, an attempt at 'kino' as the kids called it, but someone was tapping him on his shoulder, asking her if he was giving her trouble. It happened before he knew it: jumping to his feet, Thomas smashed his head into the intruder's face, sending him reeling into the nearest table. In less than a minute, he was being dragged outside by three or four men, being pelted seven different ways to hell.

Sonya had heard enough, seen enough slides. 'Like I said, it's not my decision,' she told Tammy earnestly. 'Colour Purple will be promoting the event but I don't run the organization. I'll have to talk to her. I can't promise you anything.' Tammy leaned back and smiled. She shook her head regretfully and as though responding to some secret signal, the secretaries cleared out of the room without a word. Sonya was getting nervous again. The meeting had continued for longer than she had expected; it was past eleven. She had tried to leave several times but Tammy had interjected, prolonged the conversation.

Shaun had called repeatedly and she hadn't answered. She hoped it wasn't about Thomas but she couldn't be sure. 'I like you, Sonya,' Tammy was saying. Sonya struggled to keep her hand from withdrawing, enclosed as it was in Tammy's. It was clammy, her grip strong. 'But you don't get to where I am without breaking a few eggs.' Their faces were almost touching now, like lovers before a first kiss. 'I need this. And you need this. This is your future we're talking about, the rest of your life. So you're going to talk to your friend and get back to me with a positive answer. *Theek hain?* I'll have someone drop you. Goodnight.'

Throughout the ride home, Sonya regretted not having done as good a job as she could have of negotiating. It was too early to tell with any certainty but from what she could make out, the Torso had taken a shine to the project after an overzealous employee at the agency had pitched the idea to him prematurely. Tammy now needed to swing this in his favour if she hoped to retain her star client. Colour Purple would retain the rights to the property and branding as exclusive media partner for the event, a marketing coup in itself. Riding on the Torso's endorsement, they could raise enough and more funds to not only set up formal housing for the General's girls, but also bankroll all expenditure for the next couple of years. But where did that leave Colour Purple?

If she was going to have to convince the General to let the Torso piggyback on their project, she would have liked for Colour Purple to gain more *tangible returns* from the exercise. She had made a hurried call to Shaun before leaving the agency, hoping to catch him at The Bend. But he had exhorted her to head straight home. There was nothing to worry about, he had told her, but Thomas had gotten into a scrap with a group of kids. He was alright, he assured her, he had taken Thomas home himself. It hadn't been Thomas's fault, he had kept repeating. More than the grief at what awaited her, more than the distraction Shaun's calls had caused when she should have been on top of her game, it was his transparent attempts at alleviation of Thomas's guilt, at preempting and assuaging her response, that angered her. The damn brotherhood of men. She would have to wait till the next day to take things up with Shaun.

To her relief, Thomas didn't appear to be in any great pain though she only knew too well that he wouldn't admit as much if that were indeed the case. He had a swollen lip, and an open gash on one side of his forehead that would undoubtedly leave a scar, but other than those blemishes he looked—. He looked good actually, long unruly hair tied up in a sock bun, shirtless, a KCCO apron around his waist. She had found him standing over a pan of pasta on the stove, stirring it absently with one hand while he read from a paperback in the other, soundtracked by '505' playing softly from the bedroom.

She liked it when he listened to her music. Holding his face in her hands, she tried to step back to inspect the damage but he wouldn't let her, wrapping an arm around her and pulling her close. He had lately become stronger, healthier. There was more weight in his frame, more muscle in his limbs. Kissing him lightly on the mouth, she told him she was glad that he was okay, that she didn't need any explanations, that she was sorry for reining him in. He hadn't been drinking, he lied. She had never asked him to stop, she pointed out. Returning to the kitchen after changing, she felt a familiar stirring in her, a rudely interrupted longing knocking on her door demanding resumption, release. Reaching around him, she turned off the stove and dug her face into his back, determined to claim what was overdue. Besides, she understood the need for atonement better than most.

# 21

In the end, it took Sonya a lot less convincing than she had anticipated, getting Thomas and the General on board, at least in theory. Perhaps they were tired of temping too, of waiting around for their big break in the city of dreams. They had met at The Bend the afternoon after her meeting with Tammy to discuss their course of action. As proprietor of the venue of the event, Shaun was naturally delighted about the prospect of a celebrity tie-in and even offered them a free round. The girls ordered G&Ts, with lime, small. Thomas abstained in classic alcoholic's overcompensation mode, fooling nobody and annoying Sonya. Not all unhappy families were unhappy in different ways.

The General understandably played things close to her chest, demanding details, the nitty-gritty, though she was vehement in her appreciation of Sonya for creating the opportunity. It had entirely been Sonya's idea to run a piece in Colour Purple on the General and her work with the girls as a thinly veiled promotional exercise for a proposed exhibition of their paintings. The response to the 'Donate' tab at the bottom of the article had been underwhelming at best but it certainly appeared to have paid off in hindsight. There was no doubt that the Torso was looking to whitewash his tarnished image by offering to become the spokesperson for a low-key, independent art exhibit but they were unanimous in agreeing that it would only be wise to overlook any ulterior motives if it would help the cause without undermining it. The question that hung over their table was this: was it worth the moral compromise, the anomie?

Sonya remembered reading about their dilemma in B-school in an essay by Michael Walzer. The American political theorist had termed it 'the problem of dirty hands', a nod to Jean Paul Sartre's 1948 play. The facts were these: the Torso, freshly exonerated of allegations of a crime he appeared to have been complicit in—if not directly committed—by all logical yardsticks, perpetrator of a thousand sexist stereotypes through a longstanding body of work they were repulsed and perversely fascinated by in equal measure, wanted to lend his celebrity status to help raise awareness for possibly the most disenfranchised section of a male-dominated society that brazenly patriarchal public figures like him had most benefitted from.

The General had long since admitted that she wouldn't be able to keep it up much longer, that she would have to concede defeat and give up on her mission soon if she didn't find a way to make her organization self-sustainable. That the Torso's involvement would attract much-needed attention and monetary support for the cause was undeniable, but it would also be an implicit vindication on their part of the actor. Not to mention, it could also backfire dramatically on them, rob them of all credibility, the next time the Torso did something in keeping with his woefully misogynistic track record. All

of which left Sonya, Thomas and the General staring down
the barrel of the world's oldest ethical conundrum: were they
willing to sully their hands for *the greater good*? They would
soon find out; Sonya had arranged for her and the General to
meet with Tammy in less than an hour.

Thomas spotted Shaun out of the corner of his eye,
making a beeline for his table as soon as the girls were out
the door, and shook his head. 'You can get it out the back of a
pharmacy two lanes away,' he told his dismayed friend. 'I'll
hook you up but you'll have to cook it yourself. All you need is
a spoon and a lighter.' Thomas felt an unfamiliar guilt, a pinch
of disloyalty, as he watched him walk away, his shoulders
slumped; Shaun had been good to him, kind. He had stayed
back to think some things through but now he looked around
the bar, disoriented. It was still early, its patronage limited
to a group of old timers sitting outside, a couple of regulars
on barstools, a tourist poring over a Bombay handbook. He
wondered how many of them would change into monsters
before they left for home, if the monster was within him or a
creation of the juice, a chemical reaction like any other.

Having never really contemplated the meaning or
existence of evil as something of and within itself, he was
surprised to realize now that he considered himself a good
man; a victim, often, of extraneous circumstances but a
virtuous man nonetheless. How had this happened? Life
was always doing this to him, speeding ahead of its own
volition and catching him unawares when he checked in on
occasion, looked under its hood. Perhaps all men thought of
themselves as good, as upstanding citizens of the world. If
there really was a line in the sand, a demarcation of right and
wrong, it would be impossible to function in contemporary
society if one believed one's self to be in the red. The most

heinous of crimes committed had been clothed in the rhetoric of some cause or the other; the greatest villains in modern history had all chosen to dirty their hands for 'the greater good'. We painted ourselves gold because the truth was ugly, human; we believed ourselves to be good because Good was beyond comprehension, infinite. When evil reared its head in our lives, amongst our good selves—as it must—we relegated it to illness, to sickness of the mind. To temporary loss of consciousness, to bouts of insanity. Because reciprocity; because no sane person would admit to a preference for vice. The idiocy of theodicy.

The mood was considerably less introspective in the conference room of Tammy Bhattacharya & Co. Introductions over, the older woman was quickly into her stride. 'I'm going to be blunt with you because I'm on your side.' The insinuation was clear: last night had been a one-off; she had neither the time nor the patience to *convert* a couple of irrational do-gooders. Sonya nodded earnestly, overcome with admiration.

'You've probably heard of the term "limited hangout". It's when a government, for example, admits to a previously unknown, *minor* mistake to deflect attention away from the possible exposure of a more serious wrongdoing.' She smiled, taking care to look the General in the eye. 'That's not what this is, in any sense of the term. My client needs a PR turnaround because he has been unfairly accused of crimes he didn't commit. Allegations that he has been cleared of, mind you. But more importantly—.' Sonya's phone rang, and she apologized. Tammy cleared her throat and continued. 'More importantly, he wants to help you because—let's call it a midlife crisis or an epiphany or whatever—he wants to give something back, to set right certain wrong turns he took with his, shall we say, *creative* direction. I'm no fan of his movies either but I'm a fan of the person beneath the persona. With his involvement, with *my* involvement, you're going to preach to an audience that needs your message the most, and you're going to raise a *lot* of money for a very worthwhile cause. I believe in what you're doing, and so does he. Which is why if you can't see the sense in getting in on this, I suggest we end this meeting here.'

Sonya and the General exchanged glances. They hadn't expected to have to make a commitment so early into their conversation. 'We're interested,' said the General, 'but what exactly do you expect from us?' A sigh of relief escaped Sonya's lips earning her a reprimand from the General. 'I'm not going to wax eloquent about him on any forum, let alone at the exhibit.'

Sonya knew that last statement was aimed just as much at her as it was at Tammy. How had she become the enemy, the *establishment*? She had only wanted to help. Why couldn't people like Thomas and the General just wake up and face facts?

If Tammy was aware of the chill in the air, she didn't show it. 'Let's get one thing clear. We're doing you a favour. And your *waxing eloquent* is not going to make a difference to my client, but *his* words will, given the right stage.' Satisfied that she had put the General in her place (and Sonya couldn't help a little schadenfreude at this unexpected turn of events), Tammy turned to Sonya. 'Now where's the writer?'

Having decided it was too much of a challenge to stay sober at The Bend any longer, Thomas went for a run. Dressed in work boots, jeans and a white shirt, he knew he looked comical chasing himself around Madhu Park but this had become routine lately: dull the need, whenever it took him, with exercise. *If you can imagine it, you can control it.* It wasn't dark enough yet for the working crowd to start on their daily penance but there were enough people in running shorts and activity-appropriate shoes to make him feel self-conscious.

Not for the first time, he wished he could afford an electronic device to shield him from society: a smartphone or a music player, something that came with headphones. Sonya was right: nothing—not intellect, not philosophy, not even talent—compensated for the certainty of knowing when your next paycheck was due. Noticing a group of teenagers pointing and laughing at him from their calculatedly casual perch on one of the park's benches, slowing down and inspecting his wrist in instinctive pretence of being late for something serious and adult-like, sweating profusely in his everyman attire, Thomas was suddenly aware of how pointless it had all been, of what a joke he had become.

The *writer.* Sonya could almost taste the bile in her mouth, the rage in her being. The brotherhood of men. Of *course* Thomas's brand of self-loathing, self-fulfilling nihilism appealed to the Torso. They were no different, the alpha and the beta—just delusional in different ways. *Of course* it all boiled down to the artist and the *voice;* the suits chased the talent chased the suits in a never-ending, self-defeating loop of I-could-never-do-what-you-do.

But where did that leave people like her: the believers, the nurturers, the enablers? Her only consolation was that the General looked just as aghast as she felt when Tammy declared that the Torso wanted Thomas to write his speech for him. It was the future, said Tammy, the *market.*

She had done an impressive amount of homework to support her theory. Surveys showed that there had been no diminishment in the Torso's female fan base over the years. It was the male vote that he was steadily losing; more specifically, the *urban* male vote. Unfortunately for him, it was also the male audience that had always determined his box office turnout. But while the Torso once represented a masculinity that the average Indian male could aspire to, his overt machismo now rendered him fantastical, improbable. Whereas Thomas—or at least his column in Colour Purple— represented the relatable, the average. The Torso could see now that he had alienated too many hardworking ordinary men by setting the bar too high, by putting himself on a pedestal that bred jealousy and animosity. But Thomas could build him a bridge between two disparate worlds. Thomas was the antithesis; the antidote to the Torso's impossible swagger.

The irony was not lost on Sonya: Thomas's brutal condemnation of alpha culture had been mistaken for humorous self-deprecation. Thomas's call to arms to his beta brethren to embrace themselves, to accept themselves for who they were, had been misinterpreted as satire, as a knowing wink: we claim we're happy with our spindly arms and our protruding guts and our indie music and our overweight girlfriends but really, *secretly*, we know who we'd all like to be.

Cheering up at the absurdity of the situation, Sonya agreed to find out if Thomas would be willing. Tammy looked impatiently at her phone. 'I'll have to ask him when I meet him,' explained Sonya. 'He doesn't own a phone.'

Marvellous, exclaimed Tammy, a true eccentric! 'We don't want this to turn into a farce,' she continued, 'There has to be some level of gratitude on display.'

The General shifted uncomfortably in her seat. Tammy nodded to one of her secretaries and turned to the screen behind her. 'Now this here is a painting we took the liberty of commissioning on your behalf. It will be presented to my client at the event as the work of one of the artists we're exhibiting. As a sort of—*commemoration.*'

Sonya stared mesmerized at the screen, unable to take her eyes off the painting. It was a portrait of the Torso in profile, bare-chested, riding a horse through what looked like a jungle. A Doberman trotted gamely by their side, head turned faithfully up at its master. The General was the first to speak. 'What the fuck is that?'

Tammy pointed at the dog. 'This here is Tiger, the love of his life.' The secretaries chorused noises of appreciation. 'And of course, we all know of my client's love for horses. This is Stallion. He has a whole stable of them in a farmhouse near Pune.' She appeared genuinely surprised at the girls' ignorance of the Torso's affection for the equine. 'It's a wonderful property,' Tammy added uncertainly.

'Leaving aside the sheer lunacy of naming a dog *Tiger*, my girls are untrained fourteen-year-olds. I can barely afford to buy them water colours. There's no way one of them could have painted that.' The General looked at Sonya for confirmation. 'No,' Sonya agreed, 'just, *no.*' It might seem like overkill now, said Tammy. But when you've been in the business as long as I have—. You'll change your minds.

Thomas wandered aimlessly through the many parallel lanes that surrounded Sonya's flat. He sped up and slowed down, stopped and stared and started again, ending up where he had commenced his journey over and over again. He had felt insulted that Sonya hadn't asked him to join her and the General at the meeting but he could see now how it was the result of the precedents he had set. Till recently, he would have dismissed the idea outright, made one cynical comment or the other. Sonya was right to worry that he might embarrass her, fail her, because he had failed himself, was an embarrassment to himself.

Night was almost upon him. Streetlamps were coming to life, oblivious to his plight. Every turn he took, windows lit up in buildings like candles on cake, calling attention to his shame. His birthday was coming up. He would turn thirty-five before the end of the month. Thirty-five years of treading the earth. He tried to think of it in terms of opportunity cost, in terms of resources consumed. Water, food, time, energy, love, sperm, despair, trees, air: what would a better man have made of it all? What if it could have been distributed to the needy instead—food to the poor, energy to the weak, sorrow to the intellectual, love to the orphaned? Was it too late to start, to join the race? Did the propensity to change come with an expiry date?

'One last thing, ladies,' said Tammy, 'the venue'. Sonya didn't think she could take anymore. She wondered how her friend was doing. Except for her little outburst at the unveiling of the Action *portrait*—as Tammy now referred to it—the General had been strangely calm throughout. Sonya wouldn't put it past her to be storing it all up in her head, waiting to explode. 'You'll understand why we can't have the event at some dingy hipster gastrobar. For one thing, these are underage girls as you pointed out, the artists. It's a PR disaster waiting to happen.'

They hadn't thought about this. Sonya admonished herself for having overlooked such an obvious impediment. 'We'll take care of the whole thing for you—the venue, the guests, the music, the catering, everything. You should both be proud of yourselves for what you've pulled off but you can sit back and just enjoy the show now. I want you both to go home and think about one thing tonight: in three weeks' time, the city's rich and famous are going to bid on the paintings of your little girls, your wards, in a celebrity auction compéred by the country's biggest movie star. And *you* made that happen.'

# 22

Standing beside Thomas at the bar, her arm around him, Sonya was swept up in an odd mixture of déjà vu and jubilation. The auction had been a tremendous success, raising more money for the girls than she had imagined it would in her wildest dreams. The future of Colour Purple too felt a little less uncertain now, thanks to the generosity of the man who stood next to her. He had agreed to write the Torso's speech for him without hesitation, under one condition: he expected to be paid for his services, and handsomely. Sonya hadn't the slightest inkling that Thomas would deposit the cheque in the account of Colour Purple, buying her enough time and resources to contemplate the direction she wanted the magazine to head in. More importantly, the speech had been instrumental in the success of the event, delivering sound bite after sound bite, currently being played on loop on news stations across the country and on the television screen in front of them.

Behind them, her friends—Sudhi, Anjali, the General— were seated at their usual table at The Bend, celebrating, waiting for the next round. But Sonya was still waiting,

waiting for one last bang that would—she checked her phone—no doubt reverberate across the nation in the next hour, if not sooner. Shaun appeared at the far corner of the bar, waving them away. He would get the beers in, he shouted; go! Making their way back to their table, Sonya paused to kiss Thomas on the cheek. 'You were fantastic today.'

The past three weeks were a haze, like wave after lull after wave of hallucinations that collapsed upon themselves after the trip to form one multi-layered, non-sequential memory. Damn Thomas. He had made the alternative her *usual*, normal. She tried to stitch the pieces together, to create some semblance of order.

Sonya and the General had admittedly been edged out of proceedings altogether by Tammy, and unceremoniously at that, once they had made their Faustian pact. Within twenty-four hours of their meeting, the project was already a looming reality, flashed across social and traditional media as a one-of-its-kind charity event that would see the coming together of the moneyed and the glamorous to give back, to *make a difference*. Mere minutes after the first press release, celebrities and ordinary mortals alike were pledging their support for the cause, promising to contribute, desperate to be involved.

A Bollywood starlet announced plans to fund building costs for a home for the girls in Juhu apropos her own childhood as the daughter of a sex worker in Sonagachi in Calcutta; numerous businessmen voiced concern for children like the General's girls and offered to sponsor their education, health, welfare. All outgoing communication from the Torso's camp dutifully acknowledged the role Colour Purple had played in bringing the issue to the forefront, inspired no doubt by an iron-clad contract Sonya had had drawn up by a friend in the legal team of the firm she was employed by till a few months ago and the logic in associating his brand with a little-known, local initiative. Colour Purple was cited as creator and executor; for all practical purposes, Sonya's fledgling organization was running the show. The Torso was just a humble vehicle, an agent for change.

Thomas and Tammy worked on the speech together, the former displaying an uncharacteristic nous for graft that both delighted and vindicated Sonya. This was the Potential she had invested in, the goodness of heart she had placed her faith in. She had always known it would pay off but there was no way she could have predicted the response of mainstream media to the event.

She was alerted to the first instance of the media's tendency to conflate fact with conjecture by her father, recently informed of her decision to *do her own thing*. Basking in the glow of their well-deserved sinecure, she had been trying on shoes with the General for their big day in a little boutique on Fourteenth Road, designed by a friend of Shaun's. 'Hurry,' crackled the voice of her father over the phone, 'they're talking about you on TV!'

The two of them ran all the way to The Bend five doors away, forgetting to change back into their own footwear. An ambitious young reporter had dug up some information on the elusive duo (the only modification Tammy had made to their contract was that the girls would make no media appearances till the event was over in order to prevent detracting credit from the Torso) and was presenting it to the world with the gravity one might reserve for war or natural disaster: yes, he could confirm that they were alumni of such and such a B-school; yes, they were women in their twenties and good-looking *(!)*, to boot. They would have to pay for two pairs of shoes they didn't particularly like but it was worth the elation.

In the week preceding the event, the media went into overdrive. Local Hindi channels scheduled all-day marathons of the Torso's movies, a celebration of a glittering career that had given Bollywood some of the most memorable (for conflicting reasons) and commercially successful moments in recent history. But Tammy's real victory was her hold over 'serious' television: news networks. The Torso's recent trials (literally) and tribulations forgotten, the question on everybody's lips was this: did the upcoming event mark a shift in his ideology? The Torso still had his critics of course but their recriminations were drowned out by the mob. Didn't every saint have a past, asked his flag-bearers, every sinner a future? Besides, how does one criticize a clearly philanthropic venture, shoot down altruism? Had he finally matured, the Nation wanted to know, was it finally acceptable to like the Torso again?

The answer would be culled from the Torso's own words (or Thomas's, if one wished to be pedantic) a few days later. To call the Torso's speech a triumph over adversity would have been an understatement. The narrative comprised all the ingredients of a Bollywood blockbuster: incipient humour, glamour, fall from grace, redemption, even tears.

It had taken Sonya two weeks and seven separate visits to local designer outlets to decide on an outfit for the event: a little black dress with a red velvet belt and matching pumps that Thomas had sullied thrice in the course of fitting sessions the previous evening. They had both jogged innumerable kilometres around Madhu Park so she could slip into it without discomfort. The General had chosen to wear a black suit over a white shirt and skinny tie, as had Thomas. Sonya thought they both looked good except when they stood too close to each other, at which point they reminded her of a pantomime. Of course none of them were dressed as well as their guests, some of whose attire cost more than the sum total of everything the three of them would earn in their lifetimes.

The event was held in Sobo, in the banquet hall of one of the most iconic multi-star hotels in the city, if not the country. Thomas, Sonya and the General had crowded into a rented Merc to arrive in style and still ended up feeling out of place, especially after Sonya was forced to make a hurried phone call to Tammy to gain security clearance. The General's girls had been chauffeured to the hotel ahead of time, chaperoned by Tammy's secretaries, for an extended photo shoot.

The Torso was predictably late by a couple of hours, as were the rest of his esteemed guests, causing Sonya to wonder aloud if she had missed some unwritten memo on etiquette regarding these kind of things. But it did give her time to sit down for a drink (or two) with Anjali at the bar and sort out their differences, trifling as they were. By the time the event got off to a start, they were all well and truly hammered, with the honourable exception of Thomas who had chosen to maintain his teetotaling façade in Sonya's presence. Sonya was too nervous to be annoyed; they stumbled into the banquet hall as one, Sudhi in tow, prepared for the worst.

None of them could have envisioned what awaited them. The room was filled to the brim with familiar faces—familiar in that strange way everybody knew everybody in the twenty-first century: faces they recognized from advertisements and music videos, news articles and the movies, faces with permanent smiles frozen on them as cameras went off in every direction. Sonya and the General were ushered onto the stage by Tammy's secretaries, and introduced to much clapping of hands. To the surprise of none of her friends, Sonya breezed through her speech, enthusiasm uncontained, joy contagious.

The General was more subdued, gently taking the audience through her journey as a researcher turned activist in a lesson in elocution that left but a few eyes dry. She concluded by calling her girls up on stage, introducing them by name, age, what grade they were in, hobbies, likes and dislikes. The room erupted in thunderous applause as they stood in a row on stage, the General in the middle, and bowed. Sonya had never felt so proud.

But the performance of the day no doubt belonged to the Torso, in what was an uncharacteristically sensitive and endearing reminder of his staying power, of the roguish charm that had helped him survive for so long in a dog-eat-dog industry in the first place.

'Namaste' he started. 'Eyes up *here*, ladies.' Sonya wondered about his peculiar LA-meets-Bronx accent. 'And gents,' he added. It reminded her of Pakistani cricketers from the late nineties but many of them had learnt the language well into adulthood, picking it up from foreign coaches and during travel abroad.

The Torso started off with a few barbs aimed at himself, slowly turning the narrative around to take a couple of lighthearted potshots at the Hindi film industry and the media that fed off it. He appeared genuinely touched when interrupted mid-speech by Tammy and Mikey to be presented an *action portrait* of him, painted by one of the girls. The image was beamed up on the screen behind him—an oil rendering of a still from one of his movies in which he had played a cop, walking away from a burning building as the flames licked the sky behind him—zooming in on the childish scribble at the bottom of the canvas: 'Love, Your BIGGEST fan', followed by a close-up of the precocious artist beaming bashfully up at him from the front row. The man in the painting looked nothing like him but the Torso almost choked up: 'Thank you, sweetheart!'—and blew her a kiss. Sonya looked on from the stage at journalists frenziedly transcribing every word, some onto paper, many onto their mobile phones.

Film artists, drawled the Torso, had a responsibility to their audience. Especially when these artists were blessed with the kind of adulation he was by his dedicated fan following. It was an opportunity to do good, to make the world a little better.

Sonya locked eyes with Thomas, standing unobtrusively at the back of the room, a bottle of water in his hand. He hadn't let her see the transcript despite her numerous pleas.

'I would like to put my hand up today and confess that I have made mistakes, I haven't always chosen the kind of roles or movies that could have made a positive impact on society.' The transcribers were going crazy, their hands and fingers a blur. 'But I'm not here to justify my choices or offer excuses. We are gathered here to raise money for a very important cause, thanks to the hard work and determination of two outstanding young women.' Sonya couldn't help a smile escaping from the corner of her lips as the Torso waited patiently for the applause to stop. 'I am aware many of you had reservations about my involvement in this event, given the criticisms levelled at my work.' Pausing, the Torso removed his Ray Bans and slung them sideways from the neck of his tee-shirt. The sense of momentousness was immense, a veritable presence that hung over the heads of everybody in attendance.

'There are more deserving candidates no doubt, people whose participation would seem less hypocritical. But I believe in taking the chance, when you get one, to say you're sorry, to set things right.' This was already the most coherent, sincere speech the scribes had ever heard a mainstream Hindi film star make. 'This is not one of those occasions.' There was a collective gasp, lowering of heads, darkening of faces. The Torso held up a hand. 'I'm not here to say sorry. I'm here to say I understand. I *empathize* with the women my roles, my movies, have objectified because I am a product, a *victim*, of the same system that dictates these economics.'

Uproar. It was the only word for it. Hands shot up, microphones pointed like instruments of war at the stage. Tammy immediately appeared beside her client from the side of the stage to quell the tide. 'We will be fielding questions later,' she declared. 'I request you to please maintain silence.'

'Cheers, Tammy,' said the Torso and flashed a grin at her, an incongruous if temporary return to nature that had Thomas shaking his head. 'I started in this industry as a nineteen-year-old boy. Less than a year into my career, the media—you guys—had already given me a nickname that has stuck with me till today. Did I take to my moniker blindly, *embrace* it? Yes. I was an impressionable kid. I thought it was a compliment.'

The tide was turning. Who couldn't relate to a tale of misplaced *amour propre* in the twenty-first century? If the late nineties saw mankind take to the internet timidly, shamefully, living out their fantasies in dimly lit, fiercely protected privacy, the second half of the noughties had exposed them for who they really were: unapologetic attention-seekers, full-blown exhibitionists. They all lived and died by others' responses to a new haircut, holiday photographs, pay raises. Sonya could see it in their faces. Like them, she had never thought to consider that the Torso might have had a heart.

'We live in an age in which everything is sexualized—cars and phones, airplanes and guitars, bank cards and even food.' That last part was vintage Thomas. 'And of course, men and women.' Sonya tried to catch Thomas's eye but he was otherwise occupied, staring intently at his muse. 'The damage that does to society, and individuals, is often irreparable. I cannot express how much I regret having contributed to that culture. But I hope your personal opinion of me will not colour your judgment today. I hope you will give happily and generously to this very worthwhile cause. My name is Shoaib Aslam, and I want to thank you all for coming.'

It was the most sensational public relations U-turn the film industry had witnessed. The Torso waved and pumped his fist in the air as he acknowledged the standing ovation, the surge of applause that refused to subside, and took his seat next to Sonya and the General. Not one to waste a moment, Tammy appeared back on stage and hugged her star client, before stepping onto the dais to announce that the auction would begin in five minutes.

Sonya now thanked Shaun as he set the beers down on their table and looked again at her watch. She had tried calling Mikey several times but his phone was switched off. Had something happened to him? Taking a sip of her beer, she diverted her attention towards present company. Sudhi and the General were exchanging friendly jibes, watched on by a morose-looking, sober Thomas. Clutching Anjali's hand tightly, Sonya told her she was sorry about the distance she had permitted between them over the course of the last few months. Anjali hugged her and landed a kiss on her cheek.

Sonya was a bundle of nerves by the time Mikey burst in, one eye on the television screen. 'Any minute now,' he announced as Sonya gave him a look. The others didn't seem to have heard, thank God. Pulling up a chair between Thomas and Sonya, he looked around for a waiter. 'Where the hell have you been?' It took him longer than he had expected to check out, he explained, he had had a few friends over the previous night and one of them had stolen all the towels.

'You were staying at the hotel?' inquired Thomas.

'Yeah, my dad's a gold card holder; we get like a, a we-we-week's stay free of cost every year.'

Sudhi and Anjali burst out laughing at the flustered young man.

'You're a dark horse, aren't you?' said the General.

Plus he had to help load the Action *portrait* into the Torso's car, added Mikey. Sonya kicked him under the table but his eyes were now riveted to the screen. 'There!'

The group turned to the television. The Torso was still hogging prime time but for different reasons altogether. The video footage showed a confused Torso being shepherded up the stairs of Santa Cruz station by a horde of lawyers and policemen, security guards and hangers-on. Thomas's music still occupied the airwaves but they could read the news ticker without discomfort from where they were seated: 'THE TORSO HELD ON POSSESSION OF UNLICENCED FIREARM | HANDGUN SEIZED FROM CAR ON WAY BACK FROM CHARITY AUCTION | POLICE ACTED ON ANONYMOUS TIP | MODEL MURDER CASE EXPECTED TO BE RE-OPENED.

Sudhi, Anjali and the General watched in stunned silence, unable to pry their eyes away from real-time drama. Deciding Thomas wouldn't back down until she met his gaze, Sonya finally turned to him and smiled as innocuously as she could. 'Have a drink baby,' she said. 'It's your birthday.'

# 23

# The Girlfriend Chronicles 16: Coffee and Cigarettes. And PMS.

I knew this wouldn't end well when you suggested meeting at Gloria Jean's. I mean seriously, when's the last time we met up at a coffeeshop? Is that even normal? I heard the rumours—just like everybody else—but I've tried my best to remain unaffected. You're my bro, my oldest friend, and I'm not going to buy into the nonsense that has been doing the rounds about you. I'm here and waiting, and you're ten minutes late and you won't answer your phone, but I'm counting on you to show up and tell me the coffeeshop thing was a joke and take us to some crazy new bar you've discovered and end the night scoring eckies off some random in the Red Light District or some such. Rock out with our cocks out, etc. Don't let me down, broheim.

You're wearing a pink shirt. You tell me it's not pink, that it's *salmon*, that the 'l' in salmon is silent because it originates from the French 'saumon'. I just want to have a drink. I want you to shave off that ridiculous hipster beard, and ditch the man-bag, and insist the barista top up our cappuccinos with a sprinkling of Ketamine. I want to go back in time to an age when you would never use the word 'sprinkling' in this context. It'll have to wait. Because you want to wait for your girlfriend, whom you're so excited for me to meet. So *she's* Frankenstein. I don't like her already.

She's not unattractive. She's actually quite nice. She's interested in my novel, she reels off football stats like a pro, and chases her espresso with a smoke and pokes indulgently at your nicotine patch. I think I like her a little bit, but then I notice you're wearing suede loafers. Did she do this to you? Does she do your shopping now? Would you like me to take her out, Liam Neeson-style? I've got your back, bro. Just say the words.

She's going to the loo. And she's taking your man-bag with her. So it's *her* bag. I'm sorry I'm such a superficial bastard but I'm so glad it's hers. So glad, that I'm going to ignore the fact that you lug around your girlfriend's bag. Holy fuck, you have a new tattoo. I love that you didn't post pictures of it on Facebook or show it off to me the moment you walked in. That's the cool motherfucker I used to know. I wish your tattoo weren't of a Puerto Riccan Parrot, though. I get that it's an endangered species, but I don't know if a tattoo of it on your neck is going to help them live long and prosper.

Fuck, my stomach is cramping up again. Fuuuuccccccck. Fucking fuckitty motherfucking fuckbiscuit. FUCK. Oh great, now my nipples are sore. I knew I shouldn't have worn my stupid polyester Chelsea jersey. God, it chafes so bad. Who thought making replica football jerseys for scrawny men with all the upper body strength of an eight-year-old was a good idea? Why the fuck did I ever think buying it was a good idea? I'm so susceptible to male wish-fulfilment. I'm every advertiser's dream consumer. God, men can be so stupid sometimes.

She wants to go to Toto's for a drink. It's just past one in the afternoon. What a couple of alcoholics. I just want some chocolate. All I want is to sit around at home in my boxers, order that pork thing with the black bean sauce from that Chinese take-out place, and watch that Sandra Bullock movie I've been saving for just this kind of day. But I'm never going to tell anybody that. Unless my stomach starts cramping again. Oh fuck, it's cramping again. I hope a bus runs me over the moment we step out.

'Dude, you look like you're going to pass out. You ok?' you want to know.

'Oh, *finally* you noticed?' I find myself saying, and realize immediately how mean that sounds.

'What? You don't like her or something?' you whisper, though she's in the loo again.

'I'm sorry man, it's just ... that time of the month again,' I say. And die a little inside.

'*What* time?' you say.

'You know, *that* time. The whole ... *menstrual* thing.' *Why do men always pretend like they don't know?*

'But you're a *dude*,' you say, as if the universe really is that cut and dry.

'It's my girlfriend, man. She's getting her thing. I'm getting them sympathy cramps. You know.'

You're silent. You're doing that thing men do. Please don't do that thing; we're bros. I stood guard while you took a drunken shit on your ex-girlfriend's car when you found out she was cheating on you. Don't do this to me.

'Did you just say *sympathy* cramps?'

'Oh for fuck's sake, don't go on like you don't know. Everybody gets them.'

'You get cramps when your girlfriend's PMS-ing?'

'Yes. Everybody does.'

'No they don't.'

'Yes, they do. It's a thing.'

'It's not a thing. But do you need meds or something?'

'I don't need *meds*, alright? Who even says "meds"? Why can't you just say "medicine" like normal people? God, I can't even stand to *look* at you. Why are you wearing a fucking pink shirt?'

'It's *salmon*.'

'It's not. It's PINK.'

'Whatever, man.'

'I'm sorry. You make it work. Salmon is good on you.'

'Really? Lisa picked it up for me. I wasn't too sure about it.'

'It's beautiful. It really brings out your eyes. I love you, man. I'm sorry.'

'It's alright, bro. Just don't mention the sympathy cramps thing around her, ok? I don't get those.'

'Yeah, *sure* you don't. Ooh, cupcakes! You want one?'

---

Tags: pms, time of the month, bromance, bro, hipster, coffeeshop, men will be boys, manchild

---

# 24

They'd been here before, he and her. The same old dance around their furniture the previous night, strains of that played-out song still lingering as he grappled with the selective memory—or lack of it—of an alcoholic: Did I hit you baby? Did I yell, did I scream, did I call you names?

It was the not knowing, the not remembering, that killed him. The blackouts, the temporary other him she claimed he turned into when he had drunk too much. What was he like, this man? Did he fuck her harder, longer, better? Was he always unpleasant? She had had good times too, with this man. This man who—from her accounts of him—slipped in and out of the shadows without warning, who visited and played house when he was away. Thomas was almost jealous of him.

He calculated that he had maybe half an hour till she woke up, till she unlocked the door and let him back in. It had probably been cold at night on this terrace, though he woke up with the sun in his face. The quilt she had covered him in, the one with the daffodils, the one they picked up on Hill Road together, was caked with vomit. Whisky-soaked chunks of barely chewed chicken lay at the feet of the stems of yellow daffodils, like a flowerbed in a postmodern work of art.

Thomas tried repeatedly to remember, to retrieve the night. All that came to mind was a vision of Sonya's tear-streaked face; her incredulity at his letting her down again juxtaposed with a sense of inevitability, of predictability, of disgust at the cliché he was quickly turning into. It reminded him of a Malayalam phrase his mother frequently used in recrimination of his father: 'Shankaran veendum thengella.' Meaning: Shankaran is back on the coconut tree again—a reference to the village drunk who, inebriated, climbed the coconut tree by the toddy shop after it closed and sat there all night, nodding off. Every village had a Shankaran. His must have broken every bone in his body in the few years Thomas had known him.

Thomas had not always blacked out after one too many drinks. He was getting older. But he had done a lot of stupid things, shameful things, under the influence. Maybe blacking out was a subconscious way of preventing shame, of denial. But the subconscious only knew so much. There was no greater guilt, no fear more fervent, no greater self-loathing than that felt by an addict trying to recollect words said in anger, crimes committed on autopilot.

Sonya was up. He could hear her morning song: Norah Jones's 'Sunrise'. Had she forgotten that he was on her terrace? Was there a part of her—even a small part—that hoped he had left the building in style, feet pedalling air and tonsils aflame as he drunkenly stepped off the ledge in the night? It wouldn't be the first time either. That other tumultuous night when he had accused her of lacking imagination? He didn't think so, for what it was worth, though he didn't remember saying it. *But if you wanted to kill me baby, you should have gone with the sleeping pills you think lie hidden in your underwear drawer.*

The door flung open, catching him by surprise. Sonya was already dressed. She looked like she hadn't slept much, but she looked beautiful in that tired sad way young widows used to do in Hindi movies, before multiplex economics required them to mourn in brighter colors. Thomas preferred the starched white of her collarless Fabindia shirt but as she had pointed out about his writing, he was a stickler for symbolism, for signposting. He tried to sit up, and asked if she had a cigarette. 'You need help, baby,' was all she was willing to offer.

'I'm sorry,' said Thomas.

'How much do you remember?' she asked, now familiar with the narrative of this particular conversation.

'Did I hit you?' he asked.

It had happened once before, violence. He had a family friend's place in the hills to himself for the weekend, and Sonya and he were staying over. They had started drinking early, in the afternoon. He could remember them going through a few bottles of Sula red, Sonya deciding to call it a night around eleven, him preferring to stay put and open a bottle of seventeen-year-old Glenfiddich in the hope that a stiff drink would somehow miraculously bless him with the sort of functional erection holidays in the hills called for. He wasn't entirely wrong.

'No,' she said now, after a moment, 'it wasn't that bad.'

The night in the hills on the other hand, had been a psychoanalyst's wet dream. Sonya told him—a week later, when she agreed to see him again—that he had spent a good twenty minutes having a conversation with his penis.

Unlike his penis however, Sonya had been in no mood for chitchat, or sex. She wanted to go back to the wine-fuelled sleep she was callously awoken from. The other him, their mysterious houseguest, was not as open to suggestions. More than the liquid courage, she had told him later, more than the borrowed bravado, it was the look in his eyes that had frightened her.

He could barely look at her now. Sonya went back in. Thomas struggled to his feet and followed her inside, his eyes scanning the corridor, the living room, for signs of a struggle, of violence, till he reached their bedroom. The bed they had shared almost every night in the year they had known each other suddenly felt like foreign territory. Like he was trespassing, though he was not sure why. She seemed calmer, her responses more muted than previous mornings after. It couldn't have been that bad, however relative these things tended to be. Yet it felt like he had crossed a line; like they had reached an impasse.

'That was the last time,' he said earnestly. 'I've quit drinking.'

'I hope so,' said Sonya.

He couldn't read her face, or her tone. He wished she'd stop scurrying about, collecting bits and pieces and depositing them all in her handbag like a worker ant on amphetamines. He wanted to hold her still, to grab her restless hands and press them against his face, to feel her heart beat against his being. But it felt like a violation of some unwritten rule, some new protocol that had been established overnight. It was strange to feel less than proprietary of her breasts, her ass, her cunt. It was strange to think that he may now need her permission to touch her, to undress her.

'Baby,' she said and touched him on the shoulder. He didn't catch what she said the first time.

'Yeah, sorry?' he responded.

'You say that a lot these days,' said Sonya. She smiled toothlessly, joylessly, her mouth straighter than the most stoical of emoticons; a smile he only knew too well from mornings like this one, a smile that made the hairs on his body stand on end. He felt scared; he felt afraid for her. His pounding head went into overdrive with memories of stories from his childhood: stories of the depths of sorrow and desperation women were driven to by men who let them down time and again, stories woven around a curious coincidence—these women, these wives and mothers and daughters, they were all women like Didi, women who cooked and cleaned and prostituted themselves in homes like his, homes bigger and much richer than their little universe.

He watched her, still busy putting away and collecting things that were probably not in need of reorganization, things that—unlike the two of them—were probably fine as they were. Thomas looked at Sonya and tried to identify a pattern; some similarity between the Radhas and the Mayammas that had fed and bathed and clothed him as a child, and her. He thought back to the stories she had told him of her own childhood—of growing up in Riyadh without Riyadh ever really growing on her, of moving back to India for college and completing management school in Bangalore in the top percentile, of campus recruitment and five figure salaries and Iranian cafés in Sobo and corporate retreats in Bangkok and he.

And he. It dawned on him like a looming asteroid, like a clear and present danger that one ceased to fear because they had gotten used to it. *He* was the pattern—he was Shankaran to her Radha, her Mayamma. He was Velayudhan, he was Ousep, he was Pachi the gravedigger who religiously donated all his money to the local toddy hall at the cost of sending his children to school, he was Lukappi the labour union goon who had never done an honest day's work in his life. The backgrounds that the Sonyas and the Mayammas of the world came from didn't matter because love, like violence, did not discriminate. Thomas went over that line in his head; he wondered about structure, grammar, and whether he could palm it off in one of the many half-hearted monthly columns he wrote to keep his head above water, till his unfinished novel came calling again, muse in tow.

But that familiar old voice was back in his head—the narrator of nostalgia, the connoisseur of contradictions—telling stories. The stories themselves—familiar as they were—had taken on a darker complexion, unearthed a greater honesty. There were deconstructions, insinuations, but no digressions; there was a greater urgency to the narrative, a sense of running out of time. 'Thomas,' said his mother's voice, 'baby, I thought you knew.'

'Baby,' said Sonya, 'baby, are you crying?'

'Why are you playing that song again?' he said. 'You've been listening to it all morning.'

'It helps. Are you okay?'

'I need to call my Dad,' he managed.

'Why?' she countered. 'You never call your father.'

'I need to ask him something,' said Thomas. 'Can I use your phone?'

'No, you have to leave now,' she said. 'I'm already late. Anjali has been waiting for an hour.'

'Ok, I'll just use the phone downstairs. Can I meet you after?'

Something was wrong. He could see it in her eyes, feel it in the air.

'I'm sorry, baby,' she said. 'I thought you'd remember that much.'

'We broke up last night,' he said. It was not a question. He must have known all along.

She nodded, not unkindly.

'But I'm *done*. I've quit. I'm sorry.'

*Words*. Where are all the damn words?

'I'm sorry, baby,' said Sonya. 'That was your exit music.'

She touched his face and turned towards the door. His backpack stood packed and ready against the wall. He followed her out and down the stairs, hoping only that she had kept the tee-shirts she liked to sleep in, feeling not nearly as devastated as he ought to have been, almost insouciant, probably still drunk. This had always been the only way this could have ended, even if she didn't know it yet. Besides, he realized with something approaching pride, Sonya had finally made the personal political.

# EPILOGUE

Later, much later, they would both look back on their time together and wonder who had been fooling whom. For like everybody else, they were but the fictions they were made of, the lies they chose to believe about themselves. Like Vandra is Bandra, like Soniya became Sonya. It would be unfair to assign to one of them the greater untruth, to weigh one down with the burden of their consensual self-deception. But it may be worth noting that unbeknownst to at least one of them, their paths had crossed once before, when they were still traversing—and were lost in—liminal routes. If liminality is what lies betwixt and between, if it's the space between ground and feet, between the slip and the fall, then she was as much his fall as he was new ground beneath her flailing feet. Or vice versa; it's hard to tell with these things.

She was only a child then, and still Soniya. He was speeding through the first real rain of the year—still more a sustained drizzle than anything more productive, not enough to calm the collective nerves of Kerala's agricultural community of which he was an unwitting patron but sufficiently stubborn in its persistence to demand his attention—enough to distinguish his journey from a joyride. She was in the throes of first love, sleepless and doe-eyed, wistful and entranced. He was in a state, he was, not a lot unlike first love, but kinder, grander. He had been driving for sixteen hours straight, Madgaon to Karwar to Manjeshwar, stopping only to roll a joint here, take a piss there. He was a little less certain of the route once he got on to the NH 47, following buses rather than relying on road signs. He wasn't chasing a high anymore, but he didn't want to forget. He had to get home before it settled, before the fear returned.

Soniya, on her part, had never felt more afraid in her life. There was blood everywhere—on her sheets, between her legs, even on the floor. It hurt to stand, to walk to the bathroom and bend over her shiny red bucket and rinse her bloody linen. But it was a curious kind of pain, one of belonging and permanence, of completion and wisdom. So even as her heart raced—mulling over everything that could go wrong if found out; her devastated father, her prophetic mother, oh the unrelenting march through her mind of possibilities!—she couldn't help but smile at the woman that peered back at her in the mirror.

His own rearview was black as night, a slate wiped clean. For the first time in his life, he felt truly alive, like life was only just beginning. How right he was! There was much he regretted, much time he had lost, and yet it all felt worthwhile just then, like stars that dotted a constellation or the literally garden-variety lights, imported from Singapore, that would lead him up the long driveway home, past acres of rubber and teak trees on either side, if he made it before daybreak. He had to make it home before the sun came up, before it diverted attention away from his Grand Realization and on to everyday deficiencies, to pitfalls of the past and previous grievances that would only distract from the Truth.

The truth was, Soniya thought to herself as she wrung out the last of the evidence, the truth was that this was the moment it had all been leading up to, the trials and tribulations of the past year. Like stars that dot a constellation, she thought, and oh must one *think* too in such clichés? 'Trials and tribulations,' she muttered to herself, 'stars and constellations.' She was young enough to admonish herself without judgment, to rate novelty over experience, originality over the moment. She looked at her watch. Somehow, in all the commotion— in their enthusiasm to surrender all defences, to touch every pore, to kiss every inch, to commit fully and truly like only children can—her watch had stayed on, in grotesque parody of her father's promise to *protect* at all times, preserving the modesty of her slender right wrist and not much else.

The watch had been a gift from her father, a Casio that was water-resistant up to 50m, on the occasion of another similarly bloody and momentous rite of passage. It was accompanied by a card, decorated in her father's illegible scribble—'to protect you when I'm not around'—that had left her gasping for air, for *space*. A few hours ago, her lungs had felt equally overwhelmed—just as desirous of *air, luxuriant air*—as she soldiered on against waves of her own creation and the overpowering scent of industrial chlorine to win Saudi Arabia's first inter-school swimming competition. For Girls. Under-13s. It should have been a proud moment, a glittering achievement, and yet, as she looked up through blue-goggled eyes at her mother who stood two feet above the pool, her first instinct was that of shame. Confused but aware that she had somehow swum past a barrier and out of familiar territory that could no longer accommodate her, take her back, she turned around and afforded herself one last look at what she was leaving behind. Her trail was marked in red, the sort of red that stopped the most important of SUVs on King Fahd road without a moment's hesitation, the kind of chrome that meant business, that demarcated and divided and ruled. She fainted before she was fully out of the pool.

His was a lineage that was no stranger to the blood-streaked trappings of Pyrrhic victories. This very journey had been afforded by one such, driving away with capital that belonged to another, stolen from his only friends in the world. As luck would have it, it wasn't the few kilograms of heroin stashed under the backseat of his Cielo that had brought about his current state—this ferment of clarity—but a rogue vial of LSD that had tumbled out of the glove compartment when he opened it to pull out his papers at the Goan checkpost. What was in the bottle, the policeman had wanted to know. Eyedrops, he had replied hesitantly. In a moment of panic, he unscrewed the pipette from the little glass cylinder and—tilting his head back—applied a generous dosage of the liquid in his left eye. 'See?' Racing through the Konkan Highway, wheels barely touching the ground, he had never seen as many colours as he did that night, never craved lucidity more. But it had been alright, it had brought him where he was now, he didn't mind if this was what it had all been leading up to.

Soniya jumped at the knock on her window—and seeing who it was—waved fervently and pointed at her watch. 'GO!' They were first cousins, had known each other all their lives but neither of them could have predicted the events of the last few hours a couple of months ago. Both their parents had been adamant in their decision, insistent that the two of them get married in keeping with tradition—a demand that had taken on a distinct urgency in the last year. The more they clamoured, the more Sonya had objected. She was only a child; they had grown up as siblings; she just couldn't see him that way. Sonya suspected that her parents had packed her off to Thrissur immediately after her boards more out of matchmaking intentions than out of concern for her upcoming medical entrance examinations.

He lived with her uncle and aunt, only a few houses down the road from her own temporary abode in her maternal home. The ruse had worked: she found herself falling for the young man—who was all grown up now—within days of her arrival in Kerala, as excited by the proximity of Man, by the strut of his legs and the smell of his sweat, as she was by the illicitness of their proposed communion. The most casual of physical contact—a brushing of arms, the meeting of feet under the table—invoked fire, drove her to madness. Stolen kisses on the balcony, in their meeting point under the mango tree, groping, touching, it had all led to this night, this unforgettable first time that would forever be etched in her memory as the start of something real, everlasting. Smiling, she watched him look cautiously around the rosebush that lined the wall for a clearing. She wished desperately that he would hurry up and leave, and just as desperately that he could stay. Their parents were ecstatic that they had come round to seeing things their way but she had been warned repeatedly about pre-marital dalliances; there would be hell to pay if they found out.

Thomas glared at the figurine gazing kindly at him from atop his dashboard. St. Jude, the patron saint of desperate causes. An embellishment that graced all the cars in his household. He had kept it when his father gifted him the car out of loyalty to his mother; finally, a promise he could keep! Grudgingly admitting to the Saint that he was lost, Thomas rolled down the windows and took the first brightly lit turn he could find to find his bearings. Not a vehicle in sight, though there appeared to be a bus stand or garage of some sort a little way ahead. He could get directions, stretch his legs. Cheered up by the prospect of resting his cramped limbs, he accelerated again, giving it everything he had. A twitch of the universe, a sudden movement, to his left. The silhouetted arc of a body in flight, scaling a wall, landing gracefully on his feet and scurrying across the road without pause. Thomas felt the sickening thud of body against metal only after it happened. The figure had been thrown up into the air, his face appearing in his windshield for one sickening moment before bouncing off the bonnet and under him. It wasn't unlike driving over a fallen branch or a speedbreaker at full throttle. Slowing down, he watched the figure in the mirror for movement, for hope. Seeing none, he sped away, convinced the scream that would haunt his sleep for the rest of his life hadn't emanated from the lips of the victim or his own.